The Kings of Innocence

Michael Burns

Tucket Publishing

About the author

Michael Burns is a marketing executive, but a first-time author. He holds a B.A. from Trinity College in Hartford, CT, and an M.S. from the University of Massachusetts Amherst. He is married and resides in Charlestown, MA.

Acknowledgements

This story is an acknowledgement in itself to many people, but I am most grateful to my family, my friends and my wife Jessica for their unwavering support throughout this project. They have been there from the start or close to it, their advice, encouragement and patience always limitless.

I must also thank Hisiya Beppu for her incredible creativity with the cover design, Ani Collum for her insightful suggestions, Kevin Penwell for his guidance through the publishing process, and especially Meghan McGowan, for her extensive editing efforts and feedback.

Contents

ISBN 13: 978-0-9797068-1-3
ISBN 10: 0-9797068-1-5

Tucket Publishing – 2007
587 East Broadway, Suite 4
Boston, MA 02127
www.leewellman.com

In prosperity our friends know us; in adversity we know our friends.
-John Churton Collins

I don't want to repeat my innocence. I want the pleasure of losing it again.
-F. Scott Fitzgerald, *This Side of Paradise*

1

I have chosen quite a few friends over the years, yet still fewer have chosen me. At least I had a say in the matter. When I was six, I asked my dad why we couldn't choose our families too. He told me to get over it. And that's when I began to understand the critical role friendships play in life. We do choose our friends and in some cases, we do it at a very young age, enabling them to be there from the beginning—the only guiding influence of our own accord. In small towns like the one I grew up in, the bond can be especially unyielding; strengthened by habit and confined circumstances. Small towns are everywhere, loosely defined as such by the people who live in them. Some are small, some smaller and some smallest. But it is the flow of life that people identify as small. The shared, recurring and proverbial routines carried out among friends and foes alike. The smallness fosters intimacy and a polarizing familiarity that tests friendships. It breeds contempt or loyalty, but rarely anything in between. To those who flee, the world beckons, a great new frontier. To those who stay, the world beckons too, one known and beloved. Though people stay and people go, *all remember*.

And that's why we go back. Returning to our roots connects us to the people and places that for better or for worse, shaped our being, cast our lot. It can bring great joy, also great regret, sometimes both. For me, one trip home exceeded all of that even, and when I consider my life's trajectory, I can't help but think of those summer days in 2002. They were in a word, defining.

My parents had gone to Ireland for a twelve-day vacation with a group of friends. They had dreamed about the trip for years, selflessly putting it off when tuition payments were top priority. My dad's friend, Barry, had set up the tee times, tours and pub-crawls in advance. Turnkey, just the way my parents liked things. They summoned me from my apartment in Allston, where I lived at the time, to watch the house and my seventeen-year-old brother Bobby. That was the plan anyway, and my ticket back.

I hurried to my apartment right after work that Friday, bypassing a trip to the gym with my roommate Tim. I had lived with Tim for three years during college and again that first year in the real world. We lived with another college friend, Pete, who was in Chicago for the week. Our place was a simple, but spacious 1,100 square-foot pad. It was a typical first apartment, featuring furniture from K-mart, beer posters and stolen street signs. The highlight was our bar, which Pete and I had picked up at a local yard sale for just $50. It was cedar with black leather trim and looked like something from the set of *Saturday Night Fever.* It must have weighed six hundred pounds, but we managed to get it in and out of Pete's pickup and up two flights of stairs. We stripped some paint along the way, scratching creative patterns into the stairwell walls. Pete sanded and refinished the bar. He was handy like that, and we squeezed it into what the real estate agent had called a "reading room." We tended to do our reading on the shitter.

That first year was like an extension of college. We finally had our own bedrooms, real jobs, some money and the accompanying responsibilities, but we did our best to drink and act as if we still had the world by the balls. We undoubtedly misled some attractive co-eds into thinking we were still students. For me it was never serious. I was just playing along in hopes of helping a friend here or there. Carmen Hill, my high school sweetheart, had owned my heart for years and marriage was inevitable, though certainly a few years away.

I packed an old hockey bag for the two-week baby-sitting stint, ever thoughtful of specific shirt and short, shirt and jean combinations. For every neatly folded polo, I was sure to add a jersey—vintage, of course. I grabbed a cold slice of pepperoni pie from the otherwise empty fridge, cradled a thirty-pack of Coors cans under my right arm and shuffled down the back stairs off the kitchen. The parking lot behind our four-story apartment building was empty except for a red Jetta, my black Topaz and Tim's green Explorer. July in Boston is a time to get away.

The drive from Allston to Belmont was short, maybe twenty minutes. In spite of the proximity, going back to Belmont was always like entering another world. The occasional visit for a Sunday dinner or a haircut was routine but just a window into a forgotten way of life. This time it was for real, a vacation of sorts that I knew would draw me in, hold me tight. I buzzed down Storrow Drive with the windows down, taking in the late afternoon sun and glancing at the busy banks of the Charles River. I continued into Belmont and down Trapelo Road, past so many familiar storefronts and old haunts. Memories played through my head like a slideshow. As I sped down Mill Street, I felt a familiar world unfold. Each of the modest colonials, spaced evenly on both sides of the street, blended into the next. I passed kids being kids in a yard. There was a mom unloading groceries from the hatch of her shiny black Pathfinder, a dad clipping hedges, and a few people jogging. Then I spotted an unmistakable form: Mrs. Rizzo power walking with her golden retriever, Greenwell, that little Michael Rizzo had named after the former Red Sox outfielder. I tapped the horn, and she waved at me with a small, plastic shit-bag in hand.

That made sense because Belmont is one of *those* towns. It's affluent, but not snobby. Founded in 1859, it is named after the estate of a major China opium dealer named John Perkins Cushing. The town's history is unspectacular; the opium connection one of the few facts I have committed to memory. It primarily served as a livestock and produce supplier for Boston until the development of better roads made it an attractive location for rich folks to build monster estates within close proximity to Boston. Few mansions still exist, but the posh Belmont Hill section of town still rivals the elite neighborhoods of Wellesley and Weston. It remains a fairly simple place, pretty but not beautiful, alive but not thriving. The population consistently peaks around 28,000, 90% of whom are whiter than rice.

There is a good mix of blue-collar and white-collar people. Many of the families have been there for generations and a fair share make their money working honest, traditional jobs. Dentists, landscapers, eye doctors, plumbers and roofers—all equally successful, good natured and moral. The sort of town rooted in traditional values like family, home and God. For the most part, the dads work, the moms are moms, and the kids are everywhere. It is the type of place where you didn't have to worry about stepping in Greenwell's shit.

It felt good to be home. I turned onto my parents' street then brought the car to a stop in front of the house. I hustled down the long driveway towards the backyard, where my brother Bobby was waiting, tossing a Wiffle Ball to himself.

"What took you so long?" he asked confidently, throwing me the ball.

2

Bobby repeatedly leveled the dirty yellow bat. Back and forth, it swung through the hitting zone. I focused in on my target, the opening between the second and third rungs of the metal stepladder, which we had positioned to serve as the strike zone. Time seemed to stand still. This was his spot, his big chance. I noticed his hands tighten around the frayed red tape of the handle. Victory was his, or so he thought, and it was déjà vu redefined. My lips gave way to a grin. Once again, I had brought him to the brink of jubilation, and once again, I was poised to rip it from his grasp with a calculated last-minute comeback. At twenty-four, I felt a momentary sense of guilt. I was too old for this shit. But brothers will be brothers. I had a reputation to protect, and it was for his benefit anyway. It would make him tougher in the long run.

I glanced to my left through the short picket fence and into our neighbor Gil's yard. The fence was an eyesore. My shoddy paint job from six years earlier was on display, dull gray paint chips peeling off every plank. Gil's perfectly manicured lawn stretched out in all directions, and his pale yellow house glistened in the July sun. There was Gil, a weary old man, bent over and tending to his tomato plants. After picking a few fledgling weeds, he rose and turned his balding round head to our stage. His tiny, warm blue eyes locked with mine. His face was grizzled and worn, layer upon layer of wrinkled skin folding over the next. With his pointy nose and fuzzy remnants of gray hair, he looked like a newly hatched bird. Three or four heart attacks had taken their toll. The ambulances came with the regularity of a mail carrier, and yet Gil always survived. He always came home. Soon he was back in his yard, shuffling along while hunched over as if he were carrying doubles at Pinehurst No. 2.

Gil always knew the score too. He could have his back to the play for an hour, watering plants, patting soil, fiddling with the dial on his transistor, yet he continuously knew the inning and count on the batter. It was a sixth sense. He also had an uncanny ability to diffuse arguments and interpret rules. His word was always gold. Generations of players had entrusted their fate to him.

Moving slowly towards the fence Gil blurted out, "This is it, Robert. You can do it, young buddy." He called him Robert. That killed me. Like some great uncle or dog-breathed math teacher.

Bobby nodded without taking his eyes off me. "I got him, Gil. A single ties it."

To inflate his hopes, I added, "And a double wins it. If he fists one off the porch, he can put to rest years of agony."

The short distance to the sun porch in right field was notorious for doubles—defined as any ball that landed on the field side of the porch's small pitched roof. That wasn't going to happen though. A left-handed hitter, Bobby would have to turn on my fastball. It stood more likely that Gil start break dancing.

Frustrated, Bobby spat, "Let's go. Throw the damn ball."

"Shut up," I snapped. "I'll throw the third strike and end this game when I'm good and ready. Besides, I want you to soak in this moment, you little shit."

"Little?" Bobby shot back. "I'm bigger than you, Sonny Boy."

I hated Sonny Boy. It had been my dad's mock name for me when I was younger, his response to my tendency to half-ass my way through chores. An attempt at inspiration, I suppose. Bobby had a point though: just seventeen, he was already two inches taller at 5'11". He had ten pounds on me too, at 175. He was bigger and probably tougher, but that didn't matter; older brothers possess an engrained intimidation factor. It's a birth rite.

Ah, but he was the Golden Child. Where I was smart, athletic and averagely handsome, Bobby was a stud plain and simple. I had graduated a year earlier from Trinity College in Connecticut, a good school. I had earned decent grades, played both varsity hockey and golf, and since graduation had been working as a Junior Analyst with a downtown Boston Investment firm. If Bobby followed that path, he'd be a grave disappointment. He was destined for greater things.

A junior to be at the prestigious Ward School, a private, boys' prep school located just up the hill in Belmont, he had been elected a three-sport captain in football, hockey, and baseball. He played quarterback, of course, having led Ward to its first New England Championship in thirty-five years. A pile of recruiting letters from Harvard for hockey, Dartmouth for football, and Yale for both, sat on the desk in his basement bedroom. He cruised in school, earning A's and B's without effort. Girls were a forgone conclusion. He was a dead ringer for one of those J. Crew catalogue models; the ones that frolic on a beach, clad in Starburst colored bathing suits with their big toothy smiles and wavy hair, playing tug of war with a surfboard while modeling a pair of $56 flip-flops. He looked the part. He had a short but perfectly full head of dark brown hair, a wiry build, and an "oh shucks" smile. Then there were the eyes—bright blue ones. Complete strangers like supermarket clerks and waitresses were always commenting on them. It made me sick. Still does.

It was only human to have some jealous instincts back then. But more than anything, I was oozing with pride. Bobby was my best friend, and I mean *best.* Despite the age difference, he understood me better than anyone did. I took great care in my role as his biggest influence. Few things in my life equaled my satisfaction in knowing that I had a bit to do with who he was and where he was headed. His quiet confidence impressed even me. He was just seventeen, but comfortable in his own skin. He'd always been that way.

When I was in high school at Ward, and Bobby was barely old enough to ride a bike, I'd sought out his company. I would voluntarily stay home to baby-sit on weekend nights. We'd have a great time playing mini hockey in the living room, watching movies, and stuffing our faces with mozzarella sticks and French fries. His maturity and my youthful exuberance bridged the age gap. And I wasn't missing much anyway, besides drinking warm beers in boiler rooms or hanging out at the movie theater parking lot. I'd make up for it with plenty of belligerent nights later in life. Bobby was just a calming influence and a damn cool person to hang out with. He made me forget about getting cut from the Varsity hockey team or getting a C in Algebra II. He just happened to be seven and dug playing with G.I Joe.

Still, there was no way he was getting his bat on this ball. With one final nod, I set into my motion. As I took a short step back with my left foot, I momentarily peeked down at the worn grass of the pitcher's mound. Kicking my left leg high into the air, my hips twisting, I felt the adrenaline rush through my veins. My weight shifted forward, and my eyes picked up the metal rungs of the would-be strike zone just as I delivered a blazing fastball. He knew it would be a heater. Gil knew it would be a heater. And I sure as hell knew it would be the heater.

The ball sailed towards the plate as a white blur, and Bobby launched into a swing from his heels. Beads of sweat trickled into my eyes, stinging them closed. Then I heard it—a loud ping—the welcome and unmistakable sound of the ball hitting the ladder's third rung.

3

We referred to Bobby's 1987 Toyota Celica as "The Breadbox" because it wasn't much bigger than one. The car was a family relic of sorts. It had been my Nana Claire's until she became too frail and too senile to drive it. When I inherited it in 1996, it had just 12,000 miles of history. Nana hadn't driven it much; save for her weekly trips to the market, to her bridge game and to other old people hot spots. By the time I passed it on to Bobby, the thing had more than a few dents, balding tires, and a cracked rear tail light—courtesy of a drunken maneuver I had made coming out of the parking lot at Great Woods after a Tom Petty concert. The Breadbox showed its age. The commute to and from Trinity, the treks to Montreal, and the weekend jaunts to the far corners of New England had taken their toll. As I opened the passenger door, I couldn't help but notice the deep orange rust eating away at the silver paint all along the seam where the door met the body of the car.

My eyes were tracing another line of rust above the back tire when Bobby interrupted, "Here, you drive." Looking up, I reacted too slowly. The keys clanked off my nose and dropped to the asphalt below. Wiping my nose, I immediately checked my fingers for blood, but found none. I gave Bobby an incredulous glance, similar to the one I'd give whenever he asked a stupid question. And he had plenty of those. Sure, he was book-smart, but his naivety was legendary. One time at the Thanksgiving table, he had asked if they celebrated Thanksgiving in California. Go figure.

I made my way around to the driver-side door and climbed in. With the car in park, I pinned the accelerator to rev the pathetic engine. It sounded like a window fan on high speed. After adjusting the rear view, I jammed the shift into reverse and backed out of the driveway. It was time to drop Bobby off for a workout.

I could have made the drive to Ward School in my sleep. Down Mill Street a mile, and then bear right onto Fuller Street. Fuller Street was a winding two-mile stretch up a hill and under thick tree cover. As I ascended, both the houses and the space between them grew in size. Towards the crest of the hill, the houses disappeared deeper and deeper into the woods. Small mailboxes marked the start of long driveways, winding back through extensive yards to some pretty damn nice houses. Many had pools, a few had private tennis courts, and all had beautifully kept grounds and unique architecture.

But these were normal, everyday people, mostly self-made and just as likely to be landscapers as real estate moguls. Whether you lived on the hill or in the less desirable Waverly Square area, you still shopped at the same Shaw's Super Market, and your kids still played on the same youth hockey and soccer teams. It was too small a place to close yourself or your family off from the rest of the crowd. It wouldn't fly anyway. People wouldn't put up with that sort of standoffishness. If the gossip queens at the rink or the Little League field didn't get you, the cold stares at the dry cleaner or CVS certainly would.

Case in point was the Austen family. Imports from nearby Newton, they had moved to Belmont a few years back. James Austen owned a chain of high-end grocery stores, not coincidentally called "Austen's." He had a store in Wellesley, one in Hingham, and the original in Newton. I guess he had felt Belmont would be a good demographic for his homemade pasta salads, tasty ready-to-eat meals, and fresh breads and cheeses. His thinking was right. He opened on Leonard Street in Belmont Center, right in the midst of the town's main drag. The center wasn't much, though it was bigger than the other two commercial areas, Cushing Square and Waverly Square. Other than Filenes and CVS, most of the center shops were small mom-and-pops: Harrington's Sporting Goods, Haley's Bookstore, Irving's Fish Market, and Nixon Realty.

James Jr. and his sister, Melissa Austen, were nice enough, albeit kind of quiet kids. Though slender and sheepish, James Jr. was a decent basketball player for Belmont High School. He was soft as toilet paper, but a dead accurate three-point shooter. I'll never forget the night he dropped thirty-six points on third-ranked Lexington in the State Tournament. That was his sophomore year and mine too. Even though I went to Ward, Carmen and most of my childhood friends went to Belmont High, so I was always up to speed with the goings on there, especially athletically and socially. I'd actually made a habit of visiting the high school cafeteria during my free periods. It was a short mile and a half ride from Ward, and their cafeteria featured something Ward's didn't—girls.

Mr. Austen overstepped his bounds. It was bad enough that Mrs. Austen walked around with her nose in the clouds, her gaudy pearls always on full display. After just fourteen months, Austen had expanded his store or "The Austen Empire," as we liked to call it. When he purchased his lot, he had actually bought the rights to half of Leonard Street's eastern block, taking ownership of some seven storefronts. He wasted no time in jacking up the rents by as much as 40%.

First, he bought out his neighbor, a cute toy store called Little Wonders. Then he gobbled up the Bagel Depot, which the Sather family had run since 1938. He gutted and converted the toy store in eight weeks. Even though plenty of residents were guilty of supporting his meteoric growth—I was a big fan of the potato salad—the venom started to show itself. The writing was on the wall, and Irving's Fish Market was next. But the town rallied together like a fraternal tribe. Mrs. Irving, ageless, though in her seventies, was a town icon. She could barely see over the display counter, but she knew every customer by name. To this day, I don't know how she carried the enormous vats of chowder to and from the kitchen. Irving's specialty was certainly fish, but you'd never know it since Mrs. Irving was always whipping up delicious soups, pies, and her specialty, Mac and Cheese. Every Friday she and one of her sons would bring all the week's leftover dishes to the Little League fields, the town rink, or the St. Anthony's Senior Center. It may have been because Irving's was closed on weekends and they didn't want the food to go to waste, but the smart money said they were just good people, people to be protected.

Eventually, somebody threw two bricks through the front window of Austen's. Not surprisingly, the cops didn't arrest anyone. Another night, Mrs. Austen came out of a basketball game only to find somebody had scratched three huge dollar signs into the hood of her Mercedes SUV. It made for quite a sight, her standing in the cold, berating officers in her white mink coat. Students and parents just snickered as they shuffled past. Again, there were no arrests. The Austen Empire had met its match. Irving's was safe.

4

I eased the car to a stop on the gravel of the Ward School parking lot. Wedged between the rink and the new multi-million dollar Lancaster Athletic Center, the lot overlooked what seemed to be an endless stretch of playing fields. It was like looking out on a lush green ocean. Seeing the vastness of perfectly manicured soccer, lacrosse, and football fields was a striking reminder of the school's wealth. For me it was a reminder of the elitist, stuck up jerks and their endowment that made such beauty possible.

My loathsome thoughts must have been evident because Bobby interjected, "You alright, Roy?"

"Yeah, I'm fine. I just don't like coming here. You know that," I responded, reflecting back on my Ward experience. My aunt Judy had worked as a chemistry professor there for twenty-two years, which enabled Bobby and me to attend for the donut. Too good an opportunity to pass up, my parents insisted. Though located in Belmont, almost all of Ward's students were transplants from Acton, Wellesley and other white-collar towns where the yards were big, the houses bigger and the egos biggest. "So, what's your plan? Are you going to run distance or sprints?"

"I'm running fifteen fifties and then jogging home," Bobby answered matter-of-factly. As if running fifteen successive sprints of fifty yards were an ordinary workout. Sprinting can be great for hockey—Bobby's favorite sport—especially if the downtime between runs is minimized. It simulates the stop and go, high-speed bursts the body goes through on the ice. It also helps develop footwork. I was still in decent shape, but fifteen fifties would have darn near killed me.

"You want in?" he asked teasingly.

"Not unless the paramedics are en route," I said. "You sure you don't want me to wait for you?"

"No, I'll run home." He stared out at the track, itching to get out there. "Is it still cool if I have some friends over tonight? Will you still buy for us?"

It made me nervous that Bobby and his friends would drink on my watch, and my dad had made it perfectly clear that I wasn't to allow any drinking or any girls in the house. Even though I was twenty-four and living away from home, crossing my dad still gave me some chills. He wasn't a modern-day pushover dad, who was into lecturing or talking through mistakes. Though he rarely got physical, he was a red-faced screamer and a very effective intimidator. He ran a tight ship, demanding respect and obedience at every turn.

Despite the risks, I had disobeyed the old man many times, and a life of fuck ups had rendered me apathetic to verbal abuse. I commiserated with Bobby. I had been seventeen once and sampled a liquor cabinet or two. I knew an empty house was a rare opportunity for high school kids. And an extended parental trip to Europe, heck, nothing beat that. No need to worry about mom and dad coming home early from dinner or a wedding on the Cape. Besides, I had gone over the ground rules with Bobby. It worried me that he liked to drink at seventeen, but whether I condoned it or not, he was still going to do it. All I could do was warn him how it could impact him athletically and tell him to be smart, never be a hero. He knew perfectly well the repercussions we'd both face if he fucked up.

"Yeah, I'll go. I'll leave you a couple of thirties in the fridge. Remember, no hard alcohol, no more than ten people, no hooking up in mom and dad's room, and absolutely nobody drives. You got it?"

"I do," he said excitedly, staring straight ahead.

"Have a good time. Get something done," I added, tapping fists.

"Damn straight," he said as he jumped out of the car. "Bud Lights!" he shouted, turning back briefly as he jogged towards the track.

I smiled as I watched him run off into the sea of green. He was just like me, and the whole high school mindset was alive and well. Five years hadn't changed a thing. I was just about to pull away when I heard a vaguely distinguishable voice. "Roy? Is that Roy McGrath?"

Turning to my left, I might as well have seen The Ghost of Christmas Past. He was sitting on the back bumper of a navy Land Rover, removing his soccer cleats. Slipping on some flip-flops, he started towards me with a big shit-eating grin. I immediately looked back out the passenger-side window for help, but Bobby was long gone, already out on the track.

Fuck. I was trapped but not for the first time. I had come across a handful of classmates and former teachers at my brother's games over the years, though I always managed to get by with a cursory exchange. I had taken to wearing a hat pulled down low and watching from the visitor side in order to minimize run-ins. It pissed my parents off something fierce.

I swallowed hard, took a deep breath and prepared for the root canal of conversations—a chat with Bradford Atkinson. "Hey, Bradford," I managed, using his real name to patronize him.

"Roy McGrath. Dude, how the hell have you been? I haven't seen you since graduation," he said, shaking his head in disbelief as he strolled up to the car. Not by accident, I thought to myself.

If my graduating class from Ward had been a bunch of pompous pricks, and we were talking mountains, Brad Atkinson was all 29,000 feet of Mt. Everest. Pretentiousness and back scratching had been brutal among my sixty-seven classmates, but I had survived it all. And that's exactly what I considered it—survival. Students and parents alike, pulling out all the stops, drawing on every last resource of influence and stroking whatever cocks needed stroking. Recently, I had warmed to my dad's assessment that I had been somewhat immature, perhaps judgmental and impatient with some semi-bearable people. Granted, I'd had a few hollow friendships and had been amicable to most, but my close friends from Ward had been the fellow Belmontians that I had known long before my mom dropped me off for that first September day in 1993.

I responded as curtly as possible. "Yes, it has been a while, Brad."

"Too long, my friend, too long," he answered while flipping on a pair of Maui Jim sunglasses and running his hand through his feathery blonde hair. He belonged on *Baywatch*. Though he was born and raised in Weston, his mom was from California and he was one of those west coast, plastic looking guys. He even had the year-round tan.

I decided to play games. "New Rover, dude?" I said in my best surfer accent while gesturing to his $65,000 SUV.

"Nah, that there is Flower's. She's out on Nantucket for the regatta. My Rover's at the shop. I'm having a new subwoofer installed. Little sis' was fine enough to lend me her wheels for the week."

Apparently, they had a Land Rover tree at their estate in Weston. I chuckled to myself as I imagined a huge tree in the Atkinson's yard ripe with Land Rovers of different colors. The estate was ridiculous, something out of *Cribs*. I had been there a handful of times for mandatory soccer team dinners. But I can't say which parent was more responsible for the Atkinson fortune. Mrs. Atkinson was heir to an expansive vineyard in Napa Valley, and Mr. Atkinson's family had founded one of the nation's oldest commercial real estate companies.

"What brings you to Ward?" Brad asked, bringing me back to reality.

"Just dropping off my brother. He's doing some sprints," I said, nodding out towards Bobby.

"He's some athlete, dude," he boasted, turning to watch Bobby finish off a sprint. "Quite the quarterback. I was at the championship game last year. Man, he made some monster throws. What an arm. And he's a damn talented hockey player too…got a bright future ahead of him. He's going to make us all proud; a real Ward legend."

"*We* are real proud of him," I said, suggesting Bobby was part of my family, not the proverbial Ward family.

That always bugged me. The way pretentious Ward pricks tried to take credit and responsibility for any and all successes. It was always "Ward this" and "Ward that," or the stupid "Ward community" and the "Ward Family," always "young men epitomizing the standards, values, and excellence of Ward" and its God forsaken code. Bobby wasn't a fucking asset. He was my brother. I could feel the back of my neck getting warm as I clenched my fists. I bit down on my lip. I wanted to get out of the car and beat the fucker's smug face into the gravel. Maybe I'd piss all over the Land Rover for good measure.

"So, what brings *you* here?" I quipped, doing my best to hide my rage.

"Oh, just a little workout with some future stars," he said. "I'm working with coach, assisting him with the summer camps. Worthington and I have been helping out every year since graduation, actually. Our names are still like gold to these wannabes when it comes to Ward soccer."

Ben Worthington was Brad's best friend and another white-headed zit. To their credit, they had been very good soccer players, leading us to the league title both junior and senior year. I had been a role player or a "sparkplug," as coach put it. I basically ran around like a hockey player in cleats, dive tackling, kicking, elbowing, and talking trash. I hated soccer, but I was just too small for football. I did relish the feeling that I was tougher than most of the kids on the field. That wasn't the case on the ice, where real men roamed, and where I was more of a finesse guy.

"No shit. How is Ben? Is he still with his dad's firm?" I asked.

"No, Worthington's heading off to Penn for Law School next month," he replied. "The bastard scored a seventy-seven, ninety-fifth percentile, on the LSAT. It looks like he'll be eating at the adult table with his pops and the other partners someday."

What a shocker.

"Come to think of it, we're having a big going away bash for him tomorrow night. His pops rented out the first floor of Sky Bar downtown. It should be a major gathering. You should come, dude. It's going to be open bar, and the tail will be All-Pro."

I may have thrown up in my mouth. I'd have rather stalked lions with a squirt gun. I stared straight ahead racking my brain for a clever response.

"Say, you're not still with that little Belmont babe with the killer rack, are you?" he continued. "What was her name?"

I blacked out for a second or two as his words set in. I felt my body twitching and the blood boiling within. I took a deep breath. My eyes burned a hole in his face. "Carmen. Her name is Carmen and, yes, I am still with her," I snapped.

"Sorry, dude. I had no idea. I ah, didn't realize you were still in love with your prom date. She's a fox," he murmured, sensing my agitation.

I'd had enough. "Listen, Brad, I need to get home and shower. I am meeting some friends for dinner," I said.

"Alright, dude. It was great seeing you. Hope you'll come tomorrow night. Don't be a stranger."

"Goodbye, Bradford," I managed. I let out my frustration with a savage scream as I swerved back onto Fuller Street and headed for home. I screamed so loud that the d-bag definitely heard me. I pictured his puzzled face looking back over his shoulder at my Toyota as my Tarzan yell rang out. My dad was wrong. These people were putrid human beings. Maybe they meant well—like Brad's backhanded compliment towards Carmen. Regardless, they were ignorant and condescending by nature, and to me, they might as well die, twice.

5

A hot shower and two cans of beer easily pacified me. I was ready for a night on a forgotten, yet familiar stage, which meant it was time to check in on Jay. The Nativity scene in his front yard was surreal, especially in July. But Mrs. Cantwell's devotion to Christ knew no boundaries; followed no calendar. I couldn't help but crack a smile. I let myself in the front door because you don't knock at your best friend's house. Something smelled good in the kitchen, and as I made my way towards it, Mrs. Cantwell's voice stopped me in my tracks.

"Hey, Roy, we're in here."

Like all moms, she had a ridiculous ability to identify unseen people with the most minimal information to go on. I wondered if the way that I had opened the door or maybe the way that I walked had given me away. Maybe she'd seen my car pull up. I turned to see if it was visible through the blinds. It wasn't, so I gave up, continuing towards the kitchen. Before I could mutter a word, Mrs. Cantwell was on me. Not only did she have ESP, but apparently, she also possessed the agility of Reggie Bush, because she managed to stuff a big fat brownie into my mouth while simultaneously enveloping me in a bear hug. I awkwardly hugged back and caught a glimpse of Jay seated at the kitchen table. Our eyes met and his rolled.

"Wow, tasty brownie. How's everything, Mrs. Cantwell?" I asked through a mouthful of moist chocolate.

"Thanks, Roy. Things are good. I'm making these for the priests. Father Flaherty loves my sweets," she boasted.

Militant Catholic would best describe Mrs. Cantwell and by extension, the Cantwell family because Mr. Cantwell and the three kids followed her lead. Her faith was enormous, surpassed only by her generosity. Jay was the oldest, so he had to set a stellar example for the rest of the gang. Going to church every single day for twenty-five years was demanding enough. In addition to the church streak, the constant pressure to volunteer for retreats, teach CCD classes and usher masses took its toll. Jay handled it all in stride because he loved his mom, and he was a good kid. Good kid, not good Catholic.

"Your friend and I were just talking about his job options. I think he should stick with teaching. It's his calling and the kids love him," Mrs. Cantwell reasoned as she shoveled brownies into a plastic container.

"I couldn't agree more. I think it's too early to bail," I replied hesitantly.

"See. Listen to Roy. If you won't listen to me, then listen to him," she said, turning to face Jay as she gestured to me with her black spatula. She held her stare for what seemed like ten minutes. I stood frozen as she packed up the remaining brownies, hung up her apron and then went over to kiss Jay goodbye. Jay didn't even flinch, all the while staring at me as if I had just announced my allegiance to the New York Yankees.

"I love you, Jay. We'll talk later," she added before planting a kiss on my cheek and heading out.

"Good talk," I said sarcastically.

"Not another fucking word. Are you nuts feeding her that ammunition?" Jay shook his head repeatedly and slammed his right hand on the table. He was visibly pissed.

"Oh, don't be such a pussy. She's right, and I'm right too. You give up on shit so easily. Besides, you are so good with kids. You really are, Jay. Give it another year."

"I don't like it. I'm done with teaching. D-U-N…Done."

The news disheartened me because Jay *was* a great teacher. His carefree demeanor might not have played well in the real world, but it was perfectly suited for the classroom. I had visited his second grade classroom in Belmont a few times, marveling at the way he worked with the students, coaching them through reading exercises and geography lessons. I also heard stories second-hand like the one my mom relayed from her friend, whose daughter Emma was in his class. Apparently, Emma was a dismal speller and had become timid when called upon. To ease her suffering, Jay brought in some of his old papers from when he was in elementary school, sharing them with the entire class. He had been a poor speller too, as evidenced by the red marks all over the old worksheets. It was a clever way to humanize mistakes, showing that everyone makes them—even the teacher.

"What are you going to do then? You can't work at Harrington's your whole life," I countered, referring to his summer job at the local sporting goods store. Harrington's was another place where I had seen his knack for making kids smile. His students were regular customers, and it amazed me the way he connected with them and other young customers. He put himself in their world, adeptly using their expressions, capturing their humor and discussing their relevant interests. It was certainly a foreign language to me, and oftentimes to the parents as well.

I looked at my friend. He had stood up and poured himself some water from the sink. He just stood there gulping it, intentionally not making eye contact with me. I stared at his narrow face. It was scruffy as usual. He'd started shaving in the seventh grade. His face was pale, except for his sharp nose, which was always rosy red. I let my eyes stop at his. It never worked. He wouldn't look people in the eye when he was ashamed, contrite, embarrassed, pissed or feeling any emotion. His slender frame seemed to wilt against the counter. Gradually though, the water rejuvenated his angular body, his slender face. He perked up, dropping the plastic blue cup in the sink. "Let's go," he said.

The only sounds during the short ride to Boyle's Pub were the voices of Joe Castiglione and Jerry Trupiano announcing the top of the fourth inning as the Minnesota Twins batted against Tim Wakefield. But I couldn't follow the game because guilt kept tapping me on the shoulder, and I was trying to think of something to say to poor Jay. I did think he should stick with teaching. He had only been at it for one year and had invested a lot of time and energy taking the required classes and state exams. More importantly, he was notorious for giving up. He had quit the college soccer team on the third day of tryouts during his freshman year at Merrimack College. Then he had quit Merrimack altogether and transferred to St. Anselm College. St. Anselm was a short stay too because he soon moved on to Boston College, as a commuter no less. God knows how many times he switched his major before settling into the teaching program at BC. He even bailed on the apartment in Allston after living with us for three short weeks, moving back to his old room in his parents' house on Spring Street.

Sometimes, I was confrontational or aggressive, telling him he was a pussy, and that he needed to sample life outside his little bubble. I also tried the hands-off technique, staying hush and hoping he'd figure it out. He bitched and moaned continuously about the lameness of never truly experiencing college life and the imprisonment of living with his parents, but in reality he preferred the sheltered existence. I wondered why I felt an obligation to get involved. He never really sought my advice on such matters, and he was one stubborn prick regardless. Who was I to call him out on character flaws? He would never have done that to me. My other friends were quick to tell me that I was too judgmental, too surly and too opinionated. I was known for being obnoxious, arrogant and a flat out jerk after a few drinks. Jay always apologized for me but never once criticized me for my behavior. I started to think that maybe I was the pussy, and the one too weak to just be a good friend. Like Jay.

Sometimes with our closest friends it's difficult to articulate why we hold them so dear. *Just because.* That's the way it was with Jay. Most people saw the exterior flaws of his personality. I did too. But in a way, his faults—like apathy and diffidence—were endearing. I felt for him. And his self-depreciating awareness of such failings was both rare and admirable. His unwavering allegiance to me was important too, though it went beyond situations related to my belligerence.

When we were in the seventh grade, we were immature like most, but particularly insensitive. Especially me. Enter Carrie Panagopoulos. It was a time when bodies were changing, and Carrie was ahead of the curve. No pun intended. She was a woman sooner than most, which got the boys' attention. Our friend, Mark Luna, had beat out some strong competition to be her boyfriend, but Carrie dumped him after just a few weeks. She made her reasoning known—he was too short.

Unfortunately, for her, Luna had shared every detail of their hook-ups, and we soon learned that her breasts were a bit hairy. This was critical information for twelve-year-olds and led to her nickname, "Hairy Carrie." Kids can be mean and we were. Luna took the dumping in stride, but Jay and I didn't let her off so easily. One day during art class, we took some markers and snuck into the girls' bathroom. Seeing messages on the back of stall doors was commonplace, and I still laugh at some of the grotesque things I read over the years. But we went overboard, drawing inappropriate pictures of her chest and scrawling her nickname all over the sinks and walls. Within a few days, we were in big trouble because Mrs. Sewell had seen Jay leaving the bathroom and put it all together once word of the vandalism got out. Somehow, she had missed me. As expected, Jay came clean and admitted his wrongdoing. He took the heat—all of it. I was too cowardly to come forward, and watched as they suspended my friend for two days and gave him twenty days of detention. And regretfully, I was okay with that. In actuality, I had been the primary perpetrator, with Jay innocently watching most of the proceedings. I thanked him incessantly for taking the fall and congratulated him on his loyalty. I was a real jerk.

Mercifully, Trupiano interrupted my philosophical trek. "There's a drive. Way back, way back…homerun, Corey Koskie," he announced.

"Fucking Wake," Jay snapped.

We were still lamenting Wakefield's inconsistency as we walked into Boyle's and settled up to the bar. The bartender, Darren, instinctively brought us a Bud Light pitcher. "Can I get you guys something to eat?"

"We'll take a pepperoni pie," I answered without gathering Jay's input.

Just then, we heard a collective gasp from the people around us. Wakefield had given up another bomb, this time to Jacque Jones. "He sure gives up a lot of jacks," Darren remarked while wiping up some bud light that had spilled from the pitcher.

"We should send him to the pen," Jay added before swallowing a huge sip.

I stirred. "Nah, he's fine. He has games like this. That's just Wake. He'll win you twelve to fifteen games, eat up two hundred innings and he doesn't get hurt. That's a commodity." I loved talking baseball, and I was always right. Jay and Darren both knew I thought so and let the defense of Wakefield pass.

"So; what's up for tonight, guys?" Darren asked, looking to change the subject.

"You're looking at it," Jay remarked, refilling his own cup. Jay could hammer beers.

Though expected, I was somewhat disappointed to hear Jay confirm his intentions to stay put. Boyle's wasn't really my idea of a night out. I peered to my right at the characters seated along the dark wooden bar. A few seats down, Doc Copeland was feebly attempting to hold his hand still enough to light up what was probably his thirty-sixth Marlboro Light of the night. A half-full tumbler of whiskey sat in front of him. Ironically, Doc wasn't a doctor at all, never had been either. I didn't recognize the two women seated just beyond him. One was a behemoth with half a dozen chins, who I had pegged as a waitress from Denny's or Country Buffet. She had a plastic red basket of chewed chicken bones in front of her and a full pint of lager. Her head arched back, and she let out a coarse laugh as her small friend with butch blonde hair whispered something through the side of her mouth. I thought the big one might fall off her stool; her whole body was shaking and rolling as she laughed. I must have visibly cringed because the one with the crew cut shot me a sinister glance. I quickly turned my gaze forward and eyed the various Boyle's T-shirts for sale on display above rows of dusty booze bottles. I smiled, remembering the time my dad had stuffed a navy blue one in my stocking a few years back. "I own that shirt," I murmured, thinking out loud.

"Huh?" Jay asked.

"Ah, nothing…so you want to stay here all night? No interest in heading into town?"

"No, I'm set. I just want to hang here, get a good taste going. I've got some action on the Giants game later."

"Heavy?" I replied after finally finishing off my first beer.

"No, small, not too much," Jay answered in a manner just casual enough to raise my suspicions.

"Yeah, right," I said. "I can't believe you're still betting on baseball games. West coast games no less."

"It's no different than football. One team wins and one team loses," he said.

"You're right, Jay. Except in football, there's no starting pitcher to fuck up your due diligence. The starting pitcher's influence is over weighted and nothing is more unpredictable than starting pitching. It's inevitable that even studs like Pedro will shit the bed sooner or later.

How do you know he wasn't drinking tequila shots until 4:00 a.m. the night before? Maybe he had bad Chinese and spent the morning on the toilet. Maybe he has a blister. Maybe he's pissed Ross and Rachel broke up. Too many factors can influence one man's ability to throw a baseball, and in turn, the outcome. Fuck that. You know what that is...that's roulette, my friend, fucking roulette."

"Fair enough. And by the way, it's *Russian* roulette."

Roulette, Russian roulette—it was all the same. I had no problem with him gambling. I was an avid better during the football season and had made my fair share of trips to battle the Indians at Foxwoods. But gambling on baseball, that was a red flag. I'm not sure what annoyed me more; Jay's naivety or the realization that we wouldn't be venturing beyond the cozy confines of Belmont.

Resigned to spending the night with the Sasquatch to our right and cheering on Russ Ortiz and the San Francisco Giants, I asked Darren for two shots of Jameson. The shot went down like Windex, but I made sure not to show it, relaxing my facial muscles, breathing deeply. "Good stuff," I managed through gritted teeth.

"Want another one on the house?" Darren asked, only after he had already refilled our glasses and slid one onto the bar for himself. I nodded like a big tough guy. "To Jay and Lauren," Darren announced boisterously.

"To Jay and Lauren," I followed.

Jay didn't say anything; instead, he smiled for what may have been the first time all day and swallowed his second helping of window cleaner, the whole time staring at Darren's chin. The second one went down easier.

"So, how *are* things with Lauren, anyway?" Darren asked. I couldn't tell if he was being genuine. I tried to study his eyes, but he didn't look up, instead he busied himself clearing the glasses and wiping the dribbles of Jameson from the bar with a dirty white cloth. I swallowed hard.

"Great," Jay answered, watching Darren's right hand wipe the bar. I braced myself for a heated conversation because Jay had more or less stolen Lauren from Darren's younger brother Matt.

I played out the forthcoming scenario in my mind. I would come to Jay's rescue, launching myself over the bar, reigning blows on Darren. The chef, Tony, would scramble from the kitchen in his grease-stained apron, hoping to drag me off his shit-beaten co-worker. I pictured poor Doc Copeland corralling his gobbler to keep it from spilling. The Adler brothers, friends of Darren's playing darts behind us, would join the melee. One would grapple with Jay while the other battled with me. I would be the big hero, sticking up for my boy Jay. He'd be so proud of me and know that despite my harsh words, I had his back at all costs.

Darren straightened up. "That's good. Glad to hear it." It was his body language more than the pitch in his voice that evoked sincerity. He was relaxed and calm. Apparently, he didn't care that Jay was with Lauren. "Listen, I like you, Jay," he continued. "We've known each other a long time. I don't give a shit what Matt thinks. I'm my own man. Besides, the kid is eighteen years old, and I seriously doubt Lauren was his last girlfriend."

I had underestimated Darren and failed to consider that he was a married, thirty-one-year-old father of two with bigger concerns in his life. That doesn't mean I didn't think it a bit ridiculous for Jay to be dating someone six years younger and just entering college. It was an after-school special alright, but that was Jay. Belmont was his domain. Living there, drinking there, going to the dry cleaner there, and picking up pizza there. Paths crossed and age barriers became seamless.

Lauren was smoking hot, and being a small town, we'd known her for years. Her bond with Jay was soccer. She was a star and headed to the University of Connecticut to play in the fall. Jay's younger sister, Meghan, had been Lauren's teammate at Belmont High. With nothing better to do on Wednesday afternoons, Jay had gone to most of their games, where he noticed Lauren's chestnut hair and magical smile. She also had a tight, athletic body and an ass like a twelve-year-old boy.

The freshman fifteen wouldn't be in the cards for a girl like her. Jay didn't wait long to make his move, inviting Lauren, Meghan and a few others to play on an indoor team with him and some buddies. It was innocent enough and Jay claimed he had no ulterior motive. Probably true since it would have been normal for Jay to take his sister under his wing and help develop her game. He was that kind of person.

By February, Jay and Lauren were secretly seeing each other, her two-year relationship with her classmate, Matt, deteriorating faster than the 1978 Red Sox. Matt and Lauren had been the high school's marquee couple. He was a well-liked kid, good looking and outgoing. Though just an average football player, he had managed to haul in three interceptions in his last high school game, the big Thanksgiving Day win over archrival Watertown. No doubt, my friends knew him as the kid who took Lauren Webster's virginity.

That spring, people caught on to Jay and Lauren. It was tough at first, but after a while, people fell back on the fact that Jay was as nice a kid as anybody—a class act not solely in it for the chance to roll around naked with the town's eighteen-year-old jewel. I trusted him. I knew he'd do right by her, and lately I sensed that he was really falling for her, thinking about making it work when she left for school. I joked that it would be the perfect excuse for us to hang out on a college campus. I wouldn't have hesitated to bust out the long-sleeve T-shirt, fleece vest and backwards hat if invited to a frat party.

I watched as Darren emptied Doc Copeland's ashtray. "That was decent of him to say," I said.

"It was, but I didn't think it was an issue anyway. We've been together for a while now. It's not as if I've been tiptoeing around. I still feel bad though. Matt definitely hates me."

"Well, it's nice to know that big brother Darren doesn't want your balls in a vice. And I don't think Matt cares as much as you think. He'll come across brand new options next year at Villanova. Besides, he would have kicked your ass by now," I said while laughing, knowing Jay would too.

"Oh, absolutely, I'm not sure I'd even get a punch in," he added.

6

By the third inning of the Giants game, I was a puddle. I caught my reflection in the dingy Coors Light mirror behind the bar. My head swayed like a teetering anvil, and my bloodshot eyes danced beneath heavy lids. I took a deep breath, opened my eyes wide and tried to hold still for a second so I could look into them and catch my bearings. I failed miserably. "Jay…Jay," I called.

Jay was busy talking to two old friends that had come in an hour earlier and sat next to us. "Jay!" I yelled, tugging his T-shirt.

"Yeah, what's up?" he finally replied, turning to me. His eyes were inflamed too. His skinny face was beet red and his nose looked like he'd dipped it in vegetable oil.

"I'm out."

"What the fuck? It's only 11:00 p.m."

"I know. But I'm shit-house and frankly, I could care less if Russ Ortiz wins this game for you." I threw down forty bucks, patted Jay on the back and gestured thanks to Darren by holding up the palm of my hand.

I staggered towards the door, where the Sasquatch and her friend were now standing. I couldn't help myself. "Hey, how do I know you?" I slurred to the butch-haired one, who looked like she enjoyed chewing sheet metal.

"Don't think you do, kid," she snapped.

"Wait, I got it…you work at AutoZone in Watertown, behind the counter, right? You sold me some wipers."

"You're an asshole," the fat one said through clenched teeth.

"My bad," I choked with a grin, stumbling outside into the warm July night. I stopped and took in the air. I hated myself in these moments. Being a dick never made me feel any better, worse actually. I thought about going back to apologize but was too weak to do so. I started up the street, feeling shame and a bit sick.

"Hey!" Someone was yelling behind me. I turned to see Jay standing on the sidewalk in front of the bar door. "You're walking, right?"

"Damn straight I am!" I slurred. "I'll get the car in the morning. Go Giants!" I turned and continued to shuffle up the sidewalk, my legs becoming heavier with each step. After a few blocks, I started to feel better. I flipped open my phone to dial my brother's cell, but then hit the red "End" button and dialed the house line—a small test.

"Hello." Bobby's voice was barely audible because of the music in the background. I identified it as "Bust a Move" almost immediately.

"Bobby, are you kidding me? It sounds like Times Square on New Year's Eve. When you answer the phone, you might want to tell everyone to shut up, and turn the music down. Is this your first rodeo? What if it was Dad?"

"Relax. They're in Ireland. It's like 5:00 a.m. over there. Do you think Dad would check in at five o'clock in the morning? Besides, we have caller ID now. I knew it was you."

The calculating intelligence made me proud because that's where he usually faltered. Street smarts weren't his strength. "Good points," I surrendered. "What's the deal? It sounds loud. How many people you got?"

"Just four of us. Everything's cool."

"Four? Including Dick Clark?"

He laughed in a hoarse voice that revealed drunkenness. "No, Dick's passed out in mom and dad's room. Besides him, it's Kevin, two honeys and me. We're playing asshole."

"Of course you are. Did everybody get home okay though, no problems? Nobody puked in the hamper?"

"No, we're good. I followed the game plan. There were just ten or twelve of us, and everybody walked, except for a few girls, and they got picked up by Jen's sister."

"Okay, good work. I'm staying at Carmen's house. I'll be around in the morning if you want a rematch."

"I'll be waiting."

I started to talk some smack but realized he had hung up the phone. A minute later, I was almost to Carmen's neighborhood, a half-mile from Boyle's. I started through the Grove Street Park. As I walked, I watched my flip-flops as they moved over the torn up soccer field. I could see tiny impressions in the shoddy soil where cleats had left their mark. I was picking up my pace when I caught sight of someone or something ahead to the right. I squinted in the dark, but the distant streetlights weren't enough to aid my feeble vision. I continued towards the opposite side of the field, towards what now appeared to be two people sitting on a bench.

"Roy!"

"Huh?"

"Hey, man! It's Campo and Ellison." I heard the familiar voice of my friend Adam Campo.

Though I wasn't in tip-top shape, I knew exactly what was going on. As I approached them, the heavy, pungent smell of marijuana became stronger and stronger. "What do we have here?" I asked, settling up to them. "Smoking trees, eh?"

"Belmont's finest weed, indeed," Adam sang. "A small hit, perhaps?"

"I don't know, man. I'm already pickled. Jay and I drank Boyle's clear out of Jameson."

"Hah. How is Jay?" Adam chuckled. "Still shagging Lauren Webster? I don't know how, she's some catch…that tight little bottom," Adam said. He sucked on the small glass pipe.

"God bless him," Ellison added.

"I know. I know," I replied, shaking my head. Without a second thought, I accepted the pipe from Adam's outstretched hand and brought it to my lips. The glass was scorching, and I had to pull it away.

"Careful. The glass is hot, dude," Ellison said.

"Yeah, lick your lips first," Adam reminded me, as though I were a first-timer.

I slathered my lips with drool and stuck the small end of the pipe in my mouth. The musky, tar-ridden taste was unmistakable. I readied myself, closed my eyes slowly and sucked hard like a human vacuum cleaner. I felt like my eyes were going to pop out of my head as I struggled to hold the smoke in my compressed lungs. Finally, I exhaled with all my might, returning my body to equilibrium. I then proceeded to laugh my ass off. Handing the pipe to Ellison, I noticed Adam clapping his hands in a slow deliberate way. "That was a fucking Jurassic hit, man. Fucking lethal."

"Hell yeah," I slurred, still beaming. Then, for no reason in particular, I raised my right hand and stood at attention before starting into the National Anthem. My friends joined me and our bellowing lyrics filled the empty night. After we closed with a screaming crescendo, I thanked my buddies for the grass and gave them both long hugs and big fat stoned kisses before stumbling through the park gate and onto Carmen's street, Payson Road. I was still giddy and found myself tracing the rays of streetlights as they splashed onto the dark pavement of the long street. It was actually quite beautiful, serene. All I could hear was the flip-flop of my flops and the faint sounds of night. It was nice to be back in Belmont, expectedly nostalgic. I had made that walk down Payson Road so many times.

I thought back to when I had been eight or nine years old, walking down that very street to Neil Cunningham's, carrying my twenty-eight ounce Easton baseball bat in one hand and my Mizuno glove in the other. I remembered my red and white pinstriped Phillies uniform, filthy from a day at shortstop. The cleats, the matching red cleats. My mom had balked at first but then gave in, and I became the only kid with red Nike cleats just like Mike Schmidt and the rest of the real Phillies.

I contemplated my reaction if someone had told me then that fifteen years later I'd be walking down the same street, drunk, baked and heading to my girlfriend's house. Gross, that's what I would have thought about anything to do with girls. One thing hadn't changed though; I was still wearing a baseball jersey, a blue Vladimir Guerrero Expos shirt—always a kid at heart, always.

Then something peculiar caught me eye. About two blocks before Carmen's house, on the opposite side of the street, I saw a shiny black Ford Mustang. I thought it a figment of my imagination, the weed playing tricks. It was not. And as I walked up to the car, I confirmed my suspicion. The Belmont Marauder Football sticker on the back windshield was the clincher. It was Matt's car.

7

I stood there dumbfounded, trying to process the information before me. Why was Matt's car in front of Lauren's house? By all accounts, they were still friendly, but if something were going on, neither of them would be stupid enough to attempt a maneuver this audacious. Lauren had to know that Jay might come by at any point in the night. Hell, they knew Carmen was right down the street, living at home for the summer, having just graduated from American University in May. If she wouldn't notice Matt's car, I certainly would, and they had to know that I might be staying over. I checked my watch. It was 11:26 p.m.

Surely, Jay had told Lauren that I was in town house sitting, and that we'd be going out. But when was the last time Jay or I had been home from a night out at 11:26 p.m.? The last place she'd expect one of us to be at 11:26 p.m. was on a stroll down Payson Road. Still, it seemed brazen. There was only one thing to do.

The house was a big white colonial with black shutters, and I realized the majesty of it as I scanned the front facade for lights.

Everything was dark. There were no cars in the driveway either, but that wasn't unusual, because Lauren's dad had split for Rhode Island years ago, and her mom often worked night shifts as a nurse at Brigham and Women's Hospital.

I started to think positively, deciding Matt had merely left his car there en route to some high school party. He had driven over with some classmates because Lauren's place, with her mom always at work, was the perfect staging area for warm-up drinking. They had since moved on and were drinking Mad Dog and Busch Light in a basement somewhere. He had left his car—predictably, since only a fool would park in front of the party house.

Just when I thought I had calmed my fears, I caught a faint flicker of light from the den to my left. I looked both ways on Payson; saw nothing but a runway of black pavement. Hesitation kills on the battlefield, so quickly I hurried across the small yard towards the bushes in front of the house. I crept even closer to the den before stopping to gather my breath and listen for voices.

The TV. Its alternating images had created the flickering light. I took another deep breath. My heart was in my throat. A few steps more and my flops hit the mulch directly under the den window. I tried to picture the layout of Lauren's den. I'd been in there before, just once or twice. I knew that I might only be able to risk one look. I wasn't down with people branding me the peeping tom of Belmont. I just wanted answers, perhaps revealed by an empty room, a few kids hanging out, Lauren and Matt cuddling, or maybe Matt on top of Lauren, fucking my best friend's girl. More heart slid into my throat.

Then I heard a familiar hum growing louder, then louder—a car engine. I ducked as the dark shape sped past the house. Fuck this. I had to get to the back window. I felt like a Navy SEAL as I quietly slid around the house, hugging the foundation until I found myself in the backyard, directly below the window. This was it. I started to ease my head up and noticed the window above was open—just a screen. I strained my ears. It sounded like Dave Letterman. His voice was faint, but he was talking bullshit about dog tricks. Then I heard a more constant and sustained noise, a murmuring of heavy breathing like someone hyperventilating. I closed my eyes and held them closed to elicit a clear thought, finally lifting my head slowly to the windowsill. Luckily, there was a Hibiscus plant just inside the screen, which shielded my presence but not my view.

There was Lauren. She was naked on the couch directly across from me, facing me. She was laying back, her torso propped up against the back of the couch. Her head was tilted back and moving ever so slowly in a fit of ecstasy. Her mouth was wide open and letting out agonizing, disjointed breaths of joy. Her arms were outstretched limply, and her body was writhing, her legs clumsily hanging off the couch. And there was young Matt Daniels, going to town, his face...down there.

I ducked. I had wood harder than an eighth grader slow dancing to "Stairway to Heaven." I shook my head in disbelief, thought about Jay, poor Jay. Then the rage set in. I clenched some mulch in my hands. Think. Breathe.

I started to rise up again, peeking over the sill. Matt was still working her over and quite well it appeared. Lauren's body began writhing more fiercely, her hips jolting in quick spasms. An orgasm loomed. But I'd seen enough. I rapped on the screen three times with surprising force: TING! TING! TING! The noise rang out across Middlesex County.

I turned and sprung into a low-bodied sprint, still playing the role of SEAL. I jumped some bushes and then clumsily hurdled over a picket fence and into the next yard. I came down excruciatingly awkward on my left ankle. Stupid flip-flops. I tore through some more bushes, prickly fuckers, and kept hobbling through a yard and onto Lewis Road. Thirty seconds later, I was back on Payson and collapsing into Carmen's back door.

8

A sudden jerk and we were moving. Higher and higher, we made our ascent. I could feel the breeze, stronger now. It ran through my hair and rocked our car slightly. Empty popcorn boxes, wax paper and pink tickets dotted the abandoned park below. I watched one popcorn box roll over itself in the breeze, then stop. Then roll again.

Without a word, Carmen grabbed my hand and squeezed, gesturing with her eyes out towards the horizon. I followed her eyes across an expansive oasis of green grass. Then I saw it, far off in the distance. One team wore blue jerseys, the other white. The white-shirted players stood in two rows, waiting with hands on hips while the blue team huddled in a circle; facing their leader, whose head moved as he barked out orders. Then, simultaneously, they each clapped their hands and began moving towards the white team. The blue team's quarterback, trailing a step behind, surveyed the white team's alignment as they spread out on the field. I recognized his stride as he confidently moved to join his teammates at the line. Then I saw the white number fifteen on his jersey. Bobby.

"Hey, it's Bobby!" I shouted, pointing with my free hand towards the football game. Carmen turned to me, the wind pushing a wisp of her honey-brown hair across her eyes.

"I know!" she said, squeezing my right hand tighter.

"Jay, do you see him?" I pointed across Carmen's body. He looked, but it was too late. The Ferris wheel had started to descend again, the playing field disappearing behind a cluster of towering pines. I stood in anticipation as we soon swung upward again, rising with the majestic pines. We came to the crest and our car stopped. "There!" I screamed, pointing again. Across from me, Jay stood to take in the scene.

"There he goes! There goes Bobby!" he wailed. Bobby had the ball, he was running to his right, hurdling tacklers, plowing through a particularly big one, number fifty-three. He stumbled a bit, broke free and began to pick up speed as he sped down the far sideline. Two defenders chased him, one angling to cut him off at the small orange pylon. Bobby put out his left hand to fend off the boy. He had twenty yards to go, then fifteen. But another lurch and we started to move again, diving back towards the desolate ground below. Bobby was gone again, hidden by the wall of pines.

I heard the crowd roar and a faint whistle blow in the distance. We came to a halt again, this time in the midst of the wheel's rusty red platform. Doc Copeland emerged in an oil-stained blue custodian uniform. I noticed a dirty white patch over his heart with the name "Doc" stitched in cursive red lettering. He nodded politely and opened the door to our car.

"Everybody out," he said in a scratchy smoker's voice. Carmen and Jay stepped from the car.

I looked skyward. Empty, the other red cars dangled above. They let out a collective squeak as they shifted in the wind. "Wait, I want to go again," I pleaded, but Doc didn't acknowledge me. He began to descend the platform's red metal stairs. "I want to go again, damn it!"

Carmen moved in front of me, grabbing both my hands at my side. She shook her head slowly, capturing my attention with her soft green eyes. "It's okay, Roy," she said, kissing me lightly on the lips. "They won."

"Ask the boss," Doc managed finally, his voice trailing off as he meandered through the trash-filled grounds.

"In there," Jay said excitedly. "It's your dad."

I turned to face the Ferris wheel and saw a small wooden booth attached to the platform. Inside was my dad, he too in a blue custodian uniform. He nodded, and the big wheel let out a scraping belch as it shifted into motion. I scrambled towards our car as it began to move along the platform and made it inside just as it started up. I looked back to where Carmen and Jay had been standing. They were gone. I looked in the red car below me and in the one below it. Both were empty. I wheeled towards the field. Empty also. The players were gone, the fans too. The lights were out on the square black scoreboard, and the hulking metal bleachers stood deserted. The car swept beneath the wheel and towards the wooden enclosure. There was a piece of red plywood fastened over the window where we had seen my dad. I swung up again. Then down. Then up. Then down. With each pass above the pines, the sun made a steady and silent exit. Finally, there was a fantastic red explosion, and it was gone.

Up then down. Up then down. Fifty times, one hundred times.

Then came a sudden halt, and I crashed to the floor, my legs tangling beneath me. I sprung up, saw that I was alongside the platform. I looked to the booth and saw Bobby. He still had on his football uniform. He walked towards me, his metal cleats clanging on the red metal floor of the platform. He reached out and opened the red door to my car.

"Let's go," he said.

I stepped from the car and wrapped my arms around him, but the bulk of his shoulder pads kept my arms from a full embrace. He patted my back with his right hand as I held onto him. The muscles in my face flexed. I fought it, my mouth quivering, but my eyes won. A few tears trickled down my cheeks. I took a collapsing breath and then stepped back, the tears drying up and retreating deep inside me. Bobby looked down at me with a knowing look. He smiled and let out an effortless laugh. We turned and together made our way down the platform's steps.

"Hey, did you score?" I asked, stepping onto the ground below.

"Of course I did."

9

I opened my eyes but bright light penetrated them, burning them closed again. More slowly, I opened them the second time. The ceiling fan in Carmen's room hummed around in a fast circle. I thought for a moment, trying to find meaning in my dream. But I didn't like where the analysis led, so I sighed and struggled out of bed. My feet hit the floor and standing up, the pain came: a souvenir from the previous night's journey. I lumbered to the bathroom, each step announcing a stinging pain in my left ankle. I located my red toothbrush and began scrubbing away my sins. I swung open the medicine cabinet and proceeded to gobble four Advil. Stepping back into the hallway, I checked the door at the end of the hall. It was open, meaning Mrs. Hill was already awake and likely gone for the day. My current attire of light blue boxers would suffice.

Mrs. Hill worked at a local toy store every Saturday. She could have taken on a more challenging job, but it wasn't her style. She was a bit of a free spirit and content with the stress-free gig. And though she and Mr. Hill had recently divorced, his successful vending machine business ensured her financial stability. In addition, he was a generous and decent man forever concerned that she and the kids had what they needed. Carmen and her mom lived just the two of them, in the spacious four-bedroom home. Carmen's older sister, Amanda, had moved downtown with her boyfriend, and her younger brother, Patrick, was out in Colorado, where he had landed a summer internship following his freshman year at Colorado State.

It was a good thing, Carmen and her mom alone together in the house on Payson Road. Carmen, ever ambitious, was already preparing to attend the graduate nursing program at Boston College in the fall. The considerable graduate school tuition and accompanying expenses made living at home inevitable. Mrs. Hill was happy to have her. It was great for me too—true carte blanche. Though my visits were infrequent, preferring that Carmen stay with me in Allston, I was armed with my own key, coming and going as I pleased. This came in handy when hobbling through neighborhood bushes at 12:10 a.m. The grand arrangement also enabled me to sleep in my girlfriend's bed with her mom down the hall. No small feat. My gratitude was legitimate, so I did my best to play man-of-the-house whenever I was around by mowing the lawn, removing storm windows, changing light bulbs and doing other jobs that required a ladder. On occasion, it provided a nice escape from my apartment in Allston.

Carmen was already showered and in the kitchen when I made my way to the fridge for a tall glass of orange juice. She gave me a big warm hug. I squeezed her tight, the top of her head coming to rest against my mouth. A few stray hairs tickled my lips. Her hair smelled fantastic, like fresh ginger. She pulled away and let her body suspend back into my arms. She looked up at me, her green eyes speaking a thousand words.

"You made quite a racket last night when you came in," she said finally. "I thought maybe you rode in on Babar."

I laughed. "Sorry."

She broke from my arms to grab a bagel that had popped up in the toaster. I watched her spread cream cheese on one half and then the other. She looked so alive. Maybe it was because my own body was still cheating death. I stalked the bagel as she prepared it. Turning to me, she tilted her head to one side and gave me the look a mother gives her child when propositioned for an ice cream.

"What?" I said, shrugging through guilt.

"So, how was the night? It sure sounded good," she said. "Let me guess, Boyle's, some pizza and some darts?"

"No darts," I said, taking another healthy sip of orange juice.

"Wow, such deviance," she added playfully. "I bet Jay was happy as a clam though."

"Yeah, he wasn't touching downtown. Wouldn't sniff it," I sighed, finishing my juice.

She put the bagel halves on a small yellow plate and started towards me, locking eyes with me as she walked. I watched her eyes. They really were captivating, so green. The darkness of her wet hair made them illuminate more. She was smiling now, her full, shapely lips wrapping around perfect white teeth. A subtle brown beauty mark above the left side of her lip seemed to hold a sexy secret—a little mischief perhaps. "One for me and one for you," she said, setting the plate down on the counter.

I gave her a loving kiss on the cheek. She snuggled up against me again, and I felt the warmth of her body against mine. I threw my right arm around her waist, pulling her in. Her body was muscular and curvaceous. I held her briefly, but her body told me she was ready to sit down and eat her bagel. I settled in at the table and opened the sports section. I scanned the box scores on page four, finding what I was looking for:

CUBS 6

GIANTS 4

Insult to injury. I looked up at Carmen, who was reading the movie section. I took a deep breath. "Carmen."

"Uh huh," she offered without looking up.

I waited, and the silence told her it was important. "Something happened last night," I said evenly.

She looked up with cold anticipation. I took another deep breath and fumbled thoughts through my head. I wasn't sure how to launch into a tale in which I watched another girl practically climax from the bushes outside her house.

"When I was walking home from Boyle's, I saw Matt's car at Lauren's."

"What? Why was—"

"Let me finish," I said. "So I see his car. I check the house and all the lights are off. No cars are in the driveway. But I notice the TV is on in the den. So…"

"So…" she blurted, hanging on every word.

"So…I decided to investigate. I went around the back and—"

"No you didn't. Tell me you didn't, Roy?"

"Carmen, I had to find out."

"Clearly you did," she said with a hint of disgust.

"Well, I snuck a quick peek in the den." The eagerness faded from Carmen's face, replaced by flat, yet titanic skepticism as if I had offered to see a musical. I continued, "I didn't really watch. Honest. Well, maybe a little, but anyway, Lauren and Matt were in there and they weren't playing Chutes and Ladders. He was going down on her like a champion."

"You watched!" she gasped.

"No, no. Well, yes, but just long enough to confirm she was fucking around. Look, the bottom line here is Jay. What do I do?"

"You don't do anything. You don't get involved," she said, as if it were obvious.

"You're kidding me, right? This is my best friend. His girlfriend, who he happens to care about quite a bit, is sleeping around behind his back—"

"I just wouldn't get involved. They'll work it out. She's a good person. She'll be straight with him. Besides, how the hell is he supposed to bring it up? Tell her you were in the bushes watching her and Matt?"

"Good point," I agreed. "I don't know. I just feel like I need to say *something*."

"Let it go, Roy," Carmen said, grabbing my right hand with hers. "Trust me. Let it go."

She stared at me convincingly. She was right. It wasn't going to be an easy transition from me to Jay, let alone from Jay to Lauren. "Okay, I think you're right. I'll give it some time," I said, feeling better.

Carmen smiled.

10

That Saturday was a scorcher, one of those unbearable New England days where the air feels thicker than pea soup. Pulling up to my parents' house, I heard the roar of a lawnmower, but it was louder than normal, like a mower on crack. I hurried to the backyard to make sure Bobby wasn't seconds away from a catastrophic explosion. I found him cutting a stripe down the center of the lawn, shirt off and sweat pouring from him like rain. He gave me an upbeat nod, then took his right hand off the mower handle and jokingly flexed like a beach hero—sun's out, guns out. He had on a pair of ball-hugging mesh shorts and no shoes. I gave him the universal throat slashing sign and gestured towards the mower. He stopped his stroll and cut the engine.

"What's up?" he demanded.

I was baffled as the roaring continued. It sounded like pit row in Loudon, NH. Then I realized it was a symphony of mowers coming from nearby yards. "Nothing, I thought you were going to blow up. I didn't get the memo announcing that today was National Grass Cutting Day."

"Yeah, I'm going to the Toro Convention later," Bobby added, not missing a beat.

"You're sweating like Greg Norman with a lead on the back nine."

Bobby shrugged. "It's the price I pay to deliver such fine work," he said proudly, motioning to the yard around him. "Best yard cutter in the house. My edge work is legendary."

"Please, I'm a magician with that thing."

"Fine, you want to finish up?"

"No, I'm good. But make sure you cut it nice and short so those bleeders you hit make it to the outfield," I barked, walking away.

I was still groggy and fearful of Bobby's imminent Wiffle Ball proposition, so I decided to take a walk. As I made my way down the hill of my parents' street, Brookside Avenue, I found myself anticipating the contour of the sidewalk. I knew every inch of it. But I was especially familiar with the bumps caused by bloated tree roots. I stopped in front of a particularly large one. It was the biggest "jump" on the block.

My childhood friend, Jimmy Wynne, and I had spent hours popping wheelies off the various undulations. I would speed up for most of them, but not that one. Rather, I would practically bring my Huffy bike to a stop before timidly bouncing over it. Not Jimmy though. He was crazier than I was and pretty much hit every jump like it was his last. I know because I would follow his lead, trailing behind as we made our way around the block. That way he couldn't see me hit the brakes and shy away like Tony Eason.

I continued on Brookside as it wound across Mayfield Road, making note of a few changes, like the new addition to Mary Dolan's house, the stumpy remains of the gigantic maple tree at the corner of Vernon Street, and the absence of Chief, the Reed family's English Shepherd.

***

The Reeds had moved to the neighborhood from rural Pennsylvania when I was very young. To say they were odd would be a colossal understatement. See rural Pennsylvania. The kids, Charles and Emily, were always painting on easels in their driveway and building shit with old tires and fallen tree branches. They wore bland clothes to match their personalities, and marched to the beat of a different bongo player. We gave them hell, especially Jimmy.

Chief was a shepherd dog and had been trained to herd animals. Big ones, I presumed. But he had struggled adjusting to life off the farm, as evidenced by him chasing anyone and anything that came by the house at a pace faster than a crawl. He chased cars, joggers, other dogs and always kids on bikes. Of course, the Reeds left him to roam without a leash, and nothing was scarier than Chief running out of their yard, barking like a rabies-infected beast.

One day, Jimmy led me past the Reed house, and Chief followed with an especially memorable Cujo imitation. I pedaled frantically and made it through the danger zone, but then something inside me went off. I started back towards the house where Charles had corralled Chief. And I lost it, saying something about Amish people and sex with pets. It didn't matter that the Reeds weren't Amish.

Jimmy laughed his ass off and told me I was a badass. But my dad had a different take on the situation after Mr. Reed stopped by the house that night. I was barely ten years old, but my dad insisted I go in alone, and my marching orders were clear. I was to apologize to the whole family and invite Charles and Emily to come over to play the next day. It was infuriating and humiliating beyond description.

The house started to loom one hundred yards away as I made my way down Brookside. My eyes locked in on the target, my small legs accelerating as hollow rants of confidence spewed from my mouth. I closed the distance in seconds and at thirty yards out, my heartbeat escalated to war drum mode. I circled the neighborhood seven times that night before mustering up the courage to stop at the front walkway. Anybody watching through a window must have been wildly amused. The house had grown ten-fold and held me in a sustained trance. Every ounce of moisture left my mouth, and my stomach tightened to the size of a pea. An unidentified force in the universe carried my frail legs towards the brick steps and the big black door on which I knocked.

The inside was a colorless world of dark wood and weathered gray carpets. It smelled like my nana's apartment building, like a mothball-filled linen closet. My dad must have told Mr. Reed the plan because he instinctively called for the whole gang to greet me, saving me the further embarrassment of asking the family to convene on my behalf. As he led us through Alfred Hitchcock's living room and into the adjacent room, the color came back on. A stack of board games, including my favorite, Battleship, lay on the bottom shelf of a bookcase full of VHS movies. A decent-sized Zenith TV sat opposite a big green couch. Two Atari controllers tangled across the tan carpet gave me additional comfort. I glanced skeptically at Charles, and he smiled. But Mr. Reed's focused stare, his arms crossed stance and the deafening silence reminded me of the situation at hand.

I mumbled through my pre-rehearsed words and, sure enough, my insecurity and vulnerability gradually took over. First, a few stray drops, and then the dam gave way, and I cried my eyes out right there in the den. Charles and Emily handled it like champs, playing down the severity of my comment. Sticking to the plan, they came over the next day, and the rest played out like an episode of the *Brady Bunch.* We discovered many common interests—catching toads, drawing and making fart noises. We became fast friends. But it didn't last because by middle school I had once again deemed myself too cool for their company. Ignorance dies hard.

11

Continuing west on Brookside and past more history, I soon came to a dead end. Looking up, I felt a buzz of energy rush through me. The sun was getting hotter as it continued to climb, and the sound of mowers roared into eternity. I followed the last few feet of asphalt to where the street gave way to woods. I stepped over a low rusty chain suspended between two concrete blocks, then moved past a "No Dumping" sign and onto a thin trail of compressed dark dirt.

I followed the trail up a slight slope, under the shaded cover of giant trees. Every few paces, I heard creatures to my left and right darting for cover among the thicket of twisted bushes. The trail gradually broadened, and twenty paces later, I was on the brink of a hidden world, called "Rock Meadow." It was a place my friends and I referred to simply as "The Field." I continued out from under the canopy, and as the ground leveled off before me, the sun was back at full throttle.

The meadow spread far and wide, climbing over small hills; interrupted here and there by several clusters of thick growth. Trails cut through the emerald land like a web of tiny black streams. In the distance, one trail split a particularly large hill in half, disappearing beyond the crest. It was like a perfect black part in a messy head of green hair.

Over 225 acres large, Rock Meadow is part of a larger stretch of preservation land that includes the Habitat Sanctuary, Beaver Brook Reservation and West Meadow. The area covers more than six miles of land in Belmont, Lexington and Waltham, and it's rather remarkable that such a vast nature sanctuary exists in the midst of thickly settled communities, within a few miles of Boston. Hikers come from all over to enjoy the open meadows, new forests and vernal pools. Rock Meadow is also a crucial habitat for many struggling bird species, but my friends and I never gave a damn about the birds.

We were more interested in finding snakes, wood frogs and foxes. Jimmy and I spent many hours sitting in the brush waiting to activate feeble traps designed to catch inquisitive prey. We would prop up an old milk crate or cardboard box with a two-pronged stick, to which we tied a long piece of rope. We tried all kinds of bait, including Milky Ways and Captain Crunch cereal, but usually opted for peanuts or carrots. Studying the trap with Mr. Wynne's binoculars, hours would pass before a venturing squirrel or rabbit finally inched cautiously towards the trap. We failed 110% of the time, but still felt we could have had our own nature show on PBS. One time, we did succeed in enclosing a small and apparently moronic bunny, but it exploded out from under the box before we had even finished exchanging high fives. Another time a skunk paid us a visit, but when Jimmy jerked the rope, the smelly little thing decided the best escape route was through our hiding spot. I practically pissed myself as the stinky black and white blur sped past my feet. Soon after that, Jimmy and I resorted to catching frogs over at Beaver Brook.

Fond memories of my childhood paralyzed me as I squinted out at the most distant hill. Chills ran up my spine and detonated on the back of my neck. As a kid, I had often paused at the entrance and waited for a band of Sioux Warriors to appear on horseback upon the far-off crest. It never happened, not once, but I never stopped expecting it. It was a place ignorant of time, a window of life through which centuries collided.

I followed the trail to my right where golden grasses bloomed thigh-high. I was eager to see my field. Smack in the middle of the conservation land was a sort of playground, an acre or so of finely manicured green lawn—a real-life field of dreams. I never once had seen anyone from the Parks Department out there with a lawn mower, but somehow the playing surface rivaled that of any Major League ballpark. Though there was no base path, no pitcher's mound and no fence, there was a backstop in the corner furthest from the trail and an old swing set a few feet from the trail just beyond left field. Excitedly, I hurried my pace and just as the steel frame of the swing set appeared, I stopped in my tracks. The baseball field of my youth was gone. I stared disbelievingly at a field overrun by wild grasses and an expanding virus of bushes. The spot where my dad had stood to lob me under-handed pitches was now a planetarium for new growth. I fought the urge to rip up every shrub and trample every shred of long grass. Even the trail itself had infringed on the sacred land, carving an ugly black scar across second base and on past the backstop. The backstop had become a growing station for slithering vines and other wretched forms of vegetation. I took a hesitant step onto the outfield and fixed my pain on the backstop.

So many times, I had stood in front of it wearing my white Jim Rice replica jersey. My oversized blue batting helmet, which enveloped my tiny head, would clumsily fall over my eyes with every vicious cut. My dad always made me take my stance right up against the backstop so that I wouldn't have to turn and fetch swings and misses. It made reaching the swing set in left field a daunting task.

When I would pull a ball that short-hopped the swings and disappeared into the woods beyond, I'd yell out, "Dad, would that have been a homer? Would it have cleared the swings?"

"You bet. Gone at Grove Street and maybe even Fenway," he'd reply. "Lock those elbows in, and step towards me. No stepping in the bucket," he'd constantly remind me. After a few hours hacking like a savage, we'd scuffle home, my rubber cleats rapping a tune on the asphalt as we walked up Brookside Avenue.

I settled uncomfortably onto one of the red plastic swings. I was more than too big, which made swinging out of the question. I slumped my feet to the ground, my knees shooting up just below my chin. I sat there and took it all in. I felt for the new generation of neighborhood kids. Sure, they still had the meadow to explore and the woods to roam, but the days of fathers pitching to sons were over. I had taken Bobby there throughout his youth, mimicking my dad's lessons and taking a few rips myself.

A minute later that nostalgia was gone, evaporated into the blue sky above and replaced with a new page in an old book. Maybe it was the familiarity of my awkward position on the swing, muscle memory festering in my cramped legs, and then revealing itself in aching clarity. Regardless, I realized that I had sat like this before.

It was Christmas morning 1998, during my sophomore year in college, and a blanket of fresh December snow covered the grass then. My transition from unimpeded freedom back into the restrictive graces of my parents' home had been particularly miserable. Sneaking into bars was always issue enough, but having to contend with juvenile curfews and the nightly inquisitions only made things worse.

After the bars closed at 7:00 p.m. that Christmas Eve, Jay, Mark Luna and I made the rounds at a few family parties. Our last stop was at Beth Kennedy's, just a few blocks from my parents' house. Jay had vanished for Midnight Mass rather than face imprisonment from dear Mrs. Cantwell. But Luna and I lingered, drinking in the basement with a handful of other misfits until Mrs. Kennedy told us it was time for Santa to appear and eat the cookies. Luna was in no condition to tie shoes, let alone drive, and the idea of hailing a cab at 1:00 a.m. Christmas morning was downright humorous. We made an executive decision and Luna crashed at my place.

Christmas morning, I awoke to the sound of yelling, escalating towards the door to my basement bedroom. Soon enough, my dad appeared in full fury, hovering over me in my bed. "You want to tell me why Kathy Luna is calling my house…worried sick about her son at 6:15 a.m. Christmas morning?" he screamed.

I stared at his crisp blue eyes as my brain sputtered to life. But the onslaught had been too sudden, and I couldn't muster up a single word.

"Where the fuck is Mark Luna?" he repeated. His face was turning red, a perfect match to his fiery hair. He leaned in closer, his eyes melting my skin. My brain flickered with each shot of adrenaline and finally sprung into action.

I sat up and surveyed the bedroom floor. "He just left. He stayed over. He should be home any minute."

My dad eased his head back an inch, maybe two, keeping his eyes trained on his pitiful son. At just 5'8", he wasn't a physically imposing figure. But my father had built his legacy on intensity, aggression and madness—lots of yelling too. A celebrated authoritarian, he believed in two ways of doing things: his way or his way. And he liked to keep people at a distance in order to maintain the effectiveness of his authority. He didn't take kindly to challenges and firmly believed he was right, even when he was most certainly wrong.

"Why the hell is his mother calling my house at 6:15 a.m. on Christmas Day? Answer me that," he ordered, shouting in surround sound.

"He must not have checked in last night," I whined, realizing my friend's innocent gaffe would ruin Christmas.

"You think you can come and go as you please, live by your own rules. The fucking joy ride is over," he snapped. With that, he whirled away and stormed up the stairs.

The phone was his kryptonite. He heard it all day long in his small two-room insurance office, located in Cushing Square. As a sole proprietor with no secretary or assistant, he managed client appointments and calls by himself—too many calls. His temper was hair-trigger anyway, so inopportune phone calls often sent him over the edge. Growing up, we had prison rules regarding the phone. The duration of weeknight calls was limited to ten minutes and if I went over, I could expect my dad to either pick up another line or share my shirt as I spoke. There were exceptions, like lengthy calls to go over a writing assignment or a problem set, but the Office of the Phone Commissioner monitored those calls. In her later years of high school, my sister, Tracy, had become adept at beating the system, flawlessly transitioning from boy talk to Thoreau whenever my dad came within earshot.

The most important rule was no calls after 9:30 p.m.—ever. It happened from time to time, usually from a peripheral friend or classmate not well versed in the rules. Hearing the phone ring at those times was like hearing the bomb sirens over London. Well, not really, but it scared the shit out of my sister and me. We would race to the phone, each of us praying it was for the other person. The goal was to intercept the call, make a quick apologetic explanation of the rules, and hang up before my dad could get to a receiver. He pulled no punches and would routinely threaten, insult and verbally murder the asshole on the other end. I was never a big socialite with the phone, so my mishaps were infrequent, but Tracy established quite a rap sheet. Many times, she had personally violated the 9:30 p.m. accords, phoning late to announce her whereabouts or to explain a broken curfew. In those instances calling was actually the lesser of two evils. Showing up unannounced at 2:00 a.m. or the following morning was suicide by absentia.

I sat in my bed that Christmas morning reflecting upon the fucked up rules. Though Bobby was too young to have phone issues and Tracy and I had fled residency, the phone was apparently still a landmine—especially at sun-up on holiday mornings. I felt helpless. I couldn't be mad at Luna or his mom. They lived by the sane standards that govern cultured society. I was trying to make sense of the situation when I noticed my mom on the stairs. She crept towards my bed. "Is Mark okay?" she whispered, coming to sit at the end of my bed.

"Yes, I'm sure he is fine. He stayed over."

"Oh, good," she sighed. "Too drunk to drive I presume?"

"Yes, I thought we made a mature decision. Obviously that backfired."

She nodded knowingly. Her big brown eyes were full of warmth. She couldn't help but show concern for Mark's well being, the root of the dilemma at hand. Like my dad, she too could be demanding and even passively authoritative. I always felt that pissing her off was actually worse than upsetting my dad. Checking into her doghouse meant a serious and legitimate fuck up. Disappointment trumped fear.

Compassion radiated from her as I sat on the bed, dreading the walk upstairs. She looked so peaceful and at ease with the situation, obviously skilled at dealing with my dad's outbursts.

"He's insane," I said, shaking my head.

"Sometimes he is, but this one isn't all on him," she quipped, her empathy dissipating ever so slightly. "He wasn't out until two o'clock in the morning Christmas Eve, deaf, drunk and stupid."

She had a point. My actions had indeed sealed my fate. Overwhelming shame took hold of me. I pictured my family enjoying Christmas Eve together, eating snacks, watching movies, and admiring Bobby's youthful exuberance as he inspected odd-shaped gifts. "Was Tracy here last night?" I asked hesitantly.

My mom smiled, her dark brown hair framing her beauty. Those brown eyes glowed, and she nodded slowly, her lips terse. "Yes, she came last night, slept upstairs. It would have been nice if you were here with your family." My mom had a way with words. She smiled again, this time unsympathetically, and left me with my pal, contemplation.

I showered until the water turned cold and then made my way upstairs. The first floor was silent, and for a moment, I thought maybe the house was empty, but then I heard the clank of a coffee mug. I crept into the kitchen with apprehension and a heavy heart. I nervously scanned the room for my dad. He wasn't there. My mom was pretending to read the paper while Tracy and Bobby sat quietly, picking at Thomas' English Muffins. Tracy broke the silence with calculated cruelty. "You're such an ass," she snapped sharply.

But I wasn't going to take her shit. Not when she knew as well as anyone the nuances of my dad's irrational temper. "Are you fucking kidding me? You *are* fucking kidding."

"Watch your mouth," my mom said without looking up.

"I see how it is, Tracy. Pretend it's my fault…turn your back," I said, challenging her. Her taut face grew even tighter, and her liquid blue eyes found mine. I focused all my rage into a death stare, negotiating whether to fire a deal-closing insult. Instead, I shook my head in disgust and looked around the table. Bobby's face was the most demoralizing. He looked like he had just read a "Christmas canceled" memo. Then we all perked up, hearing my dad's ominous footsteps echoing above as he made his way towards the stairs.

"Why don't you just leave?" Tracy finally sneered.

The words stung. I looked at my mom. It probably killed her not to say anything, but she was preoccupied with saving Christmas. She stared heavily. Bobby made the pushing out a poop face, fending off the tears that soon began streaming down his cheeks. I died an invisible death, making eye contact with each of them before heading down the kitchen hall towards the front door. I could have gone out the back, but I wanted to make sure my dad got a damn good look at me leaving. We met in the front hall, and I stormed past him before slamming the door on Christmas.

I walked to my field, but in all my bravado, I had forgotten to grab a coat and spent the next two and a half hours shivering on one of the red swings. Legs cramped, I sat. And I sat.

I thought too. But the answers were elusive. My dad seemed to wake up some days with a metal thorn in his ass and a film of cough syrup on his lips. Other days, he was carefree, gregarious and kind. Still, the simplest actions and events seemed to set him off, especially with me. Behind the hostility hid a heart full of good intention and unconditional love. I wondered if his lapses could be pinned on something simple: an Irish temper.

In the December chill, I evaluated the factors and personalities at play. I considered my own polarizing personality and couldn't help but think that my antagonistic ways were not by accident. But I did not absolve myself from criticism. I had to be accountable for my actions and in this case, the selfish binge had ultimately led to the early morning phone call. My liberties clearly had consequences. It was hard to tackle such complexity. I was mad at my dad. I was mad at myself. I hated that my mom was hurting and that young Bobby had witnessed the ugliness unfold. The only solution was to get the hell back to Trinity, where I could live on my terms, without causing pain to those closest to me. Time would heal the wounds. It was the easy way out and one my family had chosen many times before.

I was content to wait out the day and perhaps the remaining few days of my break on that swing. If my legs weren't half frozen, I might have sucked it up and walked the mile and a half to Carmen's house. I closed my eyes and held them shut for a few seconds. With each compression of my chest, the frigid air filled my lungs. I opened my eyes very slowly, desperately pretending that I would miraculously find myself in Carmen's living room with a beer and a roaring fire. Instead, I caught the dull reflection of a winter sun spread thin over a field of snow. I closed my eyes again, opened them methodically. Did it again, then a third time and a fourth, but it wasn't working. Each time, the pasty landscape greeted me. A stick stole my attention. It was a thick, two-foot long twig frozen in the snow a few feet before me. The top half shot almost straight up, seeking freedom from its lower half, which was firmly entrenched in a heap of icy snow. I wondered how a branch could have come to rest in such a precarious position. Perhaps a chance gust of wind had lodged it perpendicular to the ground, a quick and unforgiving freeze then fastening its fate. I sauntered over to the branch and reached down to rescue the lower half from the clutches of a submerged misery. I gave a haphazard tug with my right hand, but it didn't budge. I pulled harder the second time while jostling the base. With surprising ease, the stick broke free from the snow. I studied the hole from which it came and noticed a few scraps of bark. I turned to chuck the thing into oblivion but was stunned to see Bobby making his way down the path. I dropped my arm and let the stick fall by my side.

"Hey, what are you doing here?" I yelled.

"I came to get you. Mom and Dad told me to find you," he shouted, his voice growing with each approaching step.

"How did you know I'd be here?"

"Where else would you be? Mom called Carmen's house, but I was right, it's too far to walk. I figured you were probably up here. I know you like it."

"Yeah, I guess I do, huh?"

He nodded with sympathetic maturity. "Hey, I got new hockey gloves and four Sega games: NHL, Madden, James Bond and Sonic III." Just like that, with naivety, innocence or astounding wit, Bobby lifted my spirits and reminded me that it was indeed Christmas.

"Wow, that's great. Maybe you'll finally beat me at NHL," I said, giving him a playful jab to the shoulder.

"You know it," he snapped, pushing me with all his might. "All your presents are still under the tree. I didn't open yours for me, but it sure felt like clothes," he said inquisitively as we started towards home.

"A nice snowflake sweater and matching scarf," I joked, knowing he'd go into orbit when he finally opened the Pedro Martinez replica jersey.

There was no "welcome home" banner waiting for me, nor a six-gun salute followed by an onslaught of hugs and kisses either. My mom greeted me with her usual warmth, embracing me and holding me close for a moment or two. Listlessly, I sat on the living room floor and opened presents, simulating gratitude when appropriate. The events of the morning had apparently never happened, a figment of my imagination. But the tension remained and it could have been sliced and packaged.

We have never been a family big on communication or showing emotion, and thus, my dad never apologized, nor did I. Rather, he let his actions hint at regret. While I opened a Foreman Grill from my sister, he rose from his La-Z-Boy and stepped towards the tree. He shuffled over to me, carrying his coffee in one hand and a medium box wrapped in shiny gold paper in the other. I stared down at his naked feet. His gray robe and the bright gold gift were visible in my periphery, but I held steady on the feet.

"Here," he said softly. "Merry Christmas."

I looked up briefly. He didn't smile, and his facial expression didn't shift in the slightest, but his eyes told a story. They were heavy with profound sadness—another muted apology. I nodded apathetically and then took the gift from his left hand, tearing off the paper. It was an Irish Scali cap. Similar to the one he had worn for so many winters. The hat I remember so fondly, molded to his head at hockey rinks throughout New England.

12

Often identified as an excellent walking city, Boston's hub-shaped layout separates into distinct and diverse sub-cultures. South Boston and Charlestown are predominantly Irish, blue-collar communities. Allston and Brighton, on the western outskirts, are student-rich, yet surprisingly diverse. The South End is overwhelmingly homosexual and renowned for its top-notch restaurants. The North End is old school Italian. Beacon Hill is fancy and quaint, home to many important people. And the Back Bay, well known for Newbury Street and Boylston Street, is an outdoor shopping oasis and home to many people who *think* they're important.

Boston is also a city rich in drinking establishments. The substantial Irish population has something to do with it, so too does the unparalleled population of co-eds. The bars range from dive to swank, genre rarely determined by neighborhood.

Sky Bar happened to be located in one of the few areas of town not claimed by any one neighborhood. Located on Temple Street, just off the expansive Boston Common, it fell at the epicenter of converging neighborhoods, namely the North End, Beacon Hill and Back Bay. The location and accessibility made Sky Bar wildly popular and famously mixed when it came to clientele.

Jay, Lauren, Carmen and I had decided to scope it out; hitting Ben Worthington's little going away party that Brad had invited me to the day before. Jay had suggested dinner, but I wasn't ready to deal with Lauren's infidelity in an intimate setting. Surprisingly, he'd agreed to venture into town. Everybody likes an open bar.

We each polished off a fifth of Captain Morgan's on the subway, but the ride in on the green line was absurdly awkward, thanks to Lauren's overly affectionate behavior with Jay. Carmen sensed my discomfort and managed to keep me at ease with reassuring glances and hand grabs.

My stroll through Rock Meadow was still vivid in my mind and my encounter with the swing had reminded me of the ruined Christmas, inspiring self-reflection. Before setting out that night, I pledged to keep my indignation under wraps and make a conscious effort to be amicable with both friends and strangers. A noble thought doomed from the start because alcohol knows no rules.

Sky Bar was a massive two-level super bar, the first floor a poorly lit trendy lounge lined with cozy purple couches and tightly packed seating areas. The ceiling depicted a perfect evening sky. Glistening metal stars and odd-shaped orbs dangled on invisible wire, creating a supernatural aura. The room was large, every nook and cranny filled with many of Boston's highbrows thanks to the hosting Ward constituency.

The crowd, donning designer this and expensive that, wasn't my kind. Normally, I would have rather been flipped over in a porta potty than be there. But for some stranger than strange reason, the thought of hanging out with d-bags like Bradford Atkinson and drinking for free appealed to me that Saturday night. I think part of me wanted to confirm once and for all that Ward was unquestionably a stable for purebred jerk-offs. The idea of exposing Carmen and my friends to this fantastical culture of privilege also had merit. Though they had seen glimpses of Ward over the years, I always sought to limit those experiences. Perhaps now, they would see first-hand the nauseating effect of navigating a lawn steeped in shit. Misery liked company.

I was feeling loose and generally unstoppable as we made our way to the far side of the long mahogany bar. Sarcasm and a sharp tongue were ready in their holsters. "Four shots of Jameson," I demanded to the smoking-hot, blonde bartender, who was wearing what amounted to a black face cloth.

"Whoa, let's settle in and grab a drink first, huh?" Carmen pleaded.

"Just this one," I said, dropping down a nice tip of $15 and ensuring our status as rock stars at the busy open bar. The outfit warranted I do so anyway.

"I suppose that sells drinks," Carmen said covertly, eyeing our server's dress.

"They might as well give lap dances," Lauren added, her eyes following a tall redheaded waitress wearing a similar giddy-up. "I mean, are we at Sky Bar or did we take a wrong turn and end up on Route 1?" She was referring to the famed Route 1, north of Boston and notorious for shady strip clubs like The Rod and Mischief.

"Get used to it, honey," Jay remarked, alluding to Lauren's limited exposure to bar scenes. Indeed, Lauren had only been to a handful of bars, mostly with us, and she was alone when it came to a good fake I.D. among her high school friends. With an older crowd like us, she didn't raise suspicions. She was also a dead ringer for her older sister, Heather, the I.D. photo being particularly good and could have confused even family members.

"Who needs a drink?" I heard a familiar voice approaching from my right. It was Luna, who I had invited to join us following his shift. Always charming, he planted a kiss on both Carmen and Lauren before tapping fists with us boys. His charm came naturally, genetically inherited from his full-blooded Italian roots. His active brown eyes were ready for action, dancing below a head of perfectly parted brown hair.

"Three bud lights and two vodka sodas for the ladies," he barked, his eyes widening when the bartender turned to fetch the drinks. "Now that's a tattoo," he said in a trance, his eyes focused on the circular maze of thorns fully exposed on the bartender's lower back.

"Everybody likes a target," I joked.

"Absolutely, I'd kill that…"

"Yeah, killing that is one thing, but bringing her home for Thanksgiving to meet the family…now, that's another story."

"That's very true."

"So, what's up? Did you get out early? It's only 9:30 p.m.," Jay asked, having not expected Luna to get there until after 10.00 p.m. A rookie cop on the Belmont squad, Luna drew the shittiest shifts. He happened to have a decent daytime gig that day, but had been due off the clock at 10.00 p.m.

He nodded. "Fran Murray came in early. I guess his wife was driving him nuts. Poor bastard needed to get out of the house. Hey, it's fine with me," he said, the bartender delivering our drinks.

"I got the tip," Jay offered, reaching out with a $5 bill.

Luna slapped his hand out of the way. "Save your money, you'll need it." There was a subtle, split-second of distress that evaporated before Luna sensed it.

At a diminutive 5'6", Mark Luna constantly fought his stature, sometimes with ego, sometimes with affability, but always with flare. He wanted you to know he was there. The last few years had been particularly tough for him. His dad had passed away from stomach cancer during our freshman year in college, and Mark had been devastated, the end coming just four months after the diagnosis. He and his dad had been especially close, he being the only son in a family with four sisters. It happened over winter break and Luna had gone back to school too soon by most accounts, insisting on showing up for second semester. Ever since the tragedy, Luna's obsession with standing tall had grown even stronger. His belief that his dad was watching over him was palpable and consuming. Everything he did, he did with purpose. Never a physically gifted athlete, he had persevered in many sports and had even made himself into an accomplished hockey player. He had walked on at the University of Southern Maine, gradually increasing his playing time and the respect of his peers each year. By senior year, he had been named captain and finished second on the team in scoring. Recently, he had taken an ultra accelerated track to land the spot on the police force. Despite an average record in his studies, he had achieved a perfect score on the police exam, seemingly through sheer will. We knew plenty of people on the waiting list for police squads in less desirable towns, let alone Belmont. Luna overcame the odds and with the help of his Uncle Ralph, a Lieutenant, he had become the youngest officer to join the squad since 1978. He was an overachiever, but sometimes the first to tell you.

Years of Luna's audaciousness had worn thin on Jay. To Jay, Luna's slap and careless remark meant Jay was a teacher with a teacher's salary, and Luna was a big shot cop, so he should pay. But Luna's police salary was not overly impressive, though he did have plenty of cash—much more than Jay or me, thanks in large part to the lump sum he had received after his dad's passing. Despite his ways, those of us close to Luna knew his heart was pure, and that he'd give his last layer in the sub-arctic if a friend needed it. Jay's insecurity over his own career and his other failed experiences probably attributed to his critical interpretation of Luna's personality. Regardless, there was a definite tension at play and the three of us were far from the inseparable threesome we were growing up.

Jay shot me a disgusted look, but I just shrugged. I didn't like playing the middle and considered both of them my best friends. We polished off a few more beers and kept to ourselves, though I did recognize more than a few Ward guys, acknowledging them with an indifferent nod or a raised brow.

As the alcohol established itself in my blood stream, the Lauren issue increasingly agitated me. For a few minutes, I studied her, watching her hesitant laugh as it revealed her faint awkwardness around us. It was a silent, nervous laugh, and actually more like an exaggerated smile. She didn't add much to the conversation, content to contribute the laughing smile at well-timed intervals.

I rarely kept my mouth shut in such situations and seemed to thrive in scenarios that allowed me to put others in their place, pointing out their weaknesses. Being judgmental came naturally and alcohol only fueled my nerve. Controlling my sharp tongue was an ongoing struggle, one I lost time and time again. People I didn't know usually hated me for it and probably described me as obnoxious or mean. I had a manipulative way of broaching sore subjects, tactfully leading victims to slaughter.

I wanted desperately to ask Lauren if she had "seen Matt lately" or if she "happened to catch Letterman last night." But I swallowed my medicine and heeding Carmen's advice, put the matter out of my mind, deciding to leave the situation in the hands of fate. In subduing my aggression, I took baby steps towards the land of better people.

It took longer than anticipated for Brad to infect us with his presence. Jay noticed him first, probably because he was keeping tabs on a petite waitress with disproportionate double D's. She was chatting up Brad and Tripp Formey, another distinguished Ward gentleman. Tripp was what I liked to call a "TASH," a tag-along shit head.

"How do I know that guy?" Jay asked, motioning towards Brad with a nod.

"Which guy?"

"That one, there, the blonde guy drooling on the girl with the rack," he replied while assertively fingering Brad.

"Do you have to point?" Luna said, pushing Jay's hand down for the second time that night.

"Seriously, hands down, Jay. You might as well ring a bell," I added, turning quickly to escape the embarrassment.

"I know him, maybe from soccer. I think he played in the Bay State Games with me," Jay followed, continuing to stare in Brad's direction.

"That's Bradford Atkinson. Ward prick," I snapped. "He's the one that invited me—"

"Here he comes," Luna interrupted.

"Gentlemen, ladies…glad you could make it." Brad swelled as he and Tripp approached our group. He gave me a demeaning pat on the back and then kept his hand there as everyone exchanged introductions.

"Hey, you play soccer, Bay State, '96 maybe?" Jay asked.

"Sure did. Won the gold," Brad replied, referring to the medals awarded to winners of the high school summer tournament for sports like soccer, hockey and basketball.

"I thought so. I was on the Northeast team. We lost to you in the finals. You had a couple goals if I remember right," Jay said.

"Four. Four goals," Brad said, proudly holding up four fingers on his left hand.

"You sure it wasn't five, Brad?" I asked flatly, not able to help myself. I've always been a master of the deadpan. All eyes turned in my direction and I reveled in the display. Brad stared at me blankly, debating his next move. I didn't flinch, took a Viking slug from my beer, keeping my eyes trained on his.

"Actually, that would have been in college, against Bowdoin. My junior year," Brad finally said, a twinkle in his eye.

"I remember that," Tripp said, finally showing signs of life—the fucking TASH. "So, did you guys go to school?" Tripp added, apparently on a roll.

I studied Tripp's mug. It was a miniature horse face and completely out of whack with his lanky 6'4" frame. Despite his disjointed figure, he was amazingly smart—a certified genius in Latin, which along with his considerable lacrosse skills had helped pave the way to Princeton. Despite his lacking social acumen, the Ward ego chip functioned flawlessly in his teeny head.

Jay looked on dubiously, his forehead wrinkling and his brows sharpening. Luna didn't flinch, but that was par for the course. He consciously ignored the ignorance, instead choosing the high road. No wonder he had been class president in high school, hockey captain at Southern Maine and self-proclaimed nicest kid on campus.

"You mean college?" Jay asked.

Tripp nodded methodically; clearly surprised that the scope of his question wasn't clear.

"Are you for real, Tripp?" I snapped. I wondered if he had purposely taken a shot, or if he was just so innately ignorant that he figured public school kids preferred digging ditches to higher education.

"Settle down, Roy," Brad finally said to break an uncomfortable silence. "It was just a question. Not everyone goes to college."

"Just like not everyone goes to an Ivy school," Carmen said in the most measured tone. She had been standing with Lauren, a bit outside the main circle, an unlikely participant in the conversation. The spotlight was on her now and all our eyes turned to her. She seemed not to notice. She calmly sipped her vodka soda and then looked up, her eyes warm, a huge friendly smile filling her face. It was an All-World poker face.

At first, I wasn't sure how she knew, but then I remembered Brad had mentioned the game against Bowdoin. She knew that Bowdoin was a Division III school and wouldn't have had Division I Ivy League schools on their schedule. She didn't know that Brad had gone to Middlebury. That was irrelevant. All that mattered was that he hadn't gone to an Ivy League school. An open wound for sure. I was proud. Jay took a second to process the remark, and then it was clear when his mind made the connection. Discreetly, he winked at Carmen, probably wishing he had come up with the line himself.

"That's right," Tripp said enthusiastically. He couldn't have given a flying fuck that his good friend had just been cleverly drawn and quartered. The reminder that he had gone Ivy and Brad hadn't gave him an unanticipated rush. He beamed as if he had just blown six yards of Colombian coke.

Poor Brad just stood there, probably sorting through his resume for something to knock Tripp off his pedestal. It was always fun to watch. Carmen had dumped chum in the water, and the feeding frenzy would be spectacular. I wanted to nudge Jay and Mark, alert them to what was about to go down, but Luna broke their momentum by answering the original question.

"I went to Southern Maine, played hockey there," Luna said. "Jay went to a few places, most recently BC. He was searching for the ultimate college experience. Never did find it," he added, giving Jay a quick jab.

"I just ran out of chicks at each stop," Jay replied.

"Hardly," I said. We all laughed except Lauren. Damn hypocrite.

"You must know Jake Willingham?" Brad asked Luna.

"Sure I do, I played hockey with him, lived with him my junior year. He's a great guy. He's actually living in Boston now with a couple of other kids from our team. I'll see him in a few weeks. A bunch of us are renting a house on the Cape in August."

"Yeah, Willingham was at Middlebury with me for a few months freshman year before he transferred to Southern Maine. Good enough kid, shitty soccer player."

"Oh, you went to Middlebury?" Luna asked.

"Yeah," Brad muttered, seemingly annoyed that it wasn't common knowledge. He probably expected people to know his soccer stats too.

"Isn't Willingham the kid who got censured? Got caught with the bong?" Jay questioned, recognizing the name.

"That's the guy. It was a Tuesday afternoon, right in the middle of the quad. The Assistant Dean of Students caught him and another stoner. Not that it was difficult to catch someone smoking up in broad daylight. He was nuts," Luna confirmed. "Wait, he played soccer?" Luna continued. "I had no idea."

"Let's use the word 'played' loosely. He was a hack, got cut on the second day, but he still bruised a few shins. Worst ball skills I have ever seen. His stamina was horseshit too. That's what happens when you rip bong hits for breakfast everyday."

"Lunch and dinner too," Luna added. "He was actually a good hockey player for us. He scored a lot of goals senior year."

"Well, at Southern Maine maybe," Tripp said, glancing in my direction with a stupid looking grin. But Luna didn't take the bait. He focused on proving himself their peer. In fact, he had consistently warmed up to Ward kids over the years. Their circle was the next best thing to him, and the next best thing was usually part of his agenda.

"I think Lauren and I are going to grab a table and order some apps," Carmen interrupted, clearly agitated with the juvenile conversation.

"I'll go too. I am starving, and I didn't play a sport in college," Jay added, always keeping his good sense of humor.

"Soccer at Merrimack," Luna pointed out, knowing full well that Jay had bailed during tryouts.

"Yeah, until I quit," Jay said. "Nice to meet you guys." I watched as he quietly followed the girls towards the tables. I could tell by his off-kilter shuffle that he was spiraling towards one of his infamous blackouts. When he made Lauren switch seats so that he could see all three TVs behind the bar, something else became clear. He had money on a game.

I glanced up at the TVs and decided it was likely the Dodger game. The Red Sox game and the Cardinal game were both close and in the late innings. He wouldn't have been able to participate in the previous conversation if it was one of those games. The Dodger game was just getting under way and thus not at a critical stage. I laughed to myself. It takes one to know one. "I'm thinking the Dodger game," I whispered to Luna while giving a nod towards Jay. Luna turned to scan the games and smiled knowingly.

"Absolutely," he agreed. "Still betting on baseball? What's the matter with him?"

"You have action on the Sox?" Tripp asked Luna, evidently able to make out part of our hushed conversation.

"No, Jay does. He loves the action, a little too much."

"We're thinking the Dodger game. There's no way he walks away from either of those other games," I added.

"He shouldn't be betting," Luna offered.

"Why's that?" Tripp asked.

"The kid doesn't have a job. He's a teacher, making no money. Wait, *was* a teacher because he's not going back. Right now, he has whatever money he has saved and the nickels he makes at the local sporting goods store," Luna added, summing up Jay's financial status.

"So, what's your deal, Mark? What do you do?" Brad asked.

"I'm a cop," he answered proudly.

"Right, no really, what do you do?" Tripp asked.

"Youngest officer on the squad," I stated.

"Wow, that's fucking ridiculous. You're really a cop. Where's your gun?" Brad asked.

I could tell they were horny with intrigue. They knew dozens of kids who had found success at an early age, no doubt through powerful family connections. A cop was something different, something unfamiliar. Brad's eyes started to glow, he was fascinated and he leaned in closer to Luna.

"It's in a safe place," Luna answered coyly.

"That's too bad. Chicks love that shit. It can't miss," Brad barked enthusiastically.

The badge came out. Luna had a real discreet, dramatic way of doing it. He'd cuff it in his hand and hold it down by his thigh before slowly unpeeling his fingers. The way a dealer might reveal his stash. Every time he did it, I half expected him to be holding a dime of bud. I swear he must have polished the thing for an hour before bed each night. As he raised his hand slightly, it shimmered like the silver stuff at Tiffany & Co. All of our eyes were on it, transfixed like junkies on their score. Keeping his hand low, Luna dropped it into Brad's left hand. Instinctively, Brad drew it up towards his face to get a closer look.

"Hey, keep it cool. I'm not supposed to be showing it off," Luna snapped while reaching out to pull down Brad's arm.

"Heavier than you imagined, huh?" I asked Brad as he subtly handed it over to Tripp. Brad just nodded, mouth a gasp, but show and tell was over.

"Are you a police officer?" a sweet voice interjected. Two girls were on us and had covertly joined our circle. One was tall and blonde, a bit too skinny, not cute. The shorter one was a snack. She had stunning brown eyes and darkish skin, an ethnic look. I sensed foreign blood. She reached for the badge before Tripp could answer her question.

"I am," Luna said. He then effortlessly swiped his badge from her loose grip. As he buried the badge in his pocket with his left hand, he reached out with his right to shake the snack's hand. "I'm Mark. This is Roy, Tripp and Brad," Luna said, introducing each of us with an exaggerated head gesture. Surprisingly, Tripp and Brad didn't know the girls, though they were wearing the open bar wristbands. I smiled and extended my hand, trying not to stare at the shorter girl's bursting cans. She wore a bright red beaded necklace with equal-sized beads, save one larger red stone that nestled into her cleavage.

"I'm Graciela, and this is Courtney. Nice to meet you," she replied, her name and accent confirming my hunch. The accent was naughty, very naughty.

Courtney barely managed a smile. I had her pegged already—the quiet, wallflower type that fucked like a dead halibut. Her timid eyes and insecure posture told it all. She had soft porcelain skin and legs up to Luna's nose, but no curves, no personality and an F+ face.

Graciela hadn't uttered more than a few words, but the book was out on her too. Confidence is easy to sense, especially in girls. Her eyes were captivating, cat-like and engaging. Her body was hard, and she knew it.

"So, what kind of cop are you?" Graciela asked, continuing her interrogation of Luna.

"I'm an officer in Belmont. Sorry about the badge, I'm not really supposed to be pulling it out…unless there's a situation."

"That sounded like a bad porn line," Graciela said.

Luna's face turned red. But always alert, he recovered nicely. "That's my other gig. I do porn."

I was anticipating a cheesy handcuff line from Brad or Tripp, but thankfully, Tripp went with a safer angle. "Graciela. What a cool name. What is that, Spanish?" he asked.

"Yes, I'm from Venezuela. I was born there, but we came to Boston when I was six."

"And how do you like it here?" he followed.

"Well, since I've been here for seventeen years now, I like it just fine," she said sarcastically. That was it for Tripp, man overboard. He stepped back and began small talking Courtney in a hushed tone.

"What brought your family here?" Brad asked, ensuring the exchange proceeded.

"My dad's work, he's an engineer. His company sent him. He works for JPG, out of Needham. He came alone for a year, and then the rest of us joined him. Actually, my brother was older at the time, in high school, so he stayed in Venezuela and lived with my cousins. He didn't want to uproot in the middle of high school, learn a new language. But then he ended up coming to the U.S. for college—MIT."

"That still must have been tough, even though you came at a young age, learning a new language and all," Brad speculated.

"Not really, I started kindergarten here in the States, so I went through the system. I did flash cards and spelling bees just like you. My folks still speak Spanish at home a bit, and my grandparents do, of course, but my accent is pretty subtle."

"It's hot," Luna replied without missing a beat.

"Thank you," Graciela said seductively, tilting her chin down slightly and flashing a hidden smile.

I considered angles, perhaps mentioning Venezuela's emergence as a major oil producer or the country's rich baseball history. Having a great passion for wildlife, I could have asked her about the rainforests there and about Jaguars. Jaguars are the biggest cats in the Western Hemisphere and their jaws are among the strongest on earth. Maybe she knew this, maybe she didn't.

Luna was quarterbacking a nice game and effectively killing Brad in the process. Luna kept up the conversation, mixing the run with the pass, a combination of sincerity and pursuit. With girls, Luna definitely liked to air it out, throw it deep—a real gunslinger. His confident aggressiveness had served him well too, but he was also adaptable and could pound the ball conservatively when the situation required. Take what the defense gave him. I also liked to stretch the field, chuck it all over the yard. Jay on the other hand, was patient and conventional—three yards and a pile of dust, a Joe Gibbs protégé for sure.

I studied Graciela as she spoke, though I made a concerted effort not to stare at her Hall of Fame rack. It was right there like a flashing strobe, and even when I looked directly at her eyes, I subconsciously felt like I was boring a hole through her chest. I think I'm not looking. Does she think I'm looking? Am I peeking? Stare at the forehead. Stare at the forehead, Roy.

As I focused my eyes on her forehead, I managed to determine the secret to her enchanting beauty—her eyebrows. They were dark and full, creating the most perfect contrast to her sullen brown eyes. The brows tilted just enough to suggest anger, but really, they framed menacing beauty that screamed untamed sex. I felt a sudden urge to take the conversation up a level, couldn't help myself. "So, do you have a tattoo?" I asked.

My question stopped Luna mid-sentence. Brad perked up too. Graciela turned to me and stared straight through me, with a hint of surprise, which quickly broke into an ominous smile. Impulsively, she reached for her mid section with her right hand, the whole time keeping her eyes on mine. She brushed her hand slightly over her waist, seemingly to confirm that her tight jean skirt hadn't fallen. Location confirmed.

"What makes you think I have a tattoo?" she asked, maintaining her smile and rhythmically batting her dark lashes.

"Just a hunch, you're very beautiful, clearly confident but you have a little edge to you—in a good way, of course." She absorbed my words. So did the others. Her reaction loomed.

"Fairly impressive," she finally managed. "But, if you're so smart, why don't *you* tell us where it is?"

I hesitated, choosing my words very carefully. Her brashness was a ticking time bomb and extremely dangerous if played too far. "I'd say it is somewhere under that skirt. But not lower back. You're too secure, that's not you."

"And you're too sweet," she whispered, her eyes a bit untrusting. She sized me up, unsure of how to handle the situation. Her eyes darted from mine to Luna's, Luna's to mine. Back and forth, they went. She was thinking; thinking hard as though sorting through a nasty trig equation. Then her eyes stopped at mine, the seductive sparkle returning to her rich brown eyes. They were powerful and intimidating. I looked deep, but had to look away after a few eternal seconds.

"Am I right?" I asked confidently, careful not to lock eyes again, fearful of melting right there on the Sky Bar floor.

"Where's his?" she replied unflinchingly, gesturing towards Luna with her shoulder, keeping her eyes trained on me. Brad backed away, choking on defeat.

"Who, Mark?" I asked, taken a bit off-guard. She nodded once.

"I don't have one, not my thing," Luna answered.

"He's a little too straight-laced. He's a cop, remember?" I added.

"Save it," Luna snapped, unappreciative of my dig. "So, what's the deal, he's right, huh?" Luna said enthusiastically.

"He's certainly perceptive," she said warmly, the tension fleeing as a cool smile filled her face. The game was up. We had passed her test. "What do you guys know about Sucre?" Graciela continued.

"Isn't that the French word for sugar?" I answered, surprised that I had retained anything from four years of high school French class. She looked at me as if I had six heads. Luna shared her confusion. "What, isn't it?" I asked defensively.

"Um, yeah, I think it might be, but I don't speak French. Anyway, it's also the name of my state in Venezuela. Sucre."

"Estado Sucre," Luna exclaimed, showing off a limited mastery of Spanish. "I remember, like Los Estados Unidos de América."

"Very nice, Mark," she replied playfully. "This is Sucre." She slowly reached down towards the waist of her skirt. She lifted up the hem of her tight white shirt just an inch or two, revealing a perfect strip of flat cinnamon skin. I glanced quickly at Luna and noticed his eyes popping as he watched in disbelief. I turned back to Graciela's stomach. She looked up at us, flashing a disarming smirk through full lips and then methodically undid the top button of her skirt. I shot a look around the bar. Courtney, Tripp and Brad were now at full attention. If somebody had yelled "fire" or "loose tiger" for that matter, I'm not sure any of us would have flinched. Graciela slowly peeled down the left side of her skirt, then gave it one last gentle tug, revealing more skin and a piece of what I surmised to be a black lace thong. I didn't dare look away. Luna nudged me excitedly, a little too hard actually, because I nearly toppled over and took Graciela with me. Then I caught a faint shade of light blue, partially hidden where skin met lace on her lower left abdomen. She pulled the waist of her panties down less than an inch and revealed more blue.

"That's Sucre, boys," she said softly, running her forefinger over the tattoo. Sugar indeed, I thought to myself. I examined the design, a sky blue circle about two inches in diameter with a perfectly centered white star in the middle. "The state flag of Sucre is divided diagonally; the top half, a white background with the state badge or arms, the bottom half this beautiful light blue color, dotted with white stars," she stated, as if she were leading a guided tour. The technical explanation did little to subdue my desire. I nodded like a fool. She continued, "The flag's stars are arranged in a circle, one for each municipality or district, which varies. I think it's about fifteen now. But the two colors are very important in Sucre. White is the color of purity and nobility and represents our white sands. Light blue is for bravery and generosity and represents the clear blue water of our ocean." She held her skirt down for a moment or two longer so that we could process her tutorial, and then as though nothing had happened, pulled up her skirt and buttoned up.

"That's really something…different, meaningful," Luna managed in an awe-struck trance.

"Yeah, thanks for sharing. Very cool," I mumbled, still fixated on how that thong might tangle. I licked my lips to make sure that I hadn't drooled down my chin.

13

With Carmen on the scene, I couldn't have gotten anything done, couldn't have closed the deal. But our relationship did allow for infidelity, just not right in front of the other person. I was careful not to get involved in anything more than casual. And I knew she felt the same way. We were going to get married some day—that much was clear. Yet, if we didn't explore other options and knock down certain doors from time to time, we'd be going into a life together blind, having never tested other waters. The few times a hook-up morphed into something more, we had an honesty policy that required we come clean and take a break. I had played that hand a few times, with the flings always dying within a few weeks. Carmen had been less exploratory—as far as I knew. But one two-month break with Eric Martin had been particularly hard, an adventure for sure. And more like a walking night safari.

***

It was the summer that I don't like to discuss. And ironically, the one that followed the ruined Christmas. Good times. Eric was also a Belmont guy and interesting by most accounts. He wasn't athletic, but into playing guitar, smoking lots of joints and an alternative lifestyle. He was a big hit with the ladies, with his model looks and unconventional interests, but dudes steered clear of him, knowing that he only cared about one thing—his next piece of ass. The disclosure thing hadn't necessarily worked out that time because Carmen had been seeing Eric on the side for a few weeks before I got wind of it. She swore on no intimacy but to this day, I mock belief.

I sensed her distance in those few weeks, as she was less than eager to hang out with me, going out with the girls with unusual frequency. One night after softball, I went to Boyle's for a few beers with my teammates. My buddy, Kemp, had forgotten his glove at the bar, so I went to drop it off at his place on my way home. But as I turned onto his street, Wayland Street, I got quite the surprise—Carmen walking into Eric's house. Fortunately, she didn't notice my car passing behind her. She and Eric were old friends, and it wouldn't have been that unusual, except for the fact that she was supposed to be in Scituate at her friend Amy's house for the night. I pulled over in front of Eric's house and parked for a good fifteen minutes, contemplating my next move. It was torture.

Somehow, I continued to Kemp's, dropped off his glove and went home. I might have slept twenty minutes that night. All I could think about was Eric fucking her, over and over again, making her orgasm like Jesse Jane.

I called her damn early the next morning. "Hey, how was the night?" I asked in an even voice.

"Fine, we just drank some wine and went to bed actually. Pretty low key," she responded without hesitation. "Did you guys win your game?"

"Yeah, we won. Hey, I can't hear you very well. Is that your phone or mine?" I asked awkwardly.

"Huh? I don't hear anything. I can hear you just fine, Roy."

"Well, I can't. It must be your cell, I hear static. Give me Amy's house number there. I'll call you right back."

"What? No, it's too early. It's 7:30 a.m. I'll call you back from—"

"Give me the number, Carmen," I said, my tone strengthening.

"What's your problem, Roy? I'll try you from outside. Why are you calling so early anyway?"

"Put Amy on the phone," I said pissed off.

"What?"

"NOW!"

Dead silence followed. She knew. All I could hear was her controlled breathing. I took a deep breath, held it. Her breathing grew louder, muffling through the receiver like a soft snore.

"How did you know?" she asked finally in a guilty voice.

"Did you fuck him? Did you?" I was yelling now.

"NO! Of course I didn't, don't be stupid, how—"

"I had to go by Kemp's house after softball. That's irrelevant. How long has it been going on, Carmen?"

"A couple of weeks, maybe a month," she said dejectedly.

"How could you? What happened to honesty?"

"Oh, please, I know you sneak around too. Remember Julie?" she asked, referring to the time her friend, Stacey, had caught me at dinner with my ex Julie Wolfe.

"That was one time, Carmen, one meaningless date. I didn't touch her."

"Right, look, I'm sorry. I really am, Roy. I didn't know what to do. You know Eric. You grew up with him. You would have flipped."

"You're right. Did you have to pick someone I know, someone I have known since kindergarten, someone all of our friends know? That kid is dead. He knows better."

"No, Roy. It's my fault. This has nothing to do with him. We haven't even done anything. Please don't do something stupid."

"He's captain d-bag. That piece of shit. Are you over there now?"

"No, I'm home."

"Do I need to come over?" I asked, my emotions starting to settle.

"No, that's probably not a good idea. We need a break. I love you, Roy, but I need some time."

I felt my heart sink. I was nervous. She knew Eric. They had a history—a strong foundation. He wasn't some kid she met on a weekend in New York or a random fling in Newport. The word "potential" rang true. I couldn't be a hypocrite, but I was bullshit about the lying. "Fine, but don't ever lie like that again. Seeing someone else is one thing. Lying is another story. Don't fuck with trust, Carmen."

She didn't say anything for half a minute. For the first time, I felt the sweat that had formed between my ear and the receiver. I wiped the top of the phone on my T-shirt. I heard her breathing escalate, subtly at first, and then the short and jabbed breaths, the whimpering, the sobbing and the rush of emotion. Through quick pulsating sniffles, she told me she was sorry.

"I've got to go, Carmen," I said after another long silence.

"Okay, I love—" she said barely audibly as I gently clicked off the phone and tossed it on my bed.

The rage was gone, and I was devastated. The next few weeks were a struggle. I drilled beers nightly, often at Boyle's with Jay, wondering where and how Eric might be giving it to her. I had resisted the urge to call her, or him for that matter, instead giving her the space I knew she needed. I sleepwalked through my landscaping job; disjointed and frustrating conversations with my Guatemalan co-workers carrying me through those hot summer days.

Working for a Belmont-based company, Santamaria Landscaping, most of the jobs were in Belmont, and I made sure the route between them took me past Carmen's house. I saw her car a few times, never his. That made sense since they were both working, he at a Harvard Square music store and she at her dad's office in nearby Watertown. Time crept by, measured in seconds. The minutes seemed like hours. I couldn't stop thinking about Carmen.

One day, I was seeding a new lawn on Slade Street with one of the younger wetbacks, Manny, when he pointed out two beautiful Monarch butterflies. Immediately, I thought of Carmen's love for butterflies and how much she enjoyed visiting the Butterfly Landing, a greenhouse full of butterflies, at the Franklin Park Zoo.

I coaxed Manny, despite significant language barriers, into helping me catch them. He was stealth and eventually caught the bigger of the two as it lay resting in a small bush. He carried it over to me, pinching the wings between his thumb and forefinger. The butterfly fluttered like mad, its small wings vibrating in his hand. Manny held it up, truly proud of his accomplishment. I patted him on the back excitedly, and he broke into a jagged smile, the gold caps on his teeth glistening in the summer sun. A few minutes later, I was able to capture the other one, placing it with its friend in a brown paper bag that had held Manny's tuna fish sandwich. I poked a few small holes in the bag with the keys to our truck and returned to my work, speeding through the rest of the lawn job, my energy infectiously spurring Manny to work quickly as well.

By 2:00 p.m., I was outside Carmen's house, the big engine of the landscaping truck idling noisily. I scanned the driveway and the front of the house for cars. I saw none, so hurried down the front walkway and burst through the front door. I released the butterflies in Carmen's room, watching them fly around until they both settled on top of the curtain rod above her bedside window. A few seconds later, I was back in the truck, where I gave Manny a knowing smile. Mission accomplished.

When Manny dropped me off, I invited him to have a beer with me. It was the least I could do, and my dad always had Heinekens in the fridge.

Short and stocky, Manny was built like a brick shit house. He had a huge round face, which was always dirty from work. He wore the same black jeans, black work boots and his filthy, ripped maroon Santamaria Landscaping T-shirt every day. He smelled like a locker full of dead rats but had a beautiful, lively smile that he showed often. Our conversations were limited, requiring the filling in of blanks around a recognizable word or two. Facial gestures and hand signals were big as well.

During our few weeks together, I ascertained that he had come from Guatemala with his older sister, Rosetta, two years earlier. She cleaned houses to help pay for what I imagined to be the roach-infested closet of an apartment that they shared. I learned of his absurd daily commute, which involved a lot of walking and two buses. Without papers, I knew he was making far less than the lame $7 per hour that I was pulling in as a family friend of the owner Ed Santamaria.

Manny was just two years older than me, and we felt like peers, sharing the same interests and passions. He loved to talk about soccer—football to him—and I always enjoyed his stories about Spanish women. But I felt sorry for him and couldn't fathom living in his shoes. I admired his courage, his maturity and his dreams, but mostly his resolve. As we drank the Heinekens that day in my parents' yard, he told me the story of his brother, who had been stabbed to death back in Guatemala.

Manny had been just eleven and his brother sixteen, when rebels, who didn't approve of their father's political influence, beat and stabbed the brother in the family's front yard. My interpretation may have been a bit off, but I gathered that Manny watched the whole thing transpire from a front-facing window. He ran out of the house screaming, but one of the assailants easily pushed him over before joining his friends in the getaway car. His brother was still alive when they sped away, but died later that day. Strangely, Manny considered his brother partially responsible. Apparently, he had become too involved with their father's politics, in a country where political turmoil ruled the day.

I listened quietly to Manny's story, stringing together words and expressions, my mind taking me to a country I imagined to be dusty and brown. I pictured a white ranch house, a grassless yard, some chickens running amuck, and little Manny chasing after a villain-filled pickup truck. I wondered if my vision was accurate, or a convoluted and ignorant visualization of a life I'd never know.

After the beers with Manny, I kept my cell phone close by throughout the rest of the day. I checked it periodically to make sure it was working properly, anticipation taking over my body. Luna and I played a few holes of golf that afternoon at Oak Ridge Golf Club, and he was particularly hard on me, watching in disbelief as I frantically ran to my golf bag whenever my phone rang. Halfway through the round, he suggested I just keep it in my pocket, which was a clear etiquette foul, but a good idea nonetheless. Carmen finally called while we were enjoying some post-round beers. I ran out of the clubhouse as the phone vibrated, leaving an eye-rolling Luna in my wake.

"Hey!" I said, once I reached the privacy of Oak Ridge's front lawn.

"Hi there, how have you been?" she asked flatly.

"Fine, I miss you, Carmen."

"Uh huh, so was it you or the Crocodile Hunter that paid a visit to my room today? It seems I have two new guests."

"Do you like them?"

"Of course, where—"

"I caught them on a job this morning."

"They're beautiful, Roy. I just hope they can survive indoors. I better let them go in the morning."

"I think they'll be fine. I suppose they need to eat. But I don't know the first thing about butterfly diet."

She laughed—the most beautiful sound I had heard in days. My body warmed, blood returning to previously abandoned vessels.

"So, how are things…with… you know, Eric?" I asked.

"Good, I guess. Let's not go there. I just wanted to call and thank you."

"Simple question, Carmen," I said, anger seeping back into me. "I can't ask? Should I pretend I don't give a shit?"

"Come on, Roy…I love you. I think about you all the time, but it's not fair. Let things play out. I'm having fun right now. I'm happy."

It was like a bayonet through the heart. I could almost feel the steel carving its way through me. "That's great," I snapped, clearly agitated. "I'll just wait around and hope things fizzle out. What if you don't…come back?"

"I can't say that I will or I won't, that's the point, Roy. I'm following my instinct, seeing where it takes me. Right now, I still love you, but I don't want to be with you. This is new. Sometimes, new is exciting. It feels good to have someone really appreciate me."

I didn't like where she was going. I regretted asking questions. I should have left it alone. Now the fury was coming back, bubbling beneath my skin, and I could feel it fuel every inch of me. I could have thrown the phone to New Hampshire, maybe Maine. I held it down by my side and stared wild-eyed at the parking lot as cars came and went. When I thought I had my emotions under check, I brought it back to my face and spoke. "And what is that supposed to mean?" I snarled, my mouth drying between heavy breaths.

"It means sometimes I feel like you just go through the motions," she said sincerely. "In your mind, you think we're definitely going to be together forever. Sometimes, I don't think you work at the relationship, work to make things better, to show you care as you did when we first fell in love. It's not a done deal, our relationship. There are no guarantees. If we want to be together forever, we have to continue to grow. I don't know, Roy. I wonder if we've maxed out."

It was a lot to take in. I couldn't really process everything she had said. Two things were clear: I wasn't putting in the effort, and she was still referring to the relationship in the present tense. At least that was a good sign. I thought about the effort thing. She was probably right. I did take her for granted sometimes, canceling plans with her to do things with Luna or Jay, failing to say or do the little things that meant so much. Recently, we had been increasingly doing stuff that I liked to do: going to Sox games, going to the driving range, drinking with my friends. It had been quite some time since I'd made a dinner, taken her to the beach or gulp, to a play.

"I could work on some things, for sure," I said.

"I know, and I know you do care, but right now I don't want to think about it. I know who you are, and I know what it means to be in love with you. That's all very familiar to me. Like I said, I'm just enjoying things right now and following my heart. I trust it."

"Fine," I said through gritted teeth. "But did you sleep with him?" I continued, my voice trailing off. She didn't answer right away. I felt the bayonet again, driving through my intestines. I could have taken a knee right there on the lawn. I felt weightless.

"That's really not any of your business, Roy."

The bayonet screwed through me, maliciously thrust deeper with each spoken word. I felt my upper body crumble, my system fail, and my shoulders sway. Like a stunned boxer, I saw a green canvas loom. I steadied myself, barely. "I can't do this," I spat, then clicked off my phone.

A few hours and a dozen beers later, I was making my way on foot from Oak Ridge towards Carmen's house. Luna had left me at the bar to attend a barbeque for his grandfather's birthday, and I had declined his invitation. As I made my way down Payson Road, I wasn't exactly sure of my intentions. I remember being madder than a swarm of hornets, stumbling drunk and ready to do something. As I neared Carmen's house, I saw two people holding hands, walking a dog, heading towards me from the opposite end of the street. Even in my drunken state, I knew who it was. The familiarity of Carmen's stroll and the limping gait of her mom's collie, Kelso, had given them away. I stopped before coming through the glow of the next street light. I made a quick right turn onto Laurel Avenue, a semi-circular street that ran behind Carmen's house and back out to Payson. I picked up my pace.

I contemplated what to do next. I should have walked home, but I didn't because I couldn't erase the picture of that fucking prick holding her hand. I continued up Laurel and followed it as it bent around towards Carmen's on the corner of Laurel and Payson. I stood on the side of the house in the middle of Laurel, flight or fight consuming me as I listened to their hushed voices. I could hear

Kelso's collar jingle as she ran in the front yard, which faced Payson. I took a few more steps and saw them embracing on the front walkway to my left. I watched Eric plant a playful kiss on her forehead, a bit awkwardly since at 6'3", he was a foot taller than she was.

I turned on a dime and was soon bolting through the back door of Carmen's house, passing by her sister, Amanda, and Amanda's friend, Molly, at the kitchen table. I continued into the front hall with my eyes dead ahead before crashing through the screen door, practically knocking it from its hinges. Then I stopped momentarily because I wanted Eric to turn and face me. As he did, I barreled into him, grabbing him by the neck with my right hand as we both tumbled onto the concrete walkway. I quickly out muscled him, burying my left knee into his chest and pinning him to the ground. I cocked my right hand over his head. He flinched instinctively, turning to the right so that his right cheek brushed against the walkway.

"Open your eyes, asshole. Open your fucking eyes."

He opened them slowly and one at a time. I saw the fear of God looking up at me. He squirmed like a snake, but he wasn't going anywhere. I cocked my fist higher, tightening my knuckles.

"Don't hit me, Roy. Please don't," he wailed. My fist shook. I released my fingers and slapped him in the face with lightning quick precision. His face ricocheted off the concrete, and when he opened his eyes again, he had a fresh red handprint on his left cheek.

I screamed, "Is it worth it, Eric? Is it fucking worth it? I'll kill you, you fucking pussy." I heard all kinds of commotion around me, especially Carmen's screeching yell.

"Roy! Roy!"

I raised my hand again, but I felt someone grab it. It was Amanda and soon enough Carmen and Molly were on me, pulling feebly to get me off Eric. My heart rate slowed to Mach 2, and I allowed them to pull me up. Eric scurried towards the street, clearly scared shitless.

"What the fuck, dude?" he shouted through tears. "What the fuck?"

I started towards him again, but Carmen grabbed both my arms, put herself in front of me and yelled, "Stop it. Just stop, you fucking lunatic."

I glared at Eric, smiling when I saw the red mark still glowing on the side of his face.

"Roy! Look at me. Look at me," Carmen yelled. I looked down into her green eyes. She was crying, tears spilling down her cheeks. I could feel my arms pulsating in her tiny hands. It was then that I realized where I was, what I had done. Easing up, I took a step back and saw the blood. Carmen's knee was bleeding badly. I followed the red trail as it trickled down her leg and into her black flip-flop.

I looked for Eric again. But Amanda and Molly had taken him out of harm's way, further down Payson where they seemed to be comforting his candy ass. My eyes returned to the blood. "What happened?" I demanded, bending down and reaching for Carmen's leg.

"Don't touch me!" she shouted, stepping back. "You knocked me over. What the fuck is wrong with you? You are an infant!" she continued through choked tears.

"I am sorry, Carmen. I'm not sure what happened. I…"

"Don't talk to me. Just leave…now…leave." I tried to move closer to her, wanting to give her a hug. As I took the first step, she raised her right hand, issuing the stop sign like a traffic cop. A cold glare followed. Not one more step. I opened my mouth, an attempt to plead, but she just closed her eyes and shook her head. "Leave," she whispered.

I left, making the lonely walk home. It then took me three months to make up for my deranged attack and win back Carmen's affection. But I did, and the mission was a success because that night was the last I heard of Eric Martin. He eventually disappeared to Chicago, the only reminder of him, a fading scar on Carmen's left knee.

14

We were still talking about Graciela's peep show two hours later, having moved upstairs to shoot pool. Luna had managed to grab Graciela's number, and I was insanely jealous. There wasn't a chance in hell of going home with a girl like that on the first night, so Luna had played it smart, opting for her number and the courteous course of action—fetching drinks and setting up what would be a hotly anticipated date.

The second floor of Sky Bar was like a wet dream for guys like us, and we were ready for it because the open bar downstairs had ended. There was a long bar much like the one on the first floor, but the surrounding décor was more in line with our tastes. Huge TVs hung on every conceivable wall and beam, surrounded by pool tables, half a dozen Golden Tee games and a bubble hockey game. Men gravitated to the scene like flies to shit and thus, girls did too. Carmen and Lauren were fine with the testosterone-rich atmosphere, finding it almost laughable.

Carmen remarked, "What, no beer pong?"

"Actually, they do have a pong tourney in the spring, during March Madness," I replied.

"Figures," she said, shaking her head.

"Yeah, probably heroes from BU and MIT though. What kind of person plays pong in a bar?" Jay added.

"The same kids who lift weights for softball and own their own pool sticks that they carry in little suitcases," I followed.

"Yes, like Gordon Mills," Jay said. Gordon Mills was a kid we had grown up with in Belmont. We had bumped into him a few times at Rooney's, a local pool hall, and he was always carrying his own stick in an oversized lunch box. We nearly pissed ourselves the first time we saw him pull it out and routinely assemble it like some cadet at Fort Bragg. Neither Jay nor I had ever seen a pool stick case to that point in our lives. We came to find out that Mills participated in a competitive billiards league in which he was the third-ranked player.

"Oh, he would be first in line, carrying multi-colored pong balls in some designer case engraved with his initials," I added.

"Absolutely, remember his pool ensemble, the tight black busboy outfit and the slicked back hair? What were we calling him?" Jay asked.

"Dr. Death!" I shouted.

"Yes, Dr. Death! What a loser. That shit was too funny." Jay was shaking his head now, completely caught up in the moment. The girls laughed too, but Luna apparently had a pole lodged up his ass.

"Guys, don't be like that. Don't judge people. Gordon Mills is a nice kid, completely harmless. His dad is on the squad with me. He looks out for me. If Gordon wants to dress up like a mortician and shoot pool with his own piece, what the fuck does it matter? That makes him a loser?" His voice grew louder with each syllable. "Who gives a fuck?"

"Relax, Mark. Relax. Get over yourself. We're just poking fun at the kid. Nobody said he was a bad kid," I snapped, annoyed that Luna was playing first grade teacher.

"Fuck that. He *is* a loser. The kid owns his own pool stick and carries it in a case. He's Dr. Death," Jay bellowed, clearly drunk and not ready to let Gordon off the hook easily.

"You're fucking ignorant, Jay. Maybe he thinks you're a loser, maybe he thinks I'm a loser." Luna's eyes were sharp. His little rant was for both Jay and me, but it was clear to all of us that he was gunning for Jay. Jay knew it too, even in his semi-blacked out state.

"I suck at pool, and I certainly don't own a case," Jay mumbled, glancing at a nearby TV to check his score.

"Yeah, but you have a gambling problem," Luna pleaded, noticing Jay's eyes shift towards the TV. You can't stick with anything—school, soccer, teaching. You work at fucking Harrington's, Jay. Harrington's fucking Sporting Goods."

Jay stared straight ahead, avoiding Luna's seething eyes. The gloves were off. It had happened quickly too, but I knew Jay wouldn't fight back. It wasn't his way.

"Mark, come on," I said helplessly.

"No, he's right. It's all true, very true." Jay's voice trailed off as he spoke, and it was clear he was hurt. "Lauren, let's go shoot some pool, huh?" Jay put his arm around Lauren and led her gently towards the tables. "Did you bring our sticks, babe?" he asked sarcastically and loud enough so that we could all hear as they made their way towards a vacant table. I chuckled, but Luna froze, did a double take, clearly annoyed that his lesson hadn't registered.

"Luna, man, what is up with you?" I asked, once Jay had settled into his match with Lauren.

"That was pretty harsh, Mark," Carmen added. "He was just joking around about Gordon; no harm."

Luna looked to the floor. He was lost in thought, and I sensed he felt terrible inside. It was during moments like this that I figured his dad was on his mind. Nobody could willingly aspire to be that perfect, that open-minded. "I can't help it. I love Jay. I just want him to get his shit together. It bothers me that he is so quick to criticize others when his life is such a train wreck. And I like Gordon Mills. You guys have no right."

"Mark, it was a joke. It was funny. The kid carries his pool stick in a personalized carrying case. That's it, a joke."

"I know, I know. It wasn't about Gordon. I guess I just wanted to get that off my chest. It bugs the shit out of me."

"Okay, but this isn't the place. Jay knows he has to figure some things out. He isn't an idiot. He's hearing it from his mom, from me, from you, that's tough," I pleaded. "And to say all of that in front of Lauren, that's not fair."

"He's got enough issues with her," Carmen added, her suggestive tone alerting Luna that there was more to the story.

Luna looked up, his eyes full of interest, maybe concern. "What do you mean *enough issues*?"

I turned to Carmen and gave her a silent lecture. She shrugged innocently like a guilty child. I looked down, focusing my attention on a particularly thick pine panel.

"Oh, come on," Luna said. "We're all friends here."

"Not a word then," I said sternly. I told him the Cliff Notes version, explaining that I had seen the car and heard a few intimate noises. I left out the part about me getting bionic wood watching Lauren as if she were some chick on the *Hot Network*.

"That dirty slut, poor Jay; he really likes her."

"I know."

"He has no idea, huh?" Luna was in a hypnotic trance, watching Jay and Lauren shoot pool forty feet away. His shoulders slouched slightly.

"Luna, I know you meant well. I feel the same way sometimes. It's so tough to get through to him though," I said.

"But I know how much potential he has. He's a hell of a lot smarter than I am. Shit, I just wish he'd stick with something."

"We all do, and he will," I added quietly. "We just need to let things go a bit. He clams up if we even address it. He hates hearing it from me, and to be honest, I think he likes it even less from you."

"And why's that?" Luna was looking up at me quizzically.

I wasn't sure how to express what I was thinking. Thankfully, Carmen did. "You have a certain way of communicating, Mark. You're fiery and confident. It rubs people the wrong way sometimes," she said in a voice that was more genial than critical. I waited anxiously through a few silent seconds. Luna nodded calmly.

"Good, let's just forget about it for now. We've got drinking to do," I announced, ready to move on.

"Yes, shots on me," Luna exclaimed, gesturing for us to move towards the bar. As we made our way, I looked up at a TV overhead and saw that the Dodgers were trailing 5–2 in the eighth. I stopped, turning towards Jay. He and Lauren were playing against two townies. As Lauren lined up a shot, Jay seemed to sense my gaze. He turned his focus away from the table of colored balls and caught my eye. For a fleeting moment, he was at ease, a radiating smile slicing across his thin face. It was a snapshot in time. Then he nodded at the TV above me and shook his head disappointedly.

After forcing down another shot, this time Crown Royal, I was ready to call it quits on hard booze for the night. Carmen and Lauren had already done so, declining the shot. I ordered a light beer, which I was prepared to nurse until last call.

Luna sensed my equilibrium disintegrating. "You alright?" he asked, placing his hand on my shoulder.

"Yeah, I'm fine. I better coast from here on in though."

"I'd say so, yeah. You look like you just swallowed battery acid," he joked.

"That's not what we just drank?"

"You probably forgot about the Captain, honey," Carmen added, gently rubbing her hand up and down my back. I paused, tried to remember, but couldn't at first. Then it came to me—the flask on the train. I *had* forgotten.

"I'm fine. Let's see how Jay and Lauren are doing."

Two girls occupied the table next to them, but they didn't appear to be playing a game. One girl continued hitting random shots, sometimes striking the striped or solid balls directly. Her friend watched awkwardly, half paying attention and half monitoring the scene around them. They were buying time. Damn sluts.

I marched towards them, whacking Luna with a quick flex of my elbow. "Are you first-timers? It sure looks like it. You're supposed to hit *this* ball," I said, grasping the cue ball from the table and holding it up. Luna tugged my arm down, but I quickly held it up again, my arm working like a spring. I looked at him with a sense of accomplishment, challenging him to try again. He declined. I could tell all eyes were on me, and I loved it. "Sorry," I slurred, flinging the ball across the table and into the red three ball.

"Uh, that's okay. We're not playing a game. We're not that into pool," one of them said shyly.

I launched into a terrific deadpan. "Oh, I see, you're just waiting to hook up." While they took a minute to calculate a response, I sized them up. One was cute. She had nice blue eyes with long lashes and a funky bob of blonde hair. But she was very petite and had the body of a fifteen-year-old. Not my type. The other girl was beastly. She was heavy, and her clothes were tight, which meant she looked like an overstuffed sausage. On a hot scale of one to ten, she was a standard three, though I suppose a four on her wedding day.

I thought about announcing her ranking, but didn't. "Hey, no worries, you still have a little more than an hour to find a mate," I said, checking my watch.

"Hi, I'm Carmen. I'm sorry," Carmen interrupted, knowing all too well that they were vulnerable to a degrading onslaught.

The sausage girl extended a hand. "Hi, I'm Karen and—"

"So, Karen, how are you feeling about your outfit tonight?" I jumped in, my voice booming.

"Come again?" she replied slowly, her eyes scanning the others for a clue.

"Your outfit, do you feel good about it? Was it your first choice, or did you leave your room with discarded shirts all over the floor?"

She giggled nervously. "Um, it was my first choice," she said with false confidence. Her eyes dropped, giving herself a quick once-over, and then she nodded cautiously.

"The shirt is okay, kind of revealing with the low neck. But it's an awfully snug fit," I spat back.

"*Excuse me*?" she said with eyes on fire.

"Don't worry, it matters not if I like it," I said flamboyantly. "No, it matters whether or not Mark Luna likes it."

"And who is Mark Luna?" she asked annoyed.

I turned to Mark and put my right arm around his shoulders. As I did so, my eyes caught Carmen's, which were popping, pleading with me to stop, to end the charade. "This is Mark Luna, right here. Belmont's finest." Luna wrestled free from my semi-embrace, and I stumbled without the aid of my human crutch. Embarrassed, Luna stepped forward and attempted to diffuse my efforts with a sincere and apologetic introduction during which he referred to me as an "asshole." True that.

I heard the other girl—the short blonde—whisper to Carmen, "He's fine, it's okay, just very drunk I presume."

"I *am* fine," I shouted. "You're very lucky to have made our acquaintance. Luna is a great find at this hour. You won't do better. Believe me."

"Nice to meet you," Carmen said evenly, placing her hand on my back and steering me away. I broke free from her and turned quickly. She faced me like a roadblock, steely eyes daring me to take a step. Luna and the girls depicted a wall of nervous expression. Carmen held her stare, the anger dissipating from her green eyes, replaced by warmth. She cocked her head slightly to the left, a lock of hair falling gracefully across her forehead, partially masking her left eye. I lowered my head like a scolded hound and headed towards Jay and Lauren's table as Luna and the girls burped out a collective gasp of relief.

Jay and Lauren's opponents were what people in the other forty-nine states refer to as "Massholes." Edgy and loud, they moved around the pool table with an almost humorous swagger, their exaggerated Boston accents evident with every word. They dressed the part too, each clad in long shorts that fell below their knees and tight T-shirts that accentuated muscles I hadn't realized existed. Two of their friends stood against a nearby wall, boisterous laughter spewing from them as they taunted and teased their buddies after each errant shot. Jay and Lauren were losing big. The table was full of their solid painted balls, while just two striped balls remained. Carmen and I sat up on an adjacent pool table.

"Hey, boss, no drinks on the table," snapped one of the kids against the wall in a high-pitched voice. At first, I didn't see that he was talking to us. But then I looked over, and he nodded like a tough guy, his eyes focusing on my beer, which sat on the green velvet table.

Realizing my mistake, I grabbed the beer and raised it in his direction. He and his cheese-ball friend nodded simultaneously like two fraternal twins. "Welcome to Revere Beach," I whispered to Carmen, referencing the notoriously cheesy, waterfront strip north of Boston.

"Oh, definitely," Carmen replied. "I'm sure the I-Rock is parked out front."

Jay misfired on an easy corner shot, drunken coordination surely playing a role. "Give it up, guy. It's not your night," someone called from the peanut gallery.

Jay played along, acknowledging his feeble skills with a forced laugh. One of his opponents lined up the last of the striped balls for a bank shot. As he crouched down to calculate the angle, an overhead light glistened off his heavily waxed black hair. He stood, then crouched, stood, then crouched. He took his pool a bit too seriously. He consulted his playing partner, who was slightly shorter, but stockier if that was possible. He too had a pint of styling gel meticulously applied to a head of blonde hair.

"While we're young, Lou, hit the fucking ball," the taller, skinnier bystander barked, continuing with his running commentary.

"I will, Sean. Pipe down."

Sean was a skinny fucker, a plain white undershirt fitting loosely over his slender frame. He wore a fitted Red Sox hat tilted to one side, the visor straight as a tabletop and pulled down over his lively eyes. He was chattier than his friend, who watched the action through hollow dark eyes. Sean's friend was enormous and a real ogre. He also wore a fitted blue cap, but turned backwards, so I couldn't make out the team.

Lou missed his shot badly. My mind started to drift, picturing the four of them piling into a muscle car with a kick-ass stereo, leather seats and the top down. I imagined Sean smoking butts, his mouth constantly moving, issuing squeaky insults at his muscular sidekicks. As the scene played out in my mind, I inadvertently found myself staring at him. The ogre's arm moved slightly, his elbow jabbing Sean. Then he discreetly pointed a thick finger in my direction. I snapped out of my haze, turning away, but kept them in my periphery. I soon discovered that they weren't looking at me, but just below me, where Lauren was bending over the table, struggling to line up a physically awkward shot that forced her to balance her upper body out over the table. She propped her ass up in the air, perfectly suspending it on full display in her tight jeans. Her red thong clung to her body, much of it visible as it spread out in a "T" over her hips. I looked away as soon as humanly possible, turning my attention to the guys against the wall. They were making no effort to disguise their behavior, taking mental snapshots, grinning, giggling and relishing in the moment. Jay didn't notice. But his blonde opponent did and gave his buddies an approving smile as he edged towards them to improve his own viewing angle. I took it all in, not knowing what to do or say. I let it go, counting the long seconds that passed before Lauren finally sent a wayward shot off the far wall.

"That's a nice try," Lou said.

"Good technique," his partner added through a guilty smile, failing to mask his intended double meaning. He proceeded to miss his shot. The jerk-offs kept laughing openly, causing even Jay to stop and look over, inquisitively trying to sort out the reason for the laughter.

He looked to me, but I just sat there, eyes transfixed on the table. Jay sank a couple of shots, making the game more respectable, and then Lou knocked in the last of the striped balls before missing his attempt to kill the eight ball. It was Lauren's turn again, and I was on high alert, scanning the room for wandering eyes. Sure enough, Lauren arched her back, pushing her ass into the air as she lined up her shot. I wondered how long this had been going on—considered if she was at all responsible, perhaps playing to the crowd. I watched her. She was completely oblivious, truly focused on her shot and unaware of the sideshow.

I could understand them looking. It was only natural to peek—maybe once, perhaps twice, but not on every shot and not with open disregard for etiquette. I felt a sobering jolt of anger run through me. I looked at each of the classless fucks, ignorant of their intimidating physique. I imagined them to be street tough, the type of kids who welcomed a fight. I tried to steady my nerve by taking a deep breath and looking away. It was a mismatch, sure suicide. When I checked in again, I saw Sean and his ogre friend still completely enthralled with the thong, blatantly sizing her up. Sean must have felt my penetrating eyes because I managed to break his concentration. He shot me a quick look, his eyes wild, and then quickly turned his attention back to Lauren. As she hit her shot, he playfully stuck out his tongue and flicked it suggestively in her direction. My silent warning had done nothing to dissuade him.

"You guys want to take a picture next time? You fucking hyenas," I said loud and clear. The words came out instinctively, carrying across the room before I could realize it. Somehow, my mouth had functioned independently of my mind, and for a brief moment, I wasn't sure if I had been the one talking.

The ogre took an aggressive step forward, his body coming to life and straightening. Sean perked up too, his eyes hardening as he stepped forward alongside his friend. The players all turned quickly, Jay and Lauren not quite sure what to make of the situation.

"You definitely weren't talking to us, right?" Sean's mouth was flapping again.

"I think he was, Sean. I think this prick—"

"What's up, Roy?" Jay interrupted.

"These jerk-offs are fucking thong-gazers. They're enjoying themselves watching Lauren shoot. Especially Tony Tough Nuts here," I said, nodding towards Sean.

"Take a walk, guy. You don't want to do this," the ogre said, stepping in front of Sean, his chin protruding as he spoke.

Carmen interceded, but I easily sidestepped her, coming to a stop right in front of the kid. He was bigger than I was—wider and taller—his hulking shoulders looming over me. I sensed the others gathering around us.

"Don't be stupid," he said assertively, his eyes searing a hole in my brow.

I was scared, shitless actually. Spasms of adrenaline zipped through my legs, and I felt my body shake, charging itself with energy. I caught some movement to my right. It was Luna walking briskly towards the table. I heard Carmen say my name, pleading for me to stop. I didn't want to fight. Well, maybe I did. Bodies continued to close around us, the whole time Sean squawking from the safety of his friend's shadow, like Ulf Samuelson behind a linesman.

"Take a walk," the ogre said again, this time giving me a hard shove to the left shoulder. The force of his jab turned me sideways. I took another step away from him with my right foot so that I had my back to him. I sensed him move forward behind me, probably ready to follow up with another push. As he moved in behind me, I stepped quickly to my left, letting my left shoulder dip, my torso also twisting to the left. Then I spun upward, my body uncorking and my right elbow flying in the lead. I felt my elbow strike his chin hard, heard a crunching noise—bone on bone.

I was never a very good fighter, having lost more than I won. But I did okay most of the time, thanks to my dad's advice to throw the first punch whenever a fight was inevitable. That philosophy worked well at Sky Bar, and the ogre fell like Ivan Drago. I knew that I had broken his jaw. The elbow is one of the hardest bones in the body, a fact that was not lost on me. But I was stunned at how perfectly I had caught him, it being a somewhat blind shot and all. I looked down at him on the ground. He was a dazed puddle of muscles and mass. I started towards him, and he began staggering to his feet, managing to get one foot and a knee on the ground, but it was too late. I belted him again with a solid right hand, flush on the nose. He fell back again, blood pouring from his nose like water from a gutter. Then my lights went out.

The next thing I remember clearly was Carmen and a burly bouncer in a yellow T-shirt helping me out of Sky Bar. They sat me down on the curb and Luna, Jay and Lauren joined us. The blow hadn't cut me, but I could feel the back of my head throbbing and ran my fingers over a golf ball-sized welt. Carmen rubbed my back, and assured me I was okay. She kept kissing the side of my face, her green eyes moist and scared.

I gradually returned to form, my senses rebooting and my surroundings coming into focus. Over my shoulder, I saw Brad, Tripp and a massive crowd huddled inside at the bar's huge picture window. Tripp looked at me intensely, the way you look at a teammate in the locker room before a big game. He gave me the thumbs up—such a loser. He must have seen the other guy.

The lights from the cop cars were magnificent, a laser show of sorts. There were two of them, parked right in front of me, just a few feet from the curb. I saw a set of eyes staring at me from the back seat of the second car. It was Sean. Hatred spilled from his evil eyes. I stared hard, a cocky smirk slowly revealing itself. I laughed and made sure he saw it. He mouthed something incoherent from behind the glass. I looked away, down at the street between my feet; noticing discarded pieces of gum, one green and one white, that had become flat, permanent spots on the charcoal pavement. I looked further out in the street and saw more pieces, more spots. I heard someone call my name once and then again.

"Roy McGrath?" An officer was standing over me.

I stood up. "Yes, sir," I said.

"Are you okay?" he asked, his tone lacking concern.

"Yes, sir, I think so."

"He was knocked out, sir. Even under normal circumstances, I don't think he is qualified to answer that question. And with all due respect, sir, I don't think you are either." Carmen's voice was edgy, but respectful.

He stared at her, acknowledging her input. He wrinkled his brow, letting out a heavy sigh. I stood there patiently. As I waited for him to speak, I saw an officer leading Luna and Jay towards the other car. They were in handcuffs. I swallowed nails but knew it was a formality at that point.

"I am fine, sir," I said confidently.

His face relaxed, then grew serious. "I have to place you under arrest." He reached for his cuffs. "Please turn around, hands behind your back. Are you aware of your rights?"

"Yes, sir," I said, staring into Carmen's eyes for security.

She provided it, but then turned back towards the officer. "Sir, I really think he should go to the hospital to be checked out."

The cuffs were heavy on my wrists. I instinctively tried to spread my arms behind my back to test the amount of give, which was minimal.

"I will monitor him very closely, miss. We're extremely cautious with head injuries."

"Clearly not," she mumbled.

"Did you say something, miss?" He begged her to challenge him again. She locked eyes with him.

"Where will he be taken?" she asked finally.

"District A-1, New Sudbury Street."

"We'll be right behind you, Roy," she said, motioning to Lauren.

"Everything will be fine, Carmen."

"Let's go, Mr. McGrath, in the car," the officer said, interrupting our Hollywood farewell.

As I approached the car, Jay and Luna pushed over to make room for me. Jay was on the far side, but his smile radiated throughout the back seat of the car.

"Gentlemen," I said a bit nervously, maneuvering into the open space. Luna wasn't smiling at all, and his face swelled badly on the right side. He barely managed a nod, his eyes fixed on the Plexiglas partition in front of us.

Jay leaned forward so I could see him. His lower lip was a bubble with dark cuts showing where his teeth had clearly cut through. "We fucked them up, Roy, fucked them up bad. I think you broke that kid's face. You should have seen—"

"Hey, do not talk. This is not the time. Trust me, okay. Keep your mouths shut. We were defending ourselves. Be smart," Luna snapped without turning his head. He continued staring straight ahead and spoke through the side of his mouth.

Jay just shrugged and sat back. Luna was probably right, and I'm glad he reinforced the severity of the situation. "Did you tell them you're a cop?" I asked, also talking without moving my lips.

He turned to face me. His eyes were ablaze. "Yes, but these are city cops. Just tell them the truth, and I think we'll be okay. This can't fuck up my career. I can't have a record."

15

The two officers walked us up the concrete stairs and into a small check-in room, which featured a worn linoleum floor. Black plastic chairs sat against the far wall to my left. The officers nodded to the uniformed woman seated behind a glass enclosure and then hustled us through heavy doors and into a wide hallway with four wooden benches, two on each side. They told us to sit on the first bench to our right. Covering the bulletin board across from us were colored notices, flyers and other memos. I strained my eyes to read them, but was only able to make out two: one promoting a Youth Task Force Golf Tournament on August 16 and one listing dates for a Crime Scene Seminar that had already passed in June. We were just outside what appeared to be a large room with people moving frantically about. Through the open door, I could see both uniformed and non-uniformed people milling around. Phones were ringing non-stop. Above the door, hung an old black and white clock, the same kind we had in elementary school—the kind with the big red second hand. It read 2:31 a.m. I followed the red second hand as it swept around the worn white face.

"What happens next?" Jay asked, two minutes and seven seconds later.

"We'll be booked, and then we'll be questioned. Remember, just tell the truth—self-defense," Luna answered.

"Bet your ass it was self-defense. That animal hit him with a pool stick." Jay's voice carried.

"Quiet. Jay, calm the fuck down." Luna looked at his friend like a concerned father. "This is my career we are talking about here. You have to be composed. Tell them exactly what happened. Be articulate and be polite. Can you do that?"

Jay looked away. "Yes, I can do that, Mark."

"Look, they spoke with people at the scene, and one of the cops stayed behind to conduct interviews. They'll have a good understanding of what went down. The one guy, Lowry, seems like a good cop." Luna confirmed we were paying attention before continuing. "Remember, when the big kid pushed Roy, he established contact. Roy, say you felt threatened, which I am sure you did. You had no other recourse but to act in self-defense. Also, Roy getting hit with the pool stick was important. It was a threat from a previously unengaged party and clearly necessitated we act in defense of our friend. We were in the right."

"Do I have to use all that official language, Luna?" Jay asked sarcastically, this time able to keep his volume under control. Luna managed a smile.

"Hey, are those punks in there?" I asked, suddenly intrigued.

"The one kid certainly isn't. He's probably getting screws drilled into his face at Mass General," Jay blurted, the excitement returning to his voice.

"I fucked him up pretty good, huh?"

Luna turned to me, hesitated, but then let down his guard. "Oh, yeah, you absolutely ruined him. It was unreal. I don't know what got into you."

"And it might have ended there if that goon Lou hadn't decided to go *Out for Justice* with the pool stick. What a fucking whack-job. You're lucky he didn't split you open," Jay said.

"Hard head," I replied, knocking on my dome. "So, what happened after the asshole hit me? I don't remember."

"It was a shit-show. Luna bum-rushed him, and I jumped in too, of course. I went after the skinny kid Sean. I blasted him with two shots, but then he kind of got me to the ground and blew up my lip with a left. Luna was nails, pummeling Lou while fending off his blonde friend," Jay recounted.

"For a while anyway, until one of them got loose and labeled me, right here," Luna added, tilting his head to expose the maroon welt that was enveloping his right cheek and eye. "The bouncers got in there just in time. We were about to get rolled."

"Thanks for getting my back, Luna," Jay murmured. But Luna stared straight ahead. He seemed to be reading one of the pink flyers pinned up on the bulletin board opposite us. A few awkward yet fleeting seconds passed, but then Luna leaned right, letting his upper body brush against Jay's. It was an intimate nudge and I assume the highest form of affection among cuffed individuals.

"You didn't need me anyway, Jay."

Jay's shoulders collapsed forward briefly, and then he returned the nudge, a childish smile covering his bleeding and distorted face. Fresh blood filled the gaps between his teeth, a slimy pink film covering the bottom row. It was the goofiest smile I had ever seen.

16

I went last, but only a few minutes after Jay and Mark. An obese cop in a snug navy uniform came to the doorway and announced my name, which was both dramatic and unnecessary because I was the only jerk sitting there. I stood up and made my way over to the navy whale.

"Come with me, Mr. McGrath," he said flatly.

I couldn't help but think about flat foot, donut-stuffing stereotypes. He definitely spent his days behind a desk, guzzling sodas and hammering meat topped pizza slices. I would have checked for the grease stain on his chest, but he turned quickly to lead me into the loud room. I followed his lumbering strides and immediately scanned the room for Jay and Luna. I saw Jay seated at a desk with one of the arresting officers, the younger, quiet one. But his back was to me, so he didn't see me. I didn't see Luna anywhere, but I did see two of the punks we had fought, Sean and Lou. They were at separate desks on the far side of the room, which I realized was huge—much bigger than a high school cafeteria. My interest in the scene must have stalled my pace and the fat cop let me know. Stopping, he turned to me and said tersely, "Let's go, Mr. McGrath."

I hurried my steps and followed his saggy ass until he stopped and stepped aside. "Stand on the feet, and look straight ahead, please. Don't smile."

I looked at him, studying his flabby face for a clue. He had soft features, exuding a jolly innocence that reminded me of Santa Claus. Beads of sweat had formed on his forehead and above his upper lip. His tiny brown eyes looked to the floor, and his instructions became clear. Two black rubber footprints were on the floor in front of me. I stepped onto them, my feet covering them almost perfectly, apparently a good fit. I stared into the lens of the machine and heard the click before turning sideways for a profile shot. I immediately wondered if I had photographed well, stupid but completely true. My chum buddy nodded silently, the sweat beads having multiplied. Before we moved on, I was finally able to see the name badge over his left breast. It read "Stone," not "Claus."

"This way, please, Mr. McGrath." I followed just a few steps before he stopped again and asked me to turn around. "I am going to remove your handcuffs briefly so that we can fingerprint you." He moved behind me, methodically and swiftly removing the left cuff. As he brushed past me, I caught a whiff of stale B.O., but I reasoned that it could have and should have been worse. "Place your left hand on your head while I remove the other handcuff."

It was probably just procedure, but I couldn't help a muted chuckle when I realized this was a precautionary step to guard against my pulling a Jack Bauer move in a room full of fifty armed officers. I flexed my wrists and shook my hands, relieved to have freedom of motion once again. But it was short-lived because he soon asked that I let my fingers go limp.

He then took each of my digits into his meaty hands, and one by one dipped them in ink and printed them onto a small sheet of paper. As he finished with my right hand, I became very anxious. The mug shot and the printing had effectively eaten away at my presumption of innocence. I was scared like Jean Van de Velde at Carnoustie. I shuddered, my left hand shaking in Stone's grasp. I tried to relax. As soon as the printing was done, the cuffs were replaced, but not without another whiff of Officer Stone's B.O. He led me to a desk, where my arresting officer was waiting.

"Sir, Roy McGrath." Stone perked up, putting on his best show.

"Thanks, Stoney."

"Sit down, Roy. I'm Officer Lowry. How are you feeling? Your head okay?"

"Yes, sir, I feel just fine."

"Good, I am going to ask you a few questions."

"I don't understand, sir. Why am I being booked like this? I was defending myself. I was hit with—"

"Whoa, we're just going to discuss tonight's events. That's all. Let me do my job. Based on everything I have heard, you shouldn't have much to worry about…but I didn't just say that. Now, I am going to ask you some questions. Answer them honestly and to the best of your ability."

I let my body relax and controlled my breathing. I felt my heart slow to a jog. I looked at Officer Lowry. He looked on patiently, his eyes wide and his chin down, as if waiting for me to give the go ahead. He held a clipboard in his lap, a pen dangling from his right hand. Despite a hulking frame and dark features, including a meticulously trimmed, full black moustache, he had a gentle way about him and seemed sincere—a cop who was just doing his job and understood the situation. His demeanor put me at ease. I nodded.

He asked me a bunch of simple questions first: full name, address, height, weight, prior record, blah, blah and blah. He scribbled furiously. Then he asked me to recount exactly what had happened.

"Okay, so I was watching my friend and his girlfriend play pool against these two—"

"Wait a second, hold up. Start from the beginning, Roy. Start with when you left your house this evening."

I stopped speaking and considered why all that mattered, but then I realized he needed to put the fight into context. I decided to make a concerted effort to downplay alcohol consumption. I hesitated, wondering if Jay and Mark would be smart enough to do the same. Mark for sure, Jay maybe not. I struggled with the words, trying to map out an appropriate and convincing version. I looked up at Lowry. He didn't seem agitated by my pause at all, inviting me to take my time. Then it hit me. It didn't really matter if Jay and Luna abbreviated their consumption. I had thrown the first punch. I had been the initiator on our side, acting in response to a physical threat. My friends had simply reacted to a clearly dangerous situation. Their consumption level was of lesser importance. My judgment was the primary concern and would be what they called into question. This all ran through my mind in a matter of seconds, surprisingly lucid considering my predicament.

I took another deep breath and spoke as evenly and in as much detail as possible, leaving out little. Lowry seemed disinterested in the whole thing. He sat back calmly in his chair, his hands enclosed and resting on his lap. The few times he did scribble on his pad, I peeked but couldn't decipher anything. He asked questions throughout, usually when I had left out a potential detail. The frequency of questions and the writing increased during my fight recollections. I exaggerated the shove, saying it nearly knocked me off my feet. When I was finished, he just sat there in his same position. I thought maybe he was asleep, but with his eyes open. Then finally, he wrinkled his brow and after giving a few short nods, he sat up.

"You can call someone now," he said flatly. "I'll remove your cuffs."

"Which phone should I use?" I asked.

"Do you have a cell phone?"

"Yes."

"Use that. You're allowed one call, but you can keep calling until you reach someone," he said nicely. He removed my cuffs, placing them back on his hip. I stretched my wrists again and pulled out my phone. There were six missed calls, all from Carmen.

She answered my call on the half-ring. "Are you okay?"

"Yes, I'm fine, Carmen. Listen, can you call Bobby and make sure he is okay? Explain—"

"Already did. He was worried, but I talked to him. I told him I'd call again as soon as I heard anything." She was speaking in quick bursts, a mile a minute. "I'm right downstairs. Did they set bail yet? The woman down here said they would try to find a bail bondsman, but since it is so late, we might have to wait until morning. Did they find one? Are you sure your head is okay. I can—"

"Honey, easy…slow down." As I spoke, another officer caught Lowry's attention, motioning to him from across the room. Carmen continued spewing words, but I lost focus, watching as Lowry made his way over to the other cop, a very tall, thin, clean-cut sort. "One second, Carmen."

Lowry spoke briefly with the officer, both of their eyes glancing towards me. Lowry then followed the cop into an adjacent room. Thoughts ran through my head, none of them clear. I spun in the chair, scanning the room for Mark or Jay but did not see them. Sean and Lou weren't there either.

"Hey, sorry, this is weird. My officer just left me here at his desk."

"Why?"

"I don't know."

"Maybe he went to get the bail bondsman. Did they do that yet?"

"Huh? No, he went with another cop, maybe his boss."

"Well, I'd say it's a good sign if he left you alone. Maybe they'll let you go."

"I don't know. I was booked. I had my picture taken, and they fingerprinted me. I assume that means I am officially under arrest."

"But you were already under arrest at Sky Bar, right? Where are Jay and Mark?"

"Not sure. Listen, when he gets back, I'll see what the deal is and see if I can call you again. If I can't, just stay there and ask one of the cops down there how to go about paying bail. Please don't go anywhere, Carmen."

"Okay, if I don't hear from you in ten minutes, I'll check on the bail. The woman down here said it is typically $40 for this sort of incident. Hopefully I'll see you very soon. I love you, Roy."

"Love you too. Carmen, thanks, I'm glad you're here."

I waited impatiently, keeping busy by studying the characters around me. At the desk to my right, an unshaven guy in his late thirties or early forties sat quietly as a stout, balding cop with frosty white hair questioned him. The arrestee looked like a truck driver and had the apathy of a guy who had been there, done that. It wasn't his first time. He wore a dirty black AC/DC T-shirt, and his hair was awry as though he had just rolled out of bed. I immediately took him to be a wife beater but couldn't make out his conversation. I wouldn't have fought him for prize money and turned away for fear he might notice I was eavesdropping. To my left, sat a kid my age or a bit younger. He was completely pickled, beyond words. He kept standing up as he spoke, his body dancing with a ghost. Twice, I heard his officer say, "Sit down, Mr. Whitehurst!"

Whitehurst continued his animated circus act. I surmised that he had been pulled over for driving under the influence. From my vantage point, driving while impaired was more like it. I listened carefully to his conversation, learning that he had been stopped going the wrong way on a downtown exit ramp for route 93 north. He claimed he had drunk only three beers at the Pawtucket Red Sox game before heading home towards Norwood. The wrong way on an exit ramp was shocking enough, scary in fact, but that was nothing.

Pawtucket is in northern Rhode Island, about twenty miles south of Norwood. But Boston is twenty miles *north* of Norwood. I listened in awe as the officer broke down the geography. He was practically laughing as he explained it. I wondered if Whitehurst was at least turning around to head south—probably not. If the skyline hadn't tipped him off, maybe the Canadian border would have done the trick.

Whitehurst was too drunk to listen, too pent up to acknowledge his gaffe. He just kept slurring that he wasn't drunk and had been making a basic u-turn. I wanted to sign him up, commission him to guide my friends and me into the Amazon. Clearly, the kid had an internal compass.

My mind wandered. I envisioned Whitehurst starring in a *Saturday Night Live* skit, "The Intoxicated Navigator." The premise was obvious. Another cop, from a nearby desk was following the action too, but he reached his threshold and interrupted the cyclical conversation by walking over and dropping a map on the desk in front of Whitehurst. He spread it out and then slammed it with his right hand, deadening a pointy crease. "Here, this is Pawtucket. This is Norwood—where you live Mr. Whitehurst—and this here's Boston," he said exasperated. He had jabbed his finger to signify each location, smirking at the other cop as he held it on Boston. "And here's the ramp at Causeway Street where you were doing the backstroke. Up here, that's New Hampshire. That's Maine."

Whitehurst looked on indifferently at first, but then something registered. He had needed the visual, the paint-by-numbers template. He finally grasped the magnitude of his directional ignorance. He sulked and sat back in his chair. His eyes met mine, and I smiled with patronizing compassion, surely making him feel worse.

I was back on the *Saturday Night Live* idea, contemplating specific "The Intoxicated Navigator" episodes, when Officer Lowry reappeared. He walked briskly towards me, though calmly and collectedly. He slowed his pace as he reached the desk. Then he smiled warmly and with ease. "Mr. McGrath, you are free to go."

I didn't move. Waiting for the punch line, I looked up at him hesitantly. "Huh?"

"You can go. There'll be no charges filed against you." He glanced around the room, and it was clear he wanted to explain more.

"Okay, what about the picture, the prints? Was I charged? What happens next?" I was completely confused.

"It was just procedure. You can go. If you'd like to file charges against Mr. Barker, that's another story."

"Mr. Barker?" I asked.

"He's the gentleman who assaulted you. Actually, he'll be facing charges regardless. You may have to appear. For now, I suggest you go."

"Thank you, Officer. Thank you."

"You bet. Stay out of trouble next time."

I nodded, making sure to look him right in the eye. I tried to keep to a cool, casual pace as I made my way to the door, but I'm sure I looked nervous, and I was practically running by the time I reached the hallway.

17

The fix was in. Luna had played his get-out-of-jail-free card, Jay and I riding the coat tails. Luna downplayed his influence and said that the facts and eyewitness accounts had been equally important. Two or three times, he explained the difference between being arrested, being charged and being prosecuted. But to me, it was one in the same, and I was happy to escape with no record.

Luna used his connections to do some homework on our opponents. He wanted perspective. We all did. I had been way off. Fuck Revere. They weren't tough Italians from the rugged north shore community. They were South Boston kids. I couldn't believe it when I heard it. By birthright, they were tough, hardnosed and Irish, from a notoriously blue-collar and close-knit neighborhood. They were the type of kids we envied from the sheltered confines of rural Belmont. Being Irish, I had always admired Southie's romantic passion for its heritage.

It had once been a fraternal community of working-class Irish Catholic families who piled generation upon generation into triple-decker homes. Consequence, loyalty and self-policing ruled its streets. In the 1970s, it was thrust into the national spotlight when the residents took a predictable hard-line against imposed mix-race busing. The subsequent interracial violence horrified the nation. But many secretly admired the resolve and fortitude exhibited by both sides. People certainly saw not to fuck with the people of South Boston, MA. Unless, of course, you had the National Guard on your side, which is what it took to subdue the chaos.

Recent years had seen an influx of new habitants to Southie. The old ways were alive and well, just confined to the background and played out in speak-easy bars, living rooms and family businesses where people still took great pride in being tough, hardworking and Irish. But younger professionals had started filling up Southie's convenient-to-town, waterfront properties in the mid-nineties, just prior to our under card battle with Lou Barker and Co.

I respected South Boston. It had the St. Patrick's Day parade. It had the no-nonsense reputation, and it had Shamrocks, lots of Shamrocks. Playing against South Boston hockey teams growing up had meant three things: the coolest shamrock-clad uniforms in the league, a wonderful lesson in profanity and the most grueling, intimidating, stick-carving game of the year. Rarely, we won.

As for the fight at Sky Bar, all of us had been white, Catholic and Irish, but the similarities ended there. Their accents were stronger, their street smarts better and their fists harder. If I had known they were Southie kids, I'm not so sure I would have swung my elbow.

Waiting for Luna was always a test in endurance. And that Wednesday was no different. He was punctual with opinion, but rarely with action. Finally, he emerged, the sports section of the *Boston Globe* in his right hand. Jay had suggested a trip to Suffolk Downs, the historic horse track in East Boston. I had been there before, but never on a weekday. Jay, with the summer essentially off, had been a handful of times already. He warned me straight up about the mid-week crowd, a cross-section of a degenerate nation. That turned out to be a conservative description. Bobby had been bored stupid all week, having accumulated a surplus in backyard defeats, so he came along too. According to Jay, the food at Suffolk was notoriously atomic, so we stopped at Rick's Pizza & Subs.

"Rick's," as everyone called it, was the town pizza spot in Belmont. There were similar places in town, but Rick's was king. Sure, Theo's had better subs, Al's better crust, and Palfrey Café a more diverse menu. The same is true in every town. The blueprint is part of small-town culture, and yet there's always one place with the best pizza—Rick's.

Rick's was located among a small cluster of businesses, on a somewhat busy street, Trapelo Road, which connected the two small squares Waverly and Cushing. Jay butchered a parallel parking job in front of Rick's, earning us belittling stares from some folks eating in the window. As soon as I stepped out of the car, the smell hit me. Rick's shared the block with an insurance agency, the town movie theater and a hair salon, making the source of the crisp cheese and garlic unmistakable. I stopped, letting the rich Italian fragrance tease my senses.

"Nice parking, Jay!" a heckler yelled from the Mobil station across the street. I knew the voice without looking. It was Brian Conley's. We all gave a wave. Brian was a couple of years older and ran a landscaping business with his brother, Tim, and their dad. By the looks of his new black pickup, business was grand.

"That a new truck?" I yelled, a passing car drowning out my voice. Brian nodded as he pulled the nozzle from the side of the truck. "Very nice, I like the new logo," I shouted, having noticed the new Conley & Sons Landscaping Services 484–7760 graphic, painted in metallic green on the passenger-side door.

"Thanks! It's sharp, isn't it? Hey, shouldn't you guys be working?"

We laughed. "I'm watching Bobby for the week."

"I'm sure he's watching you," he shot back, waving goodbye as he climbed into the truck.

There was some truth in that. On my way into Rick's, I glanced up at the movie theater sign, where unevenly spaced black letters spelled, *My Big Fat Greek Wedding.* To the right, "630" and "900" appeared, reflecting the only two show times. I shook my head. The theater was old, but not charming. Rather, it was dilapidated, dirty and small with a flat seating plane that made for impossible sightlines. It had been a hot date spot back in middle school. Luna had once hooked up with Jacqueline Weir in the back row during a showing of *The Prince of Tides.* He still talked about it as though it was some great accomplishment, which I suppose it was, at the ripe age of thirteen and with his peers lurking in nearby seats. The seat itself became a biohazard of sorts, one that we avoided during subsequent visits.

It made sense that *My Big Fat Greek Wedding* was playing because the theater was always six to eight months behind the times, and *My Big Fat Greek Wedding* had premiered in January. Other than elderly folks looking to save a couple bucks and unlicensed, horny adolescents, the place didn't draw flies. The extreme disparity in clientele made for a surreal scene, old ladies who snuck in their own chocolates surrounded by teenagers looking to get into somebody's pants.

I caught up with Jay, who was waiting for me at the door to Rick's. "What's the over/under on people we know?" he asked jokingly.

I checked my watch. "I'll go with six."

"And the percentage that Luna will engage in a meaningless conversation?"

"One hundred," I said flatly.

Luna was a politician that way, friends and acquaintances routinely referring to him as "The Mayor." He loved bumping into people and engaging in casual, rhetorical conversation. It was all genuine too, not an act. But Jay and I were lesser beings, preferring to watch and enjoy the unintentional comedy of it all.

As I entered Rick's, my taste buds kicked and screamed with anticipation. And the atmosphere only accentuated the experience. Forget about traditional pizza shop décor—bright lights, orange tabletops and snack racks. Rick's was dim and it was cozy, a labyrinth of dark wood and deep tones constant throughout. Construction workers huddled in shaded corners while local executives in ties lined the long wooden counter, slamming down slices next to filthy plumbers and sweaty teenagers.

We sauntered up to the high counter, where Bobby and Luna were ordering two large cheese pies. Toppings were sacrilegious at Rick's, suffocating the trademark three-cheese blend. We grabbed a booth against the sidewall and settled in for the agonizing wait. I fiddled with the hot pepper shaker while my friends compared hunger credentials. The smells were tantalizing, and it was inevitable that I'd burn the roof of my mouth. It happened every time. Our light conversation barely registered, anticipation killing our ability to form coherent conversation.

I quietly studied the faces around me, making evaluations as if I were at a poker table. Jay's face looked worn. He seemed lost in thought; his hollow eyes a lifeless façade to something amiss. I wondered if he had caught on to Lauren or if his career plight had finally gotten to him. Something was up. Bobby's demeanor was in stark contrast. His eyes were alive, and I could feel his energy. He didn't have a care in the world—a picture of innocence. He was so at ease around us, dodging our insecure needling, dishing out his own insults and letting his personality take hold.

As expected, Luna couldn't sit still. His eyes were darting around the small room looking for familiar faces as he eavesdropped on conversations. "Sorry you don't recognize anyone, Mark. We can come back later if you'd like," I said sarcastically.

"Maybe we should," he replied.

"Here it comes," Jay interrupted. "Establish the LZ."

I turned to see Nick Wainright carrying over our pies. We all sat up in our seats and readied our area, quickly and carefully rearranging napkin dispensers, the pepper and our drinks to create a landing zone. "Nick! How goes it kid?" I asked excitedly. "Did you sling these pies yourself?"

"Hardly," Nick muttered.

"What *are* you slinging back there, Nick?" I replied with a shit-eating grin. Nick smiled awkwardly and then looked at Luna.

"Don't look at *him.* I asked the question, Nick. Officer Luna doesn't care anyway. Do you Luna?"

"I don't know what you're talking about," Luna said.

Nick stood stiff, scared and expressionless. He fit the stoner profile: curly black hair was his defining feature, tangling and weaving in a sloppy heap. His T-shirt fit loosely over his bony frame, and a white, sauce-stained apron hung from his neck like a leash, the waist ties freely floating along his legs. As he finally shuffled away, I saw the predictable swatch of plaid boxers revealed by jeans that seemed one quick movement away from becoming ankle bait.

Patronizing Nick was always fun. He was a punk, and I hated his guts. Bobby did too, but he'd already made it known with an ass kicking. Throughout middle school, Nick and his delinquent friends had given my cousin, Tammy, a particularly hard time, bringing her to tears on numerous occasions. Tammy was a year younger than Bobby and suffered from a developmental delay. She and Bobby were close, so she confided in him about Nick making fun of her. Expectedly, Bobby flipped out, pulling a Kermit Washington on Nick one day after school. Bobby was suspended for a week—a big deal back then and a joke considering the circumstances.

Nick's family was a shit-show. His dad was a non-factor, stories of his whereabouts mostly exaggerated speculation. His mom was a chain-smoking real estate agent with a leather face and a propensity for sealing deals on her back. She was town trash. Nick's older brother, Andrew, had fled to Florida, where he was supposedly working for a chain-link fence company. Like Nick, he was an All-American dickhead. Some felt they were victims, just by-products of their environment. Not true.

By high school, Nick was selling drugs, but not on school grounds at Belmont High because that was a Cardinal sin, punishable by public stoning or something worse. Even Nick knew this, so he had somewhat ingeniously come up with a clandestine, transaction-rich alternative. He leveraged his role as pizza delivery boy to make sales. And sales he made, hand over fist.

We all stared down at the simmering pies, bits of cheese bubbling in sizzling pools of oil. We feigned patience. I tried to buy time, taking a sip of my lemonade and sitting through a few seconds of silence.

"Fuck this," Bobby said, swiping at a slice with one hand. As he began to lift it, the flimsy tip succumbed to physics, a glob of sauce and cheese falling back onto the pan.

We broke out into childish laughter. I quickly forked up Bobby's lost pile of gooey cheese and deposited it on my plate. Bobby was not amused. "That's unfortunate, Bobby," Jay said gleefully.

"That's mine," Bobby whined.

"Sorry, rules of engagement." I blew on the orphaned piece of cheese and then cautiously sucked it off my fork, taunting Bobby with each embellished chew.

"Bobby, that's amateur hour, an F-. Watch a pro," Luna boasted, pulling the crust with one hand as he cradled the tip with his other. "That's how it's done here at Rick's."

"Fuck off, Luna," Bobby snapped. He repeated Luna's technique, opting this time for the biggest slice on the pan. Per usual, Jay went last and opted for a modest slice.

"So, *slinging*?" Bobby asked during a brief pause in the action, referring to my banter with Nick. "We are in Belmont right? Shit, is this East Baltimore? If it is, that's fine. Just let me know, so I can adjust my lingo accordingly. *Slinging*...that was priceless."

"That it was," Jay added.

"Whatever, I heard it on BET."

"Roy, people sling rock or blow, not marijuana," Bobby said.

"I like it, and I'm going to continue using it."

Bobby smirked. "Fine, sling me another slice...*dog*."

I laughed half-heartedly. "Fuck Nick, I want to strangle his ass. You need to bag that kid, Luna," I said, changing the subject.

"Unfortunately, as a department, we can't let personal vendettas dictate our police work. Besides, he's small potatoes. We've got some information on his supplier, a guy in Arlington. He might go down and soon. He's been on our radar for three or four years. He sells to Belmont, Arlington and Cambridge."

"Even so, Nick's not the brightest bulb. And everyone knows his gig, I'm surprised he hasn't been busted yet," Bobby added.

"Yeah, extra pineapple," Jay said.

"That's not how it works. This isn't the movies, Jay," Bobby responded.

Jay and I liked to pretend that people who wanted a dime bag with their pizza asked for extra pineapple on their pie. In reality, Nick knew who his drug customers were, and when he didn't, he had a stash of shit in his delivery car anyway. He'd even go in for a hit or two if he wasn't too busy. Bobby told the story of one particular night when Nick had delivered to a party and gone in for a pull but then stayed for a few too many beers. Bobby and his friends then rifled half a dozen pizzas from Nick's car. The munchies were a powerful thing, vengeance too. It didn't matter to Nick because Rick was his uncle and surrogate father, and a sympathetic one at that. Nick was steeped deep in job security.

"I know where he keeps his stash," Bobby mumbled without looking up, instead sizing up another monster slice.

"You do?" Jay gushed overzealously.

"Whoa, keep it in your pants, Jay. You have enough issues between the gambling and the drinking," Luna counseled.

Bobby leaned in, looking slowly to his left and then to his right, finally leaning in even further. "Luna, ear muffs," he demanded. Luna pretended to cover his ears with his hands, as he always did when we discussed illegalities. "He keeps it here," Bobby said in a hushed tone. His face was just inches from mine. He smiled wide, pizza oil glistening on his lower lip. His big blue eyes were shining, lashes flickering. "In the basement," he whispered.

"No shit…it makes sense actually. Nobody would ever suspect it," Jay exclaimed, sighing. "Wait, where in the basement?" Jay continued after a beat. I looked up at him, and our eyes met for the briefest of moments. He shrugged.

Bobby went on. "I guess there's a dropped ceiling in the supply closet. You know, one of those white panel setups…"

"Yes, thanks, Bobby. We're all familiar with dropped ceilings," I said.

"Also known as a suspended ceiling in some construction circles," Jay added, jumping on the opportunity to dump on Bobby.

"Thanks, Bob Vila, appreciate the tutorial," Bobby quipped.

We all leaned back in our seats. A brief silence followed before Bobby reached for his slice and took a bite.

18

As we pulled off Route 1A and into the incredibly vast parking lot surrounding Suffolk Downs, I was amazed to see so many cars on a weekday. We parked and then hurried past a few dejected souls, likely already relieved of their week's paycheck after just a few races. Nearing the clubhouse entrance, we passed by two kids our age, who were cooking kielbasa on a small legless grill. They raised their plastic red cups at us. "Good luck," one shouted.

"Smells good," I called, nodding to them.

"I didn't know people tailgate here," Bobby said, shuffling to catch up.

"They don't, that's an anomaly," I said flatly.

"Good, then we don't have to worry about flying footballs," Jay said calmly. Everyone laughed—Bobby so hard that he actually had to stop walking. I couldn't help but offer a wry smile.

***

The previous fall, Jay and I had gone to a Boston College football game and tailgated like rock stars on Shea Field, a very exclusive grass parking lot reserved for BC alums and their guests. It was a place rich in arrogance and also Brie cheese. We had made the rounds after the game too, stopping by numerous tailgates until settling in at a particularly lively one hosted by our friend Colin. We played flip cup and Beirut well after the 3:00 p.m. game had ended.

Beirut involved two teams of two at opposite ends of a long table. In front of each team rested ten half-filled cups of beer, arranged in a triangle. Each team attempted to throw ping-pong balls into the other team's cups, with players required to chug sank cups before returning a toss. The first team to wipe out the opponent's cups won and earned the right to shout drunken insults. Most people played with one ball and alternate shots—one team shoots, then the next. I preferred to play with two balls and another adaptation, which allowed players to fight for all loose balls as they careened off cups and bystanders. This meant no alternating shots and very little sportsmanship. My faster, chaotic version of the game forced players to drink their beers quickly and make shots on the fly.

Jay and I instituted these high-tempo rules that day on Shea Field. We ended up with our shirts off, schooling various BC students, and horrifying any, and all passersby. The BC alums, in their Polo sweaters and tassel loafers, were surely pissed that we had taken over their sacred ground. They watched in awe.

When our dominance on the Beirut table had run its course, we put our shirts back on and staggered into vinyl chairs, settling in for cold hot dogs and scraps of potato chips. Two young kids were tossing a football to our left. I watched as they lofted the ball high into the dark sky, which was faintly illuminated by a few towering light stanchions. Despite my drunkenness, I quickly discerned that the kid closest to me had the better, more accurate arm. Within seconds, the blue ball came bouncing my way. I scooped it up. It was youth-sized and fit perfectly into my right hand. The kid with the good arm was already standing over me, an innocent grin enveloping his freckled face. Maybe age nine or so, he wore a baggy maroon Boston College sweatshirt. Instinctively, I hopped up out of my seat and motioned for him to run a pattern. He smiled with recognition and then sped off to my right for fifty feet before cutting across to the left, his eyes turning to me as he made the cut. I lofted the ball into the night and it dropped a bit too far out ahead of him, but he accelerated and made a nice running catch. He jogged the ball back to me, clearly insinuating that he wanted to run another play.

"Looks like you've got a new friend," Jay said, holding the bag up to his mouth to swallow the chip shavings.

"You got anyone to cover you?" I asked, scanning the surrounding tailgates for his buddy. I didn't spot him, but my little receiver didn't even turn to look.

"He sucks," he snapped.

I laughed. "Go ten feet, turn, I'll pump fake, and then turn to go deep."

"Got it," he said excitedly before racing away. He ran a few more routes and with each passing throw, my enthusiasm grew and so too did the velocity of my throws. The kid was good, snatching pass after pass, even the errant ones.

"This time, go straight out at that trashcan, and then make a sharp cut left towards the cars." He turned to consider his path as I spoke.

"Watch this gun," I bragged to Jay. Jay sat up a bit in his chair, his eyes shattered with exposed blood vessels. The kid ran a perfect pattern, even over emphasizing the sharp cut with a head fake. I gripped the rubber ball a little tighter this time and waited anxiously for him to arrive at the spot. And then I uncorked a missile. The kid turned for the ball but never saw it because it sailed over his head, a blue blur camouflaged by the sky and headed straight for Helen Emerson.

What happened next went down in slow motion. It's the same way with car accidents—the few that I have been in anyway. Time stands still, the pending impact frozen right there in all its clarity. Someone or something must want to be sure we have a good, long look at disaster, and yet altering it is always impossible.

I saw her cutting between two parked cars, inching her way along their length, from front to back. She was likely heading to the group tailgating nearby or maybe towards another tailgate across the open area in which we were playing. Just as she emerged from between the cars, the ball was there, a tight destructive spiral. The eerie pause followed. Then her face exploded, and she crumbled to her knees. Jay leapt—no catapulted—from his chair. It would have made NBA scouts drool. I sobered up in a nanosecond. I hurried over to the woman. She was on her back, struggling to sit up. Her glasses had snapped at the bridge, one piece dangling lensless from her left ear, the other piece somewhere in the grass. Blood trickled from between her eyes, where it looked like the compression of her glasses, not the ball itself had opened a gash.

"I am so sorry. I am so sorry," I managed, mouthing it to nobody in particular.

"What the hell is the matter with you? You asshole! Look at my wife. Jesus Christ. Look at her." The man she had been walking with was now a volcano of anger. He knelt over his wife, who looked at least sixty, maybe older. He gently held her cheek in his hand, turning as he screamed. There were two choices: one involving her, the other me. With every word, he raised himself as if he were going to get up, but he fought the urge, instead remaining on one knee at his wife's side. I stood over them briefly before hesitantly crouching in to help. He flailed an arm towards me, grunted, and made it very clear that my assistance was not welcome. As I moved back a few steps, her blue eyes met mine, questioning me without anger, but with conviction. I wanted to dig a hole and tunnel my way to Mongolia. I felt one hundred eyes fall on me and sensed just as many fingers point in my direction. Finally, a few people came over to help her to her feet and then into a folding metal chair. A crowd gathered, young and old.

With his wife finally settled in the chair, the man stampeded in my direction. "What is wrong with you?" he shouted.

"Sir, I am so sorry, it was an accident. I was playing catch with a boy." I turned to point at my playmate, but he was AWOL. Later, Jay and I joked that he had, in fact, been just an aberration. Either that or he had high-tailed it off that field. The man's breathing grew more exaggerated as I searched helplessly for the kid in the maroon sweatshirt. "I was playing catch, sir. Obviously I didn't *mean* to hit your wife."

He didn't respond, instead shit-beat me with his eyes and then looked back at her again. Looking at her must have triggered something because before I knew it, he had the front of my shirt in his right hand. He twisted the cotton clockwise and pulled me in close. He was a small man with grayish white hair and a moustache to match. That and his hunched posture exposed his age, but his bones seemed strong, not frail. I immediately assumed he was Irish, a safe bet all things considered. I liked him.

I could feel his anger, his arm twitching as he tightened his grip. He moved in, his nose just a few inches from my chin. I could hear each breathe, and stale, it singed my nostrils. I prepared to get my ass beat by grandpa. There would be plenty of witnesses too, plenty of people to spread the word. I deserved it and had already decided to take the beating and keep my arms down.

"Look, sir, all I can do is apologize," I said frustrated. Another hand flashed across my face, and I flinched, but it was just Jay. He grabbed the old man's forearm. Not good.

"Hey, get your fucking hands off my friend."

Good old Jay, loyal to a fault. His eyes were hot. It was a side of him I rarely saw. "Whoa, Jay, it's alright. Jay! Jay! Jay!" I yelled.

The crowd was buzzing too. Shouts and pleas filled the air, the noise growing into a blur. Jay let go, but he quickly shimmied his body in between us, the man losing his grip on my shirt. Without hesitation, Jay put his arms on the man's shoulders. "Sir, come on, don't make this worse. It was an accident."

"Dick!" It was the woman. And she had gotten his attention. His shoulders relaxed in Jay's hands. He released a loud sigh, a demon escaping.

He returned to his wife and we followed him, emotions in check. I watched disbelievingly as another man brought over a frozen steak, covered in plastic wrap, for her to hold over her face. I wanted to make a joke about always packing extra sirloin, but didn't. The woman held the beef firmly to her face. I needed a camera. The steak shielded one of her eyes, but the other found me. She looked on with disgust. My remorse was off the charts. I winced pathetically as if I too felt the pain.

Within a couple of minutes, I was huddled over the roof of a white Nissan with the husband, who introduced himself as Dick Emerson. His lawyer friend, Ted, joined us while Jay looked on from a few feet away. Ted asked for my license and began frantically jotting down my information on the back of a game program. I watched as he wrote, all in caps, seemingly to emphasize the seriousness of the situation.

When we were done, I felt at ease, proud to be accountable and face the consequences. It sure beat getting my ass kicked up and down Shea Field by Jim Leyland's long-lost twin. After Ted finished writing the last digit of my phone number, I asked if I could issue a proper apology to Mrs. Emerson. The two men looked at each other. Ted nodded. "I think you had better," Dick said curtly.

I walked slowly behind him towards his wife. With each step, I felt the eyes of too many. I bowed my head in shame, unable to make eye contact with any of them.

"Helen, honey, he wants to say something," Dick said, a bit too sweetly as if I were there to perform last rights. Dick moved to the side. I looked up as she pulled the thawing meat from her face. Those fragile blue eyes waited, anticipating explanation. She blinked twice and I looked at Dick, who just furled his brow. A heavy silence enveloped the field, except for the distant sound of traffic on Beacon Street. I fixed my eyes on her again. She seemed alert and comfortable.

"I'm so sorry, ma'am. I can't begin to explain, but it was an accident. I am so sorry."

She didn't smile, but her eyes warmed slightly with the glow of forgiveness. She nodded slightly and in a low voice said, "Okay." I determined right there that she would be just fine. And she was because I never did hear from her, Dick or Ted.

Memories of the Emerson incident had faded by the time we reached the concourse inside Suffolk Downs. The fourth race of the day, our first, was about to start. With just a few minutes before post, we didn't have time to do any research, though I use the word "research" loosely. For me, it usually consisted of scanning the race form for each horse's previous results, record at Suffolk and success against other ponies in the field. Jay and Luna had similarly lame and inadequate techniques.

In this case, we each picked a horse to win based on its name or a lucky number. Except Jay, who boxed a trifecta—a wager that attempts to identify the top three finishers in any order. Being a rookie, Bobby went along with my pick, agreeing that the number five horse, Itchy Unicorn, had the most creative name on the board and was capable of a decent payout on a $10 bet at twenty to one odds.

After making the mindless wagers, we hustled outside and found a spot along the fence that rimmed the track. I leaned over the top rail of the white wooden fence and peered down to the left. A cluster of brown and black ripped around the final turn like a storm hell-bent on destruction. Dark bits of dirt spewed in its wake, spraying out in all directions. A few horses slid to the outside, pushed wide and into obscurity. I strained my eyes, squinting with all my might. I felt bodies perk up all around me, a massive rush of energy filling the air. Eighty more yards. A giant wave of adrenaline rolled over my shoulders and the hairs on my neck stood up. The dark mass rocketed towards me, each combatant an indistinguishable shape. People screamed their heads off. Wild freakish excitement came to life through deranged shouts and expletive-filled demands. Fifty yards remained.

"Come on you fucker," Luna yelped.

"Run you bastard, run," a man behind us followed.

It was no place for a child. "Where's the five?" I shouted, but nobody answered me. "Where the hell is the five? Come on five!" I screamed at the top of my lungs.

The cloud of dust drew nearer and so too did the sound. At thirty yards out, the rhythmic smacking of hooves grew louder and louder until I felt as if I would be trampled by the onrushing stampede. As they sped towards us, I was finally able to pick up the yellow "5" flag in the midst of a lead pack. Without realizing it, I was soon in the air, short frantic leaps of excitement carrying me airborne. "Do it, five. Do it!"

The public address announcer shouted the leader names into his microphone, but at track level, it was just white noise. I jumped one final time, this time higher, propelling myself with a rung of the fence. Then a dusty blur roared. A yellow image flashed before me, but only after a flash of red and then green. As the leaders swept over the finish line, a wave of hot air passed through my hair. Then disgruntled agony revealed itself with a few muffled remarks. The exhales were so plentiful you could hear them. A handful of orgasmic screams shot up in random locations. My shoulders slumped, and my body gave way. My load was blown. I looked to the scoreboard to confirm what I already knew to be true. A digital gold "2" lit up the black square next to first, then a "7" next to second and finally a "5" next to third. In the now silent infield, the public address announcer's voice was finally audible, crystal clear, in fact. "The winner is number two, Hungry Felix, followed by number seven, Dream Weaver and number five, Itchy Unicorn."

"Anybody have anything?" Luna asked apathetically, ripping up the ticket in his hand.

"I thought I had Itchy Unicorn…until he stepped in that fucking pothole," I snapped.

"Oh, is that what happened? I thought maybe a sniper got him," Bobby added, countering with his own frustration. "I thought we had something, big brother."

In our haste to get a bet in and get down to the rail, we had rushed through the crowd without taking in the scene around us. As I leaned my back against the fence and tore up my ticket, a bizarre world finally unfolded before me. "Look at this place. This is the armpit of the earth," I remarked.

"Why does everyone look so angry?" Bobby asked naively.

"I'm sure they have their reasons. Lost their job, lost their family, lost something," I speculated, watching grizzly, hard looking men shuffle away from the rail in disgust.

"Or their mind," Jay added.

Within minutes, the trackside viewing area was empty. A concrete yard dotted with green wooden benches sat abandoned, discarded white tickets tumbling in the light breeze. A few men sat silently on the benches, some in pairs, their potbellies disguised by windbreakers and their balding heads by mesh hats. Most wore jackets and polyester pants despite the ninety-degree weather. I looked up to the grandstand and saw a huge green façade framing rows of empty wooden seats. Every twentieth seat or so was occupied by people studying their race forms, pencils in hand, through thick-rimmed glasses. It was as if they were in the midst of an SAT test for the elderly. A few heads popped up periodically, perhaps for a breath or perhaps to stare out at the grass canvas surrounding the track itself. I fought the urge to yell out, "Time is up, pencils down."

Steel green pillars held the roof in place, a dark ramp adjacent to each pillar leading to the concourse. Shadowy figures lurked in the darkness. As I watched, a sense of yesterday manifested itself. I let my eyes wander through the green seats again and looked for a sign, any sign that signified that it was 2002. There wasn't one. It just as easily could have been 1949.

"Let's get some beers," Luna said, bringing me back from my moment of solitude.

"And me too?" Bobby asked.

"You bet, but hang here, Bobby." I gave him a light jab to the gut and started towards the concourse before he could fire a return shot. "Study the next race," I shouted over my shoulder.

"What do I look for?"

"Cool names."

"Study their history at Suffolk."

"Check for well-known trainers."

Jay, Luna and I simultaneously offered suggestions, confirming that we didn't know how to handicap a race.

While we waited in the beer line, I continued the surveillance of my surroundings. Glancing up at the dirty white ceiling of the concourse, I noticed a series of colorful banners hanging from the rafters, carefully spaced out in rows like the championship banners at Boston Garden. Each banner recognized a famous horse and the year it had run at Suffolk. Every color of the rainbow was represented, the row of banners stretching all the way to the far end of the building. I was surprised by how many names I knew and by the sheer number of star ponies that had run there. Superstars like Seabiscuit, Whirlaway and Cigar.

As I read the banners farther away, my feet instinctively scuffled along in the slow-paced line. I was trying to read a distant green banner when a throaty voice startled me. "What can I get you?"

I turned to see a woman's unblinking brown eyes. She was wearing a standard blue concessions shirt with a "Peg" nametag resting over her A-cupped left breast. The crisp shirt snuggly enveloped her elderly frame. A spiky, blonde dye-job framed her raisin face. She gnawed on a wad of white gum, her lower lip moving in a perfect reverse circle with each chew. I froze, fixating on the gum as it tumbled in her mouth.

"What'll it be, honey?" she asked impatiently.

"Two Bud Lights," I managed. I tipped her three bucks, then waited for a special thank you, but got none. She just casually brushed the bills aside.

Luna was already on his way back outside, the sun hitting him as he emerged from the dim concourse. Jay waited for me. He cocked his head upward, towards one of the many TV monitors listing odds for the fifth race.

"Who do you like?"

"I don't know yet, maybe three–four–nine, definitely the three," he answered without looking away from the monitor. I looked up to check out the numbers myself. The three was ten to one, the four was the favorite at three to one, and the nine was a long shot at thirty-two to one.

"That'd be a nice payout if you hit the trifecta," I said, nodding my head with approval.

"What, like a grand, you figure?"

I agreed with another nod. "Let's head out. We still have sixteen minutes until post," I said, anxious to remove myself from the suffocating gloom of the concourse. We hadn't taken a step or two when I felt a sharp smack on my back. I jerked forward and beer spilled over the plastic cups, flowing down into my hands. I turned, expecting to find Sean or Lou Barker.

But it was John "Rock" Rocatelli. "Jesus, Rock. You scared the shit out of me."

"Roy, what brings you to the Downs? I know why this guy is here," he said, slapping Jay on the arm. Rock clearly liked to supplement his greetings with physical contact.

"I'm off this week, watching Bobby. There's not much else to do. I can only play so much Wiffle Ball. And my golf game is shit."

"Yeah, mine too. You guys hit anything yet?"

"No, we just got here. We will. It's early." Jay looked to the ground as he spoke, undoubtedly intimidated by Rock's personality and his equally imposing physical presence.

"I hope so for your sake, Cantwell," Rock snapped with an edge that revealed Jay was in the hole. He was Jay's bookie.

Rock's father and Rock's uncle ran a substantial sports booking business out of Medford. Their connection to the Italian mafia in

Boston was openly known but never discussed. At twenty-six, Rock had no choice but to join the family business. He knew too many potential customers.

A year older than us, Rock had been a star fullback who went on to play football at Curry College. Luna and I also knew Rock from hockey. He was a likeable, overly gregarious kid. Like most of his family, he was enormous, a bear of a kid, though not mean-spirited. But he certainly had a mean streak, and I had seen it on the ice more than a few times. He was the type of kid who went around slapping backs, but not realizing his own strength, he left welts and bruises on his victims.

Rock's older brother, Anthony, was a completely different animal, and feared, to put it plain and simple. Big, but not as big as Rock, he was a surly, impatient prick whose very presence killed chatter. He had been in the family business from the beginning, and we speculated that his responsibilities went beyond collecting money. I tried to keep my encounters with him to a minimum. His rap sheet read like a short novel—decorated mostly by breaking and enterings and assaults on people who owed money or looked at him the wrong way.

His temper had landed him in jail back in the early nineties. In broad daylight, he had beaten a debtor, Jared Latimer, within inches of his life, right in front of Jared's home. Anthony's weapon of choice had been the shovel Jared was using to clear his walkway. It led to a conviction for aggravated assault. Conveniently, none of Jared's neighbors or the four eyewitnesses could recall much detail, but an off-duty officer had caught the tail end of things, and his testimony, along with the shovel and the brutal wounds, provided ample evidence to send Anthony away for eighteen months.

Though the main shop was in Medford, the family owned a small hardware store in Belmont, where both Rock and Anthony worked. Rock was usually out front or at the register, his friendly face greeting customers and handling transactions. Anthony lurked in the shadows, confining himself to the back office, where we assumed he cut up bodies and banged strippers. More likely, he was just doing paperwork and running the numbers. Regardless, when he strolled through the store or yelled for Rock from the back, he sucked the life out of the place.

Rock folded his massive arms, revealing a barbed wire tattoo that encircled his left bicep.

"Still juicing, Rock, huh?" I asked sarcastically.

"You wish, buddy. This is all natural, just the peck deck at Gold's," he snapped back, glancing down at his arms. "I'll bench press you right here." He reached for me teasingly, but I jumped back to avoid his grasp and an accidental death. "What happened to your face, Jay?" Rock asked, finally noticing the dark red scar on Jay's lip. "One of my guys get to you already?" he joked. He grabbed Jay by the ear and quickly put him into a headlock, half of the beer splashing from Jay's cup. Rock gave Jay a playful noogie and when Jay broke free, his hair was a static mess.

"Easy, Rock, that's a $4 beer," I said, getting a kick out of the whole thing. I looked to Jay, expecting to see him laughing too, but he wasn't.

"We got into a little scuffle the other night. It was a fucking donnybrook," I offered, my voice trailing off as I glanced at Jay. Something was still eating at him. He'd been acting peculiar all day. I wondered again if maybe Lauren had come clean about Matt. Jay was always internal about things, insecure by nature and probably embarrassed as hell. I couldn't wait for Rock to leave, so I could talk to Jay. My heart sank and I felt pain. I could feel Jay's too.

"What? How'd you do?" The news surprised Rock, and he was eager for the details. I hurried through them for what seemed like the fiftieth time that week. "No shit. I'm glad you guys are okay, you fucking savages. Good for you, representing well."

I nodded, but I was growing more and more distracted by Jay's wilting demeanor.

"Say, Jay, take a walk with me? I'll buy you a new beer," Rock said.

Rock had caught me completely off-guard, out-dueling me in my attempt to get Jay alone. Jay shrugged, and before I could say anything,

Rock slapped me on the back again and led Jay back towards Peg's beer line.

The fifth race was moneyless for us too. The number six horse, No Wake, won easily. It wasn't until the break before the sixth race that I saw Jay again. Bobby was the one who spotted him, pointing to three people sitting on the far edge of the grandstand, far down to our right. I couldn't make out much detail, but I could see Jay sitting in a chair next to Rock. A man in a dark shirt stood in front of them. His back was to the track, his right foot perched up on a chair in the row below. Every few seconds, he leaned in, waving his finger at Jay before falling back.

"Luna, I don't like this," I said quietly.

"It can't be good," Luna shot back, squinting to make out the unidentified character.

"Who are those guys?" Bobby asked innocently.

"One of them is John Rocatelli. I haven't a clue about the other guy, but considering where we are, I bet he's one of John's bosses," I answered. "Luna, it makes sense they'd have a key guy here at the track, no?"

"It wouldn't surprise me. I'm sure half the people here are customers. What the fuck has he got himself into now?" Luna asked, more pissed than concerned.

"He must be down big," Bobby mumbled, showing his ability to discern the situation at hand.

"I hope they cut him off," Luna snapped.

"That's not likely. Those guys don't give a shit. They'll bleed you dry," I countered. It was true. Some small-time bookies would refuse to take action if your debt was substantial. It was a way for them to protect themselves because most outfits needed the collections to pay out winnings. It was a simple system of checks and balances. They'd freeze your account, set up a payment plan and stalk your ass, day and night. But not the Rocatelli family. Their business was big enough and stable enough to let debt slide and let it breed.

Luna hit a perfecta on the sixth race, correctly picking the top two finishers, but they were both favorites, so it only paid $46. Still, not a bad take on a $4 wager. He went to cash in. After the race ended, Jay stood and shook hands with Rock and the other fellow. I took this as a good sign. He hurried down the steps two at a time and then disappeared down a ramp. A minute later, he strolled out from the concourse. He was still ten yards away when I asked, "Everything alright?"

"Yeah, why?" he replied casually.

I looked at Bobby, who just shrugged. I pushed further. "Who was that guy with Rock? What was that all about?"

"Oh, that was Terry. He works for the family. Rock wanted me to meet him."

"Why?"

"No reason. I guess I'm just moving up the ranks on their customer list. Big spender, I suppose."

"Oh, I see, he was updating you on their member rewards program."

Jay smiled. "Yeah, exactly, pretty soon I'll qualify for the microwave."

"Bullshit," I said angrily, instantly killing the humor vibe. "What's going on, Jay? How bad is it?" I looked him dead in the eye.

Jay looked down, took a deep breath and then looked back up at me. I saw fear and hopelessness in his eyes. I swallowed a lump, the kind that makes a noise as it passes through your throat. Jay took another deep breath.

"How bad, Jay?"

"*Bad.*"

My brow wrinkled, my eyes widened and my head tilted slightly downward. I was waiting on more information. I focused my eyes on his. His eyes wandered left, then right towards Bobby and then finally back at me. "Seven grand," he whispered dejectedly, his eyes leaving mine once again.

"Wow," Bobby gasped.

I literally felt life escape from my body and vanish into the summer sky. Then my legs buckled under an invisible pressure that felt like Rosie O'Donnell. Unconsciously, I mouthed the words, "$7,000?"

Bobby stood with his mouth wide open, his face frozen with fear. I struggled to say something, but just mouthed the words yet again. "How did this happen?" I finally managed.

"I chased. Got down $1,500, started increasing my bets to make it back and then chased it all. Lost $2,500 on the Sox last night—fucking bullpen." His matter-of-fact tone was way too indifferent, disturbing, in fact.

I was seething, my breaths becoming shorter and louder. I shook my head with disappointment, outrage. I wanted to grab him and squeeze the apathy from his being. I took a purposely loud, harsh breath through clenched teeth. I turned away, looking out over the fence at the track and beyond. Dark green grass spread far out to the north, a few well-kept flowerbeds spotting the landscape. I followed the lush grass to the end, where it melted into a steep rocky cliff on which sat a large white house somewhere in East Boston. I tried to gather my thoughts, but there weren't any. I was completely shocked, speechless for the first time in my life.

"It'll be fine, Roy. I'll figure something out."

When I turned around, Luna was approaching. Jay saw him coming too. He shook his head slightly, pleading with Bobby and me to keep quiet. I frowned, consenting with my eyes.

"Jay, what gives?" Luna spat. "What was that all about?"

Jay sighed, licking his lips. "I'm down a bit. Rock and his buddy were just setting me up on a payment plan," Jay said calmly.

"Shit, how bad?" Luna asked.

"Fifteen hundred bucks, nothing too major," Jay replied. "It's no big deal. They were cool."

I wanted to come clean, lay it all out there, exposing Jay as the fucking idiot-of-the-week. Instead, I bit my tongue.

"Fuck, Jay! Not that much? Fifteen hundred fucking dollars! It's not as if you have a steady income right now..."

Jay braced himself for what was coming. Luna flipped open his race form and looked at the near page, but he wasn't reading it. Rather, I could see that he was fighting to stay mum. He breathed tensely through his nose. Then he looked back up at Jay. "Listen, Jay, that's a lot of fucking money," he said seriously. "You need to call it quits. Okay?" Luna paused, waiting for Jay's eyes, but they came and went. He continued anyway, "If you need a loan…I can help you." Luna's face was sincere now, his eyes soft.

Jay nodded dispassionately. He wouldn't take money, especially from Luna. Part of it was insecurity—the acknowledgement of defeat that came with relying on Mark, but I also think he just didn't want to burden someone else. He was too unselfish.

We continued with the beers and the bets, but it wasn't the same. Conversations were brief and lackluster, limited to short remarks and rhetorical questions offered through dead lips. Jay played ignorance, studying his racing form oblivious to the mounting concern. It was such an infuriating act, a tired one too. I was lost in thought, subscribed to worry. His debt, Lauren, his career. Walls were closing in on him, and it was only a matter of time before he'd break. I pondered what to do, knowing there wasn't much that I could say. His whole life he had taken beatings, absorbing many of life's punches. More often than not, he had cowered and chosen to walk away. That was easy with college, Lauren or a job, but not with the Rocatelli family. It was all very reckless to me. That word kept creeping into my mind. A word Jay knew well.

He never wore condoms—the last of the bareback riders. He also considered seatbelts, prescription meds and sunscreen a waste of time. But chief among his carelessness was his drinking and driving. I was just one of many people who had tried to intervene over the years. Pleading with him not to drive at the end of a night was a chore, and a grueling bout with his stubbornness. But one driving episode trumped all others. It's a story most people write off as fiction. It's not.

***

It had happened on January 19, just a few months earlier. The scene was the legendary New England Patriots/Oakland Raiders playoff game, "The Tuck Game" as it became forever known. The name obviously originated from the controversial non-fumble call involving quarterback Tom Brady. The 8:00 p.m. game was also memorable because it played out in the midst of a nasty blizzard. What started out as a standard first-round playoff game eventually became the greatest game in Patriots' history and the game that spawned a dynasty.

We had arrived early at 3:00 p.m. and before the snow. We did our tailgating routine, double fisting beers and vodka cocktails. The plan had been for me to stop drinking upon entering the game, figuring I'd be okay to drive Jay's Tempo home five hours later. Foxboro was simply electric that night, the stage and the weather creating a supernatural atmosphere. The snow was falling in sheets, the field completely covered by kickoff. I spent most of the first quarter on my feet, my excitement and anticipation swelling with every play. It was about that time that Jay got up from his seat and announced, "I have to go."

I thought nothing of it, assuming he was off to the bathroom, but as his words settled, I realized his intent. I turned to see him hustling up the metal steps, heading for the concourse. I chased after him, snowflakes blinding me as I climbed, but I didn't catch up to him until he was at the stadium's exit. A security guard in a bright orange coat stopped me and warned me that if I left, I couldn't come back in. I hesitated, turning to look back at the dark concourse behind me. I heard the deafening roar of the crowd—another Patriots' first down. I looked beyond the security guard and saw Jay stumbling up the walkway that led to our parking lot. He cast a lonely and indistinguishable silhouette against the white backdrop. Fuck it. I stepped out into the raging storm, turning my back on what would become the greatest comeback in NFL playoff history. Yes, I left *that* game. I ran after him, catching up to him at the edge of our lot. Hurrying alongside, I shouted some choice words, none of them printable. It was just white noise to Jay, just like the crowd and the cars sliding down Route 1. As he went to open the car door, I grabbed him and threw him up against it.

"What the fuck are you doing? You're leaving?"

"Yup," he said oblivious to my fury.

I thought about punching him in the face, wrestling the keys from him and firing them into the surrounding woods. But I didn't. Instead, I released him from my clutches and stepped back. "I'm not getting in that fucking death mobile. What are you going to do, leave me here?" I asked, spreading my arms wide to reveal the winter wonderland around us.

"I sure am," he said matter-of-factly and then used his sleeve to brush heaps of snow from the windshield. He opened the door and climbed into the car. I stood there helplessly in disbelief. He was really prepared to leave me, freezing in a snow-ridden, deserted parking lot outside Foxboro Stadium. I couldn't find words. He rolled down the window, big flakes instantly blowing into his face. "Last chance if you want a ride."

"Fuck you. You're a fucking asshole!"

He shifted the car into drive and pulled away. I watched astonishingly as he turned left onto Route 1 and sped north towards home. I felt like crying but didn't. I remained there in the frigid January air, the snow drifting down. It was an incredibly bizarre moment and a quiet one. Snow is strange like that, the distinctive insulating effect it has on sound. Another cheer interrupted the silence, and I turned to see the stadium, which looked like a giant bowl of jellybeans nestled into a glacier.

I considered my predicament. My mind was a mess from the booze and the desertion, but I tried to weigh my options. Jay's fate was irrelevant. In fact, I was rooting for a fatal crash. I didn't want to bother Luna, my roommates or anyone else during such a significant game. The driving would have been too treacherous anyway. I certainly didn't want Carmen driving in whiteout conditions. I did know some other people at the game, but I wasn't keen on waiting for them for three hours in a damn blizzard. I called a cab.

The long ride back to Allston was a nightmare, a suicide drive through the teeth of the relentless storm. I was nervous like Alex Rodriguez in the midst of a meaningful at bat. A hellish, spinning crash wasn't just a possibility. I fully expected it. The seatbelt was so deep beneath the seat that I imagined it tied to the muffler. I pictured the different ways my body might pinball at impact. The cabby and I followed the game on the radio, cheering as the Patriots embarked on the fairy tale comeback. We skated down the highway, and an hour and $165 later, I walked into my apartment. Pete and Tim might as well have seen Tom Brady. Jaws dropped. I quickly made up a story about Jay getting violently sick and puking up his kidneys. Pete and Tim bought it because an alternative explanation made even less sense. They said terrible things about Jay, and I agreed.

I sank into a recliner and watched the Patriots' defense get the ball back. That's when the storm knocked the cable out and that's the fucking truth. We looked on in horror, stunned by the wretched timing. The Patriots were driving. We raced into my bedroom, and I frantically unplugged the cable from my tiny twelve-inch Sony before connecting a rabbit ear antenna. I was able to secure the image, though fuzzy as it may have been. The three of us huddled on my bed like three homosexual men and watched the tuck call, kick one, kick two and the Patriots' miraculous victory. Just before Adam Vinatieri had come on to kick the game-winner; I mumbled dejectedly, "I was at this game."

The greatest win in Patriots' history brought to me in black and white on a twelve-inch screen. The next day I contemplated writing Jay out of my life. I went back and forth with the decision, ultimately determining that Drunk Jay was an altar ego, a different person who made judgments mutually exclusive of the real Jay. The decision to leave the game was utterly inexplicable. To this day, I don't know why he left. He doesn't either. It took him a good three weeks to muster up the courage to call me and attempt an apology. I heard his pain and his embarrassment through the phone, but I didn't say much, just demanded that he stop driving drunk. He did for the most part and hadn't driven drunk in the sixth months leading up to that day at Suffolk.

With only two races left, we needed something to salvage the day, something to free us from the melancholic spell cast by Jay's debt. "Let's check out the ponies," I suggested, pointing at the walking ring, where the horses paraded in a circle before each race.

We ambled over to the ring, the fence surrounding it lined with spectators. We squeezed into a gap and settled in. Handlers led a few of the horses for the ninth race around the mini track. I watched the big heads bob as they strutted past. Other horses remained in the paddock, where attendants rubbed them down and saddled them.

Up close, it was amazing to see the discrepancies. Some were giants, others dwarfs. Some were black, some brown and some gray. The gaits were different and the eyes were different too. Some seemed anxious, even jumpy, others seemed calm, disinterested. All of them had freakish muscles that rippled with every stride. The information was in surplus, but interpretation was the challenge.

The number three horse, a medium-sized chestnut one, sauntered by, his golden mane dancing as he jerked his head from side to side. He seemed uncomfortable about something. I crossed him off in my form. A small brown horse, number six, came by next. He strolled by, head down, shoulders relaxed, a sticky white liquid dripping from his lips. I wondered if his tranquil nature was a good thing or a bad thing. I decided calm was good, but too calm was bad.

"Number ten is a monster. Look at the size of him," Bobby gushed, eyeing a huge black horse with a blue "10" flag meander by. He seemingly glanced in our direction as if to acknowledge Bobby's comment.

"He knows it too," Luna added. "The cocky fucker, did you see that look?"

We all nodded. "Hah, look at this. His name is Happy Hour," I exclaimed, pointing at my racing form.

"Great name," Luna said, making a check mark next to the "10" in his form.

"Are they all boys?" Bobby asked, raising a very good question.

"Most are," said a stranger to our left. I turned to see a short man in his fifties, gnawing on an unlit cigar. He had slick black hair and stiff blue eyes. His face was bumpy and worn, certainly not the kind you'd want to kiss. He dipped his right leg awkwardly and turned towards us. "You'll see a few girls now and then. That's one there, the seven, she's a mare," he said, pointing with his cigar at a very ordinary looking brown horse to our right. "She's not much of a race horse though."

"What's a mare?" Bobby asked from his spot closest to the man.

"A mare is a girl, four years or older. Fillies are girls, under four. Not too many horses, boy or girl, race after four. Nope, most are just babies."

"Colts," Jay followed. "Boys are colts until four, and then they become stallions. A lot of them breed when they're three years old. Imagine that."

"Unless they get castrated, then they're a gelding," the man continued, his smile revealing gap riddled rows of surprisingly white teeth. He was impressed with Jay. They exchanged silent pleasantries, instantly accepting one another into some sort of secret society—one for degenerates with useless knowledge.

"So, what do you look for?" I asked cautiously. The man looked at me, his emotionless blue eyes confused and void. "What signs for a winner?" I added, gesturing with my right thumb towards the ring.

He frowned with arrogance, quipped "Different things." He then ran his left hand over his greasy hair, pulling back and stretching the wet helmet.

"Big is good, right?" Bobby followed eagerly. "Like that number ten horse, he's a fucking specimen."

"Not always. Sometimes size is a deterrent; slows them down. That big son' a bitch over there, you like him, huh?"

Bobby nodded hesitantly as he watched Happy Hour strut down the far side of the ring.

"He'll be lucky to finish. He's got a serious sweat going," the man barked.

"Huh? I don't see any sweat," Luna snapped disbelievingly. I stood on my tiptoes to get a better look across the bushes lining the inside of the ring.

"It's in his ass," Jay added calmly, drawing a pencil line through the name Happy Hour on his form.

The man smiled again, but Jay didn't see it. "This guy knows his stuff."

Jay laughed sarcastically. "Hardly," he said.

"Wait, his ass? I don't get it," I said clearly annoyed. I liked to be in the know.

"When he comes around, check out his ass-crack. You'll see it," Jay replied, his head still buried in the form.

"Oh, the white stuff," I said pointing to the number one horse, a black beauty with huge ears that ambled by us, his ass discharging a creamy white substance.

"Exactly, yes, that's sweat," the man acknowledged, reaching up again to run his left hand over his slick-back hair. It was at least the fifth time he had done so. I checked his back pocket for a Fonzi comb, but didn't see one.

"I thought that was cream, like an ointment," Bobby said a bit disgusted by the sight of a foamy white liquid dripping down the horse's hind legs. Luna made a face too, like the one a child makes before eating Brussels sprouts. And similar to the one I'd made after learning he had slept with Alyssa Brandt in high school.

I started crossing off horses with the white shit, which eliminated half the field of twelve. Happy Hour was especially sweaty, a nasty vanilla frappe flowing down his crack and covering his hind legs.

We all decided to go with the number four horse, Deleted Scenes, a twelve to one brown stud with a noticeable jump in his step and leg muscles that would have made Earl Campbell jealous. His ass was dry.

But he finished third after a good start and a game finish. Luna had him across the board and pulled in a respectable $26 for the show.

By the last race of the day, you could sense a collective fatigue infiltrate the crowd. Hope had lost out to despair for many. They went through the motions of picking one last horse—one last chance to salvage the day. Dejectedly, I turned my racing form to the last two pages and slowly scanned the names. My eyes stopped at the bottom of the left-hand page. "You've got to be shitting me…it can't be…check the seven."

Luna looked over, smiling and then doubling over in laughter. Jay had ditched his form, but eagerly leaned in for a look at mine. I firmly stuck my right finger on the big black "7" and held my form up to Jay's face.

"No way, there's no fucking way," he gasped.

"Yes way." It was right there on the page: Holiday Kid. I shook my head in awe, utter disbelief. It wasn't the least bit unusual to find a name with personal significance—your street name, a variation of your own name, a school name. It happened all the time. This was different. The irony was unworldly.

"I don't get it. Who is Holiday Kid?" Bobby was laughing too, but half-heartedly, like someone weary that the joke was on him.

Jay put an arm around Bobby's shoulders, abruptly cutting his own laughter short and transitioning into a rich, self-depreciating tone. "Bobby…*I am*…The Holiday Kid," Jay admitted, his eyes closing.

During college, Jay had often been lonely, unhappy and bored beyond belief. Jumping from school to school hadn't helped. Neither had his closed mindedness and some wet fart roommates. It reached a pinnacle when he finally settled in at Boston College. By then, he had thrown in the towel, like a sweat-pants-wearing George Costanza. He had moved home with his parents and younger siblings, commuting to and from campus and purposely avoiding any social involvement. It made for tremendous humor, Luna and I constantly referencing his new "dorm" and his new "roommates," making jokes about the one who cooked and the one who didn't allow female guests. Jay lived a life of solitary existence that was and still is unimaginable, especially in light of the contrasting environments at places like Trinity. On one hand, there was Jay, sitting down for family dinner and then fighting to watch *Walker, Texas Ranger* instead of *The Adventures of Little Koala.* On the other, his peers fighting over stale slices of pizza and easy co-eds.

Without residency at BC, Jay's social opportunities had revolved around the mostly shady characters who also called Belmont home. Boyle's became a sanctuary. The comatose social scene meant no ass either. For those two years at BC, Jay survived biblical hook-up droughts. His only respite came when girls returned home for long weekends—holidays like Columbus Day and Martin Luther King Day. Those were his Super Bowls and he prepared for them accordingly. New outfits, fresh haircuts and an infectious enthusiasm became his calling card. With resolve, determination and an unparalleled willingness to settle, he found success.

Unfortunately, Luna and I were rarely around to witness his exploits, our hockey obligations keeping us on campus. What we missed in person, we heard about in hilarious detail through Jay's handwritten newspaper articles starring "The Holiday Kid." His adventures became engrossing must-reads, Luna and I following our hero through each agonizing obstacle in his constant and unrelenting pursuit of tail. I found myself racing to my school mailbox during the days that followed holidays. Fervor peaked after the big holidays, which drew more candidates, higher stakes and the likelihood that the Kid had struck. The coverage went something like this:

HOLIDAY KID GETS IT DONE

Associated Press (Belmont)-

Columbus Day brought torrential rains and a saturated contempt to the residents of our small town. As co-eds piled into cars and cramped buses with their sights on home, they were oblivious to the melancholy that awaited them. Some returned home for the first time, no longer the naïve, timid freshman they had left as just weeks before, but now poised, omniscient and promiscuous. Yes, college girls ready to show the world their newfound assurance. Lurking in the shadows waited the centerpiece of the despondent populous. Patient, calculating and ready to pounce on false confidence, sat our friend and confidant, The Holiday Kid.

The Holiday Kid ventured out Friday evening to the scene of so many victories, The Derry in Harvard Square. With him trailed his trusting sidekick Kyle Mooney. Kyle wore a horrible red turtleneck and brutal black jeans that threatened to impede the Kid, but our hero likes a challenge. That night the Kid played hard, darting in and out of conversations, spending like a drunken sailor and lobbing compliments without prejudice. He went home empty handed, save for a drunken Mooney and two slices of Sicilian pepperoni, but he knew it was just one battle in what would be a weekend-long war.

Saturday found our hero at the home of Kate Redmond, again with Mooney by his side. With history as our witness, the Kid surely thrives at local house parties, where he can comfortably operate with intimate knowledge of all attendees. After carefully evaluating response and vibe, the Kid got cozy with one Tiffany Rapp, who looked rather hot after her first forty days on the University of Vermont campus. Shortly before midnight, the Kid effortlessly guided Ms. Rapp into an upstairs bedroom, which appeared to be that of a young girl. Various stuffed animals covered the bed and Power Ranger posters covered the walls.

The Kid got down to business, tenderly kissing and petting for the state-mandated time before going for her shirt, which came off without incident. After fondling Tiffany's undersized breasts, the Kid moved assertively for the pants. He fought off one staged denial and then proceeded with great success to remove the jeans and pleasure his guest. He had high hopes for a return serve, which he soon received. Her work was suspect, but the Kid doesn't require excellence these days, just mediocrity. In the end, the Kid cuddled up, and then both he and Tiffany returned to the party where he went on to kill nine more beers.

On occasion, an ex would come home for a random weekend and Jay would fight like a rabid dog for a piece, any piece at all. Even then, such occurrences seemed to fall on a holiday, albeit a lesser one like Earth Day. I specifically remember him landing Nancy Mandel on National Secretary Day, and I have the article to prove it. Her dad had been in the next room, snoring on the couch, meaning Jay had to keep her pants on and maneuver his hand in tight space. The article spoke of the Kid's inability to perform up to snuff due to the restraints of a pants-on approach. He feared for his hard-earned reputation, arguing that the performance was a statistical anomaly, a hiccup in what had been a fine career.

Holiday Kid, the horse, was forty to one, a true long shot, but he could have been ninety to one or three-legged and he still would have been our guy. Our excitement was subdued when Holiday Kid emerged from his paddock. He was unimposing—puny really—and looked more like something you'd see at a town fair carrying girls in pigtails. He walked quickly around the track as though he were in a hurry.

"He's smaller than the jockey," Bobby said derisively. We watched as he skipped by, feeling a bit reassured when we saw that he had a clean ass.

"It's not the size of the horse in the fight, it's the size of the fight in the horse," Luna countered stoically.

"You'd know, right, Luna?" I quipped. My joke drew hearty laughs. "Fuck it, we're on him. Let's go ten bucks each," I suggested.

"Done," Jay said and handed me the cash, followed by Luna and then Bobby, reluctantly as if I were being trusted with his college fund.

Once at the window, I threw in an extra $10, just because. That made $50. We hustled over to the track level viewing area, but couldn't get close to the fence, so I stood on tiptoes and watched as the horses entered the starting gate. A post-Armageddon silence fell over the track. I could hear Jay breathing over my left shoulder. Finally, the bell rang, like one in an elementary school, followed by a quick clang as the metal gates slammed open. Just like that, the serenity was gone. Incoherent shouts spilled into the air.

Holiday Kid stumbled to the first pole, squeezing in amongst a cluster of horses. They moved as one around the first turn and then the second, just a few lengths off the two leaders. He was in there somewhere, hidden by his taller peers.

"Where is he?" Bobby yelled, leaping into the air for a better view.

"He's in that pack," I replied.

"Damn it. He'll be stampeded, the little shit," Bobby snapped.

As they neared the third turn, the two leaders seemed to lose ground to the pack and when they came out of the turn, everything was in disarray. The previous leader, number three, was now fifth or sixth. A new pack of three horses burst into the lead.

"Ugh, come on, Kid." I heard Luna's dejection sweep past me. He had hopped up on a picnic table and was watching with a tepid look of displeasure. I took two quick bounds and joined him on the table. I picked up the unmistakable figure of the Kid as he floundered along and drifted back.

"No!" I shouted.

He held his not-good-enough pace into the fourth and final turn, struggling to maintain his spot ten lengths back. But as he made his way into the turn, the jockey gracefully guided him towards the rail. It was a thing of beauty, like a car—in this case a Dodge Neon—shifting lanes on an empty highway. The lead horses fought for every inch, almost colliding as they roared around the turn and onto the stretch. Heads bobbed back and forth, eyes wide and white. One of the lead ponies, the number six, couldn't take the torrid pace and slipped back, other horses passing him. Then there were two. They battled down the track, the crowd frenzied. The Kid hung tough, skipping along the rail unbeknownst to the top two and the delirious spectators.

Jay jumped up onto the table, Bobby too. The table lurched forward, briefly stealing our attention until we restored balance by shifting our feet. Jay let out an ear-piercing scream inches from my left ear. "Here he comes! Here he comes!"

It stunned me, rattling my head. I leapt involuntarily, watching as miraculously, the Kid kicked it into another gear and ripped down the stretch, still hugging the rail. You couldn't miss him. It was a remarkable burst as if he'd been shot from a cannon. His momentum soon became the crowds, fans pointing at the Kid. Gasping with horror, they realized the two leaders were about to have company. People all around us glanced down at their forms, trying to identify the name of pesky number seven. He closed to two lengths, then one. The crowd was frantic, so many of them banking on the other two—the popular favorites. People fought valiantly for their ponies, urging them on with spit-spewing screams. Hold on.

My body movements became strictly impulsive, my knees colliding with others as we fell all over each other. It was like standing in a canoe. With thirty yards to go, the Kid shot past the favorites. They hung in for a stride or two but couldn't keep up. Holiday Kid blasted past them and sped over the finish line.

I jumped in the air with my arms raised high. Bobby and I embraced, probably tighter than we ever had before. Luna joined us for a group hug, our arms intertwined and our feet still bouncing. Jay stood in the midst of us, the circle of euphoria closing in around him. He stood proud, his feet firmly on the ground, his arms raised in the air and his hands in tense fists. He screamed like a warrior, raw emotion pouring out of him. I saw a few faces below staring up at us. Some smiled, amused by our celebration or perhaps familiar with the feeling of hitting a long shot. Others looked on with disgust, not amused by our unruly reaction and bitter about their own fate. We tightened the circle around Jay, our sweaty bodies sticking to him as we continued the emasculating celebration.

"The Holiday Kid strikes again!" Jay yelled, his words echoing across the retreating crowd. A bearded man in a white shirt turned briefly as he walked away. Jay's eyes caught his, and to this man and to everyone else, he yelled it once more, "The Holiday Kid strikes again!"

19

Cashing a $2,000 ticket was no walk in the park because any payout over $600 was taxable and required paperwork for Uncle Sam. But we weren't prepared to report shit. Elderly citizens were exempt from the tax and lucky for us, we might as well have been at a casting call for *Cocoon III*. There'd be no shortage of arthritic lowlifes willing to cash our ticket for a percentage of the winnings. The unwritten rule for such services called for 10%, but we'd decided to hold firm on a little more than 6% or $125.

We took our search seriously, sizing up each prospect with a critical eye. Luna found the first legitimate candidate, a thin old man clutching a black wooden cane. His face was tired, cheating death. His skin had no hue, except for rosy lines that formed where it wrapped tightly over his sharp cheekbones. He stood at a plastic trash barrel, a foot-long hot dog resting on the cover. He struggled to tear open a mustard pack with his cane-free hand and whatever teeth he had left. He gnawed off a piece of the packet and spat it to the ground before spreading the golden sauce over half the dog. He took a bite that barely registered, nibbling on the tiny nub that protruded from the bun. It was painful to watch.

Luna, the best man for the job, made his way over while we stayed back at an unthreatening distance. Luna seemed to make small talk, flashing his trademark smile. Luna then opened another packet of mustard and gracefully covered the other half of the dog. The man grinned with delight, revealing a mouth full of yellow teeth. Luna said something else and the man gazed in our direction, squinting to evaluate us. I stood up straight and made myself look innocent by changing the complexion of my eyes. The man snapped off another feeble piece of hot dog and chewed it with his mouth open. Luna spoke again, gesturing with his hands in a helpless way. The man shifted his weight, tightening his grip on the cane and slamming it against the barrel. "Then find someone else," he barked, pieces of bun shooting from his mouth.

I quickly went on the counter attack, B-lining for another elderly fellow in a red corduroy hat. I launched into my spiel, the man with the cane following the action while he continued working on the hot dog. Within seconds, I had a deal. "Excellent, $125 it is," I said in a loud voice.

The man in the red hat nodded repeatedly, looking over at Bobby and Jay and even giving a friendly wave. I led him towards my friends, the man with the cane growing more and more agitated by the moment. Just as we passed the man with the cane, he motioned to Luna, who was still standing silently a few feet away from his mark. "Okay, I'll do it," he grumbled.

I stopped and the man in the red hat did too. "Just a second, sir," I said, turning to Luna, who gave me an affirmative. I broke the news. "I'm sorry, sir. I think my friend has already found someone."

"Ah, come on. What the fuck? Get your shit together," he snapped, quickly altering his mood. I handed him $10 for his trouble, and he stomped away towards the beer line.

Luna waited while his new partner finished the dog and then followed him to the window, keeping back to disguise the operation from track staff who didn't give a fuck anyway. I watched it all unfold with Jay and Bobby, each of us eager to get our hands on the cash.

"What was that? What just happened there?" Jay asked, still confused by the negotiations.

"I told my guy that we had a $1,000 ticket; told him we'd pay $125 for his services," I explained.

"No you didn't. You didn't. That's dirty."

"Hey, it's his fault for not asking to see it."

"And if he did?" Jay asked.

"I hadn't thought that far ahead."

Luna returned with the stake and we fussed over it like amateurs. We hurried out of the stadium, whooping and hollering as we crossed the increasingly vacant lot. Luna grabbed my arm as we approached the car, pulling me in tight. His eyes were intense, sincerity pouring through them. "You know what we're doing with our money, right?"

I did. My money was Jay's the second Holiday Kid had crossed the finish line. I couldn't possibly have expected the same sympathy or generosity from Bobby. He was too far removed. Luna was the wildcard. Though he was famously generous, he was equally strong-minded. When he wanted to impose a lesson, that's exactly what happened. I wasn't sure if he felt handing Jay money encouraged behavior and veiled hard truths. I thought maybe his patience had run out; thought he might be poised to let Jay fail and in doing so face such truths. But I had underestimated him and should have known better. I beamed with pride as if I were the beneficiary. It was inspiring to feel the tight bond that connected us.

Mark pulled almost $500 from his shorts and handed it to me. "Here," he said. "You give it to him. And make sure he takes it."

We dropped Bobby off at the gym, where he insisted he'd get in a workout despite his buzz. Minutes later, Jay brought the car to a stop in front of his house. He and Luna had grown up as neighbors, living directly across the street from each other on Spring Street. Luna had recently moved into an apartment with his sister in nearby Watertown, but he was still a fixture at his mom's place, where he often checked in on her. Luna dismissed himself with fist taps before climbing up his mom's long driveway and disappearing behind the house.

Jay and I stood outside his car. I had agreed to stop in for another beer, expecting Mrs. Cantwell to call us into action, as she would surely need assistance with dinner preparations. The prospect of a hot meal was reward enough. I had already predicted tuna casserole or Swedish meatballs, two of her staple dishes and both delicious.

"Jay, hold up a sec," I said, pausing on the sidewalk. He turned after scooping up a Nerf football that someone had left on the front lawn. He underhanded it to me, and I corralled it, noticing a chunk that had been removed by a dog or a feral sibling.

He moved in closer, and I pulled the cash from my pocket. "Here. This is Luna's and mine. You know what to do with it."

He jerked back, completely taken by surprise. He stared at the money and then laughed insincerely, a muffled gasp of nervous energy. "No way, not a chance."

"Come on, Jay. Take it. We didn't even earn it. We both want to help. It's nothing, really."

"You know me better than that."

"Take it." I held it out, waiting for him to meet my hand with his own.

He sighed, the frustration burning up inside him. "This is my thing. I don't want you guys involved."

"We already are, Jay."

He shook his head with conviction, the full power of his stubbornness rearing its ugly head.

"Don't be a prick. Take the money. I'm not going to stand here all day. Take it, or I'll walk in that door and give it to your mom."

"You wouldn't."

"Really, well, *you know me* better than that." I took a step towards the walkway to the front door, dropping the football.

"You're an asshole. Fine, fine, I'll take it."

"Good." I turned it over to him but held it tight as he tried to pull it away. The resistance surprised him. My hand overlapped his, and I tightened my grip, looking up into his eyes. "Jay, don't fuck this up. This is a lot of money. This is for a payoff, not for a parlay. Do the right thing."

He swallowed hard. "I will."

I let go of the wad, and we stood silently for a few more seconds.

"Mark?" he asked quietly, clumsily kicking at the football.

"Without hesitation, he came to me, in fact."

Jay looked up towards Luna's house across the street. "He's a good friend," Jay acknowledged.

"Of course he is. Don't ever doubt it."

Jay kicked at the football again, dribbling it with his right foot as if it were a soccer ball. "It's just…when I'm around him, sometimes I feel like such a piece of shit. Like I have let everyone down, you know?"

I nodded slowly, sensing a talk coming on. I wasn't good at such open communication, except with Carmen. With everyone else, I felt vulnerable sharing and receiving so much. I wanted to change the conversation and get back into a comfort zone, but I realized Jay needed me, so I gave in. "That's not true. We don't think that. And you've got a lot of people around you that care about you: your family, your friends, Lauren."

"You can scratch her off that list."

Impulsively, I went into play dumb mode but just as quickly realized that I couldn't fake it. He'd have called my bluff. "Yeah, I sort of knew," I said ashamed, struggling to look him in the eye.

"What? You knew…about Matt? And did you think maybe you ought to tell me?" His tone escalated with every word, the anger blossoming.

There was no way, unless at gunpoint, that I was busting out the details. Never. "I saw his car at her place the other night, *late*. I didn't want to say anything right away. I wanted to give her a chance to tell you herself. I swear I was going to tell you by the weekend if she didn't."

"Oh, so you had a timeline. Come on, Roy."

"Hey, for all I knew, they were just hanging out." The images of her amateur porn hour appeared vividly in my mind, and I couldn't wash them away.

"Well, they weren't. They hooked up a little. Sounds like they might be getting back together or at least things are heading that way."

"Jay, I am sorry about that and for not saying anything." I caught his eye and he actually held, focusing on mine.

"It doesn't matter. I suppose you had good intentions. It wouldn't have changed anything. It is what it is. When it rains, it pours. My life sucks." Just when I thought it might wind down, he pulled me back in. He continued, "Sometimes I think I should get the fuck out of here. Start over. Look at me. I live with my parents. I work at fucking Harrington's. I just got dumped by a high school girl, and I'll have to check the list on the fridge, but I'm pretty sure it's my night to do dishes."

"It's kind of funny actually," I said.

"I wasn't finished. I have $223 in my savings account. Even with this, I'll still be in the hole to the mob for $5,500. I drive an '87 Ford Tempo on which my dad pays the insurance, and my greatest asset is a fucking Springsteen box set. It's all really fucking pathetic."

That was enough for me. I was sick of listening to the bullshit, woe is me crap. I didn't harbor much sympathy for people who complained about such trivial shit. I had lived and breathed it at Ward and was way too familiar with people who gave too much of a fuck about the wrong things.

"Jay, forget about the trappings of success—everyone's obsession with owning a titanium-shafted driver and a summer home. It's all shit. I thought that I wanted those things—wrinkle-free Italian suits, a flat screen TV with PIP. I still do sometimes because it's hard not to. But it's all wrong. And it doesn't ensure that we won't get a text-only obituary. Perceptions aren't measurements. I wouldn't trade my friends for every last drop of oil on the Saudi peninsula, my mom for Phil Knight's debit card, and not Carmen for a villa in Italy either. People like us, we have so much, yet we take it all for granted. It's time to appreciate each friend, each student, each loved one. Fuck, each experience. Days like today. Show me the balance sheet worth more. Show me the car, the job, the hemisphere, the anything. Still, we wake up dead set on maximizing public appraisal and showcasing the unseen. We follow shadows, shuffling along like a parade, too stupid to be naive, too ambitious to be bold."

My face twitched. It felt weightless. I tried to recalibrate my emotions but couldn't. It had been quite a rant, one of fortuitous momentum. I knew what I had said, and yet I couldn't recall a single word. Jay was speculative, lost in thought, likely trying to interpret my feelings, which I had veiled with analogies and the hypothetical.

"Well, Socrates, you're right, very right," he said after a long pause. "I suppose it is difficult to keep everyone's perspective in…perspective."

"Good, can we get a beer then?"

"Yeah, let's do it." He gave the football a hard boot, sending it bouncing across the yard and into some bushes. I followed him, my heart pounding with nervous delight. "Don't forget your soap box," he quipped without breaking stride.

20

It was a dead giveaway: a hardware store open for business until 9:00 p.m. It made no sense. I suppose it was a necessity in order to match hours with the bigger superstores like Home Depot. But that seemed more coincidental than anything else, proven by the fact that the Rocatelli store had maintained the late hours for twenty-five years, dating back well before Home Depot burst onto the scene.

We arrived at the small parking lot off Belmont Street and pulled into a spot next to a navy Camry. The lot had once been a gas station, the name "Peterson Gas" still faintly visible on the storefront, even though the giant red letters had long been removed. The sheet of ghostly dirt and grime that covered the little white building failed to adhere where the letters once hung, leaving a perfect stencil. Three old pumps, stripped of their nozzles, stood like motionless metal droids. We walked along Belmont Street, past Cotter's Beauty Salon and Kramer Insurance, both of which were closed.

I followed Jay through the door, glancing up at the ridiculous green sign that read simply, yet appropriately "Hardware." As we entered the musky interior, a little bell that hung overhead jingled to announce our presence. Jay stopped at the shiny gumball machine immediately to our left and deposited a quarter. An oversized ball clunked its way down the passage and dropped into Jay's hand when he lifted the latch. "Yellow. I always get yellow," he whimpered.

I dug into my pockets but came up empty. "Grab me one, will you?" I asked. Jay stuck another quarter in the slot and watched as I gently turned the knob with a measured, slow twist. I flung open the latch and let a big red ball fall into my hand. "It's all in the wrist, baby," I said.

Jay frowned with sarcastic frustration. He jerked another quarter from his pocket and placed it in the slot. I nodded with encouragement. His eyes stayed on mine as he spun the knob with a slow, tender twist. I nodded some more. He opened the lid and a big green ball slid out into his hand. I couldn't help but laugh, but Jay wasn't amused. He reached into his pocket again.

"Jay, come on. Let it be. You can have mine," I said, pulling the partially chewed mass from my mouth and holding it up. "Seriously, let's pay the man and get the fuck out of here. I'm thirsty."

Jay returned the quarter to his pocket and followed me down the narrow lane that led towards the register area. The uneven, wide wooden floor panels creaked with each step. The sound was somewhat comforting and strikingly similar to the one produced in my parents' attic. As we made our way down the aisle, we walked by dusty metal shelves filled with every conceivable gadget, tool or supply. We passed fertilizer, lighting stock and can upon can of paint. Every square inch of shelf was covered, and the wall space was equally full, garden hoses, rakes and extension cords hanging from bent nails. Not a single item had a price sticker affixed to it. That was the Rocatelli way. Pricing was discretionary. If you wanted a price, you simply asked. This led to notorious fluctuations and inconsistencies. Some patrons took it upon themselves to proactively suggest a lowball price. My dad was particularly successful in that regard. Other customers merely grimaced to solicit an immediate discount, especially from Mr. Rocatelli. He was

"Big Rock" to those he knew and the nickname was appropriate, chosen both for his mountainous physique and because he commanded unparalleled respect. Gentle and gregarious to a fault, he was most concerned with treating people like family and solidifying his public image in town. Despite this genuine, albeit ironic persona, we had all heard the stories about his famed temper.

We were there to see his son, Anthony, who had inherited the temper but not the grace. Positioned to be a prick, he was the cold-blooded face of his father's business. He excelled in that role and being that it was after hours, Jay and I knew that we would see him, not the old man. Big Rock seemingly stayed behind the scenes on the gambling front anyway, distancing himself from both scrutiny and the strong-handed tactics required by the business.

I stopped at the register, where a high school kid, Ronnie Giordano, was flipping through a *Maxim*. He didn't acknowledge us. I smacked the bell on the counter, which was littered with a key ring display, lip balms and all kinds of other trinkets. Ronnie nearly fell of his stool, the sharp ring startling him. He finally looked up at us, perturbed by the interruption. I glared hard. "Hey, Tony Tough Nuts, is Anthony around?"

"Yeah, he's in the back." Ronnie jerked his head to the right, towards the back of the store, his eyes still focused on the article. Jay smacked the bell a second time on his way by.

Apparently all the ringing roused Anthony's attention too because he appeared in the doorway leading to the back office. "Is everything okay, fellahs?" he shouted.

"Yeah, Ronnie was sleeping, that's all," Jay answered. We didn't like Ronnie, a pompous little shit. He imagined himself important because of his job and the perceived power that came with it. But he was a tool. Anthony looked past us, narrowing his dark eyes on Ronnie, who was now paying close attention. I turned and caught Ronnie's reaction. He slid off the stool, lowering the magazine behind his hip and straightening up some papers in front of the counter.

"Fucking kid," Anthony snapped, motioning for us to follow with a quick tug of his finger.

I had only been in the back office once before. I had been eight-years-old then and accompanying my mom on some errands. At the time, the hardware store sold Topps baseball cards, a colorful box always positioned next to the register. My mom was next door at the salon, where previous visits had shown my distaste for women's magazines. Rather than watch me launch into wrestling stunts from atop the leather chairs, she gave me a couple dollars and sent me card shopping.

I bought the last four packs and took residence on a folding chair next to the register, where people like Mr. Lombardo would sit when they were visiting Big Rock. Like every other kid that year, I was on a mission to find a Jose Canseco rookie card. I rifled through the first pack and then the second. Cards passed through my hands rapidly, good players like George Brett and Don Mattingly irrelevantly shuffled away like minor league scum. My eyes were on alert for one thing and one thing only: that familiar green and gold image. The only pause was to acknowledge the occasional Red Sox card, perhaps a Marty Barrett or a Wade Boggs. A minor consolation, I adeptly separated the Sox cards at the back of the pile. The final two packs were my last chance, so I changed my technique. I methodically made my way through each pack, slowly sliding each card over the next, revealing one millimeter at a time. Each and every time, I was disappointed. I sunk into the chair while an All-League puss spread over my face.

Big Rock emerged from the shadows of an aisle where he had been helping a customer. His omniscience was legendary, not that I knew that word back then. "No Canseco, huh?" he inquired.

I shook my head side to side, tightening my puss.

"Looks like we need a refill too," he said, glancing at the empty box on the counter. "Come with me, Roy."

I looked around to confirm that there were no other Roys in the store. Then I slid off the chair and took a few short, frightened steps towards Big Rock. He reached out and rustled the hair on my head. His stubby fingers felt powerful. "Come on. Let's see if we can't find another box."

I took indecisive steps, following him down the long wooden aisle. His khaki pants fit snugly on his hips, his trunk-sized legs lumbering with each short and hearty stride. The floor below squealed with each transfer of his weight. I was sure that he was leading me to a scary place. Even a richly naïve child like me knew that the door at the back of the hardware store led to a forbidden land. I stopped in my tracks a few feet from the door, hoping that I had come far enough. The door was slightly ajar, but I couldn't see much except a long table covered with manila folders and magazines—nudies for sure. I inched a step closer, my curiosity trumping apprehension. I leaned slightly to my left, rising on my toes and trying to peer around the door. I still couldn't see much, Big Rock's wide rump blocking my view.

"Let's see, what do we have here?" He turned and seemed surprised to see me standing there below him, as I had fully penetrated the room. The smoky smell was overwhelming. Musky and dense, it smelled much worse than my Uncle Paul's car, which was essentially an ashtray on wheels. Wide-eyed, I scanned the small space, taking mental photographs that I could relay to friends. To my surprise, there were no human limbs cast about, no machetes adorning the walls and no bloody workbench. I was gravely disappointed. Instead, it was a typical office, with shag blue carpet, some cheap, dark wood furniture and a vinyl table on which sat two decks of cards and a dirty ashtray. Paperwork, newspapers and an empty potato chip bag littered a metal green desk. Framed pictures of Anthony and John hung crooked on the wall behind it, surrounded by photos of golfers and other people pinned up with pushpins. Next to a picture of Anthony's Little League team, there was another framed picture. It was a large, black and white one of a beautiful woman standing on a crowded street. Her smile was radiant, even in black and white. Her slender body looked full of life as she posed playfully, holding a shopping bag while dipping her hips. I edged closer to it, captivated by her striking dark eyes.

"She's beautiful, isn't she?" Big Rock asked. I nodded, embarrassed as hell. My face swelled bright red, and I felt it get warm. "That's Mrs. Rocatelli," he continued.

I looked up at him quizzically and then moved in even closer to the photo. The Mrs. Rocatelli I knew didn't look like that. She was a wrinkly old woman with a nest of black hair. She wore lots of gold jewelry and smelled like kitchen cleaner.

"That's in New York City, Times Square, Memorial Day 1952. Maybe the best weekend of my life," he said, letting out a raspy sigh. "I was in Korea a few weeks later, fighting on Hill 122. We were the first major marine ground action in the war."

I nodded my head, engrossed by his solemn voice. "Did you shoot people?" The words were out before I could stop them. He looked down, sizing me up. I waited patiently for his response, watching as his brow wrinkled and his face turned dispassionate.

"Just a few bad guys. It was either them or me." Big Rock's eyes went empty, fixating on the picture and the memories therein. "That was a long time ago."

He turned back towards a huge bookcase that ran the entire length of the sidewall. He scanned the shelves, each filled with cardboard boxes. I was dying to know what lay in each. I saw the name Sony written on quite a few stacked at the far end. They were too small for TVs, but not for boom boxes or Walkmans.

"Here we go," he said excitedly, pulling a small red box from the top shelf, where I noticed a stack of twenty or thirty boxes just like it. He opened the box and pulled out a short stack of cards. "This here is the 1986 Topps Traded Set. It's not for sale yet. It has all the rookies and players traded during the season."

I had heard about the Traded Set from Jimmy, who had explained that it was expensive, rare and only sold in real card shops like the one in Arlington. Big Rock sorted through the deck, his stubby fingers snapping each card behind the next. Then he stopped, studying a card before letting an enormous whale grin take hold of his face. He looked me right in the eyes and held up the card. "Do you know this guy?"

"Jose Canseco!" I gushed, wanting to swipe it from his hands, but thought better of it, my manners on high alert. I waited patiently, rocking slowly on the balls of my feet. He handed me the Canseco card, and I immediately held it up to my face, studying each and every detail, brushing my thumb over it slowly with adoration.

Big Rock knelt down on a knee, letting out a groan because the maneuver had been anything but fluid. "Here, take this too. You'll find a Bo Jackson, a Will Clark, a Bobby Bonilla and lots of other rookie cards. Keep the set together though. It's more valuable as a whole. Besides, Jose Canseco may not be the best of the lot when all is said and done. Barry Bonds is in there too. His dad Bobby was quite a player. I bet the kid won't be half-bad either."

I was stunned. Though besides Bo Jackson, I wasn't overly excited about the other cards, just the Canseco. That was the prize. I nodded my head furiously and then thanked him.

Before I could turn to run next door, Big Rock called, "Roy, wait just a second." He was still on his knee and his tone was sharp. I froze and then turned slowly. "Listen, you can't tell your friends. You can tell your mom and your dad, but this has to be our secret. There are too many little boys and girls in this town and not enough of those boxes. You're a good kid and your father helps me with my insurance. You understand what I am telling you?"

I got the message loud and clear. "Yes, Big Rock, I won't tell a soul. I promise."

"Good boy." Shuffling to his feet, he smiled and then watched me dart through the store waving the shiny red box.

Almost twenty years later, I was anxious to see what had become of the back office. But I moved with calculated steps, weary of change. When I reached the doorway, I couldn't believe my eyes and laughed openly. I stood transfixed, casting my eyes on the same green desk, the same cheap furniture and, yes, the same damn photos. Mrs. Rocatelli was there, as beautiful as ever. The baseball cards were gone though, replaced by cardboard boxes, likely filled with iPods and laptop computers.

"Whoa, what happened to you?" Anthony asked, seeing Jay's lip.

"Ugh, had a little fight the other night," Jay responded proudly, as if it were a common occurrence. I smiled at that.

My attention soon returned to Mrs. Rocatelli, a nostalgic comfort connecting me to her. Anthony watched me closely. A biting silence followed—the kind that begs of conversation. I didn't oblige. Anthony placed a cigarette in his mouth and lit it with the same hand. He didn't ask if we minded, though I certainly did. He sat back in his swivel chair, taking a drag and then another before exhaling a big putrid cloud of smoke. I didn't look at him but knew he was still following my eyes, which remained glued to his mom's picture. He jerked forward in his chair, catapulting his weight towards me with a thud. Then he leaned in, placing both elbows on the desk. I didn't bite. For some messed up reason I wanted to test his resolve. It was juvenile and purposeless, but fun nonetheless. He tightened his eyes, probably wondering if I was on something. He turned abruptly in the chair to identify the source of my infatuation, his fidgeting growing with each passing second. He looked at the black and white photo, then back at me, seemingly to calibrate my line of sight.

"Do you mind if I use your bathroom?" Jay interrupted, pointing over his shoulder at Anthony's personal restroom.

"Huh? Sure, go ahead." Jay disappeared into the small bathroom behind me. Based on proximity, I hoped it wasn't a shit.

I decided to speak. "That picture was taken fifty years ago, Times Square, right, Anthony?"

Anthony swung around again to analyze the picture, probably in search of a landmark or something that gave away the location. There wasn't one. He swallowed another long pull of nicotine and looked on quizzically. "Yeah, how—"

"Your dad told me about it, a bit about the war too. He's got some great stories," I said, my nonchalance off the charts.

"And when was this?" Anthony demanded, clearly agitated. The sight of him squirming thrilled me. My goading uncooperativeness was working, deflating his monstrous ego.

I stared right into his menacing eyes, sizing up his despicable character. I hated him. He was an arrogant prick who took too much comfort in the life his dad had afforded him. He lacked his brother's humble innocence and his dad's charming sincerity. They were both kind and genuine people operating in a not-so-nice business. Anthony abused the power, leveraging it to intimidate vulnerable people like Jay.

"A while back," I mumbled, careful to offer little insight. I heard a muffled flush and a few seconds later, Jay returned from the bathroom.

Anthony anxiously sucked down his cigarette and then lit a new one with one hand again. I figured it was his greatest skill. He immediately inhaled two monster drags and exhaled a cancerous cloud that made Jay cough, but Jay did it subtly. I preferred the more obnoxious, exaggerated kind of cough that cast guilt on the smoker.

"So, you have some money for me, Jay?" Anthony barked. He was suddenly at ease.

"I do. I have $1,500." Jay handed Anthony a wad of bills.

"Good, when will I get the rest, the other $5,500?"

"Soon."

"When is soon?"

"Next week."

"No, that's not good enough." Anthony leaned forward to extinguish his half-smoked cigarette in a large glass ashtray. "I need it by the weekend."

Jay looked on the verge of tears or a shit in his pants. He knew not to argue though. He looked at me, pleading with his scared eyes for me to say something, but I just shrugged my shoulders. Getting involved would have made him look weak and that is exactly what

Anthony wanted. He thrived on that shit, like a wolf exploiting the weakest member of a herd.

Anthony furled his lip and made an Italian tough guy face. He held it, narrowing his shadowy eyes. They were void of compassion. He was an imposing figure, and as I sat there hanging on his next word, I felt stupid for challenging him moments earlier. His face was clean-shaven but pockmarked and beaten. He combed his black hair back tight, though it curled slightly over the back of his neck. He wore a thick gold chain, which I automatically assumed held a golden horn or an oversized cross—maybe both. His shirt was a long-sleeve, white waffle shirt that clung to his muscular frame, especially his arms, undoubtedly the focal point of his workouts. He struck me as someone who liked to look in the mirror and who absolutely and unequivocally took himself and his collections seriously.

"Jay, I understand that it sucks, but it's not my problem. I wish it didn't have to be this way. But I have a business to run and people to pay. I can't have you carrying this shit. This is your thing. Figure it out. Find the money."

"I'm trying—"

"Trying isn't going to cut it. Sunday, the whole fucking thing. I have been more than lenient," Anthony insisted.

"I appreciate that," Jay murmured.

Anthony didn't acknowledge Jay's forged gratitude, but lit another cigarette instead. "Anything else?"

I was upset but helpless. Silence lingered like the stink of dog shit. I tried to sort out a solution, which was useless because my mind wouldn't focus. The good-idea part of my brain was in hibernation. Jay remained in his seat, probably hoping that, in doing so, a resolution would be born in his still obedience. But it didn't happen.

"So, what's Bobby thinking for schools?" Anthony asked.

"Huh?"

"Your brother, what's he thinking for college? Hockey? Football?" The question wasn't just from left field; it was from beyond the left field bleachers. I was caught off-guard, insulted really, that Anthony could ponder something so trivial. That's when I realized that it was just a transaction to him. There was no room for sympathy or understanding. To be good at his craft, he couldn't entertain such concepts. Though it bothered me, it made sense and further clarified the dire situation Jay faced.

I ran my tongue against the roof of my mouth because my mouth had gone dry. I breathed slowly through my nose, the room so quiet that I could actually hear the warm air pass through my nostrils. I felt hot and knew Jay did too. He was a notorious sweat hog, always pitting out.

"He's not sure yet, probably an Ivy School. If I had to guess, I'd say he'll play hockey."

Anthony did one of those nods with his lower lip protruding, the kind Robert De Niro would do to signify reserved approval. "Good for him."

I didn't elaborate because I didn't feel like it and didn't see the point. Jay squirmed slightly, probably to adjust the distribution of his pit stains. It was time to go. I leaned forward slightly, easing the chair back with my ass. Jay jumped to his feet. Anthony came around the desk on the side closest to me. He brushed past me and walked confidently to the door. Jay lingered for a second or two. In my periphery, I thought I saw him move towards the desk, but by the time I turned back, he was striding towards the door. I shot him an inquisitive glance, but he didn't see it. We both moved through the door and shook hands with Anthony. I made sure to squeeze extra tight as though it would let him know that I was a badass. I then held his hand in mine for longer than what was acceptable and soon enough, he jerked his hand away.

I followed Jay down the aisle and past the register. "Wake up, Ronnie," I jeered, making my way past him. As we approached the door and the looming stillness of a summer night, I slowed my pace. "Jay, I'll catch up. I want to throw some action on the game tonight."

"Whatever," Jay mumbled, his patience running thin.

I walked briskly back down the aisle, my feet moving so quick that the wooden planks didn't have time to squeal. Anthony was at the register, signing something for Ronnie. He saw me coming, looking up to see what I wanted without saying the words. "You got a second?" I asked.

"Sure, what's up?" Anthony said cheerfully, placing a blue pen down on the counter. I moved down the aisle a few feet towards the back office and turned to see if he'd followed. He stepped closer, relaxed yet curious. His dark eyes widened with anticipation, inviting me to speak.

"Listen, Anthony, I know this is business, but can you help the kid out?" I asked.

Anthony raised his hands and held them out, palms up. "How?"

"I know you're still taking his action. Can't you cut him off? I know Jay. If he doesn't have the money—and he doesn't right now—he's going to chase."

"Not my problem," Anthony hissed coldly, his eyes seething.

"Yeah, but you can cut him off until he's paid up. Isn't that how it works?"

"Not with us. We take the business, especially with people we know, people in good standing. Shit, that's when we make the real money. We want people to chase. He's *your* friend. Tell him to back off."

"He won't listen. If his back's against the wall, that's his only option."

"Fuck that. His family has plenty of money. If he's in a bad spot, he's got plenty of resources," Anthony said, his irritation growing.

"Oh, so you want him to go to his dad? Are you nuts?" I demanded sharply, but then realized I had been a bit too aggressive with my tone.

"Listen, frankly I don't give a flying fuck where he gets it."

"Well, fine, maybe he will have to come clean with his dad. I can suggest that if you agree to cut him off. That way I can tell him chasing isn't an option," I responded with what I thought was a fair compromise.

"You're not hearing me." Anthony took a step towards me, lifting his chin in the air and glaring down at me from an angle. "This is not a negotiation. Jay Cantwell owes my family $5,500, which I will have in my hands by Sunday. That's it, end of story. You understand?" He moved in even tighter, his bulldog breath burning my face. He stayed in close, his beady eyes twitching as they monitored mine.

I backed away, partly because I was scared, but also because of his breath, which suggested he had recently eaten a shit burger. I shook my head dejectedly. I thought about telling him what a fucking d-bag he was, what a loser he was and what a useless existence he led. Fortunately, I didn't. I bit my lip, staring so hard that his ugly mug fell out of focus, a blurry mass of evil.

21

Jay was outside sitting on a dark green *Boston Globe* newspaper box. His feet swung casually, bouncing quietly against the box's Plexiglas window. "Did you get it in?" he asked, hopping down.

"Huh?"

"The bet..."

"I wasn't placing a bet, Jay. I was talking to Anthony. I asked him not to take your action."

"Yeah, I figured as much," Jay said. "He told you to go fuck yourself, didn't he?"

I kicked at an invisible pebble. "Yeah, he did. Jay, you should lay low until this debt goes away. You paid a nice chunk today. Chasing the balance is only going to make things worse. It's the least you can do."

"What in the hell is that supposed to mean?"

Annoyed, I started towards the car. I exhaled loudly. "It means we just gave you $1,000, and I think I speak for both of us, when I say we'd appreciate it if you didn't turn around and piss it away. That's what it means." My cadence grew with each word. I felt enraged, at a threshold.

"Hey, I didn't ask for that money. I appreciate it, but I am not going to let it dictate what I do. You can have it back."

"Why are you so stubborn?" I inquired calmly. He didn't answer. He sped up his pace and turned into the lot. "Hey!" I called.

"Fine, I won't bet. Enough already," he shouted, swinging open the driver-side door. I walked sheepishly to the car and settled into my seat. I wasn't interested in pushing the issue.

"We're going to Boyle's," he demanded.

"That sounds good to me," I said, relieved that he was finished talking too.

We didn't say a word through the first two beers. I followed the Red Sox game on the TV to my left, though my mind was certainly elsewhere. Doc Copeland was at the end of the bar playing out his recurring role. I strained my ears to eavesdrop on the slurred conversation he was having with himself or Walt Sheehan, seated to his right. All I could make out was something about Doc's niece. The owner, David, was behind the bar that night, a stroke of good luck because I'm not sure Jay could have dealt with Darren in light of what was going on with Lauren. Despite the silence, I never felt awkward around Jay. It was a comfortable void. The kind you don't necessarily notice. Boyle's was dead, save for the group of UPS guys playing darts in the corner and the miscreants like Doc. It was more depressing than ever. I watched the UPS crew, wearing their brown uniforms, as they slapped high fives and touched fists after good throws, dropped f-bombs and shouted insults after the bad ones.

David brought over a fresh pitcher, topping off my glass with the remnants of the first. "This one is on me, boys," he said, turning away before we could thank him.

"You're right," Jay said, his voice sharp. I turned to my right to confirm he'd said it, but he was looking straight ahead. I looked forward and caught his gaze in the dusty Coors Light mirror behind the bar.

I spoke to his reflection. "I'm glad you think so."

"I can't chase it," he added.

"I know you want to, but that will just put you right back where you started. It might be time to come clean with your dad."

He broke off my reflection, taking a sip of his beer. Then, out of nowhere, he smiled a devilish grin. "Nah, there's another way."

"Oh? I can't wait to hear this."

"It's ingenious, it really is."

I took down half my pint. I tried to identify the ludicrous plan forthcoming but could not. "Alright, go ahead."

He leaned in tight, lowering his head and speaking down towards my legs. "Okay, we leave here, we go down to Rick's, we park in the back or down the street, we bust in, and we swipe Nick's stash from the basement. Then we sell it off and just like that, I have two, three, maybe even four G's."

I laughed it off, shaking my head and smiling, completely under the impression that Jay's plan was a joke. But then I saw the dead serious look on his face and my shoulders stopped convulsing. My head stopped shaking. He wasn't kidding. "No…fucking…way," I said slowly. "That's just about the worst idea ever, right up there with the New Coke and prohibition. Are you insane? Do I look like a fucking bank robber to you?"

"Keep it down. Who said anything about robbing a bank? And by the way, I liked the New Coke."

I stared at him long and hard. He just sat there with all the confidence of an innocent child. I shook my head some more but simultaneously began mapping out the caper in my mind. "Is that what you've been thinking about, sitting here like a damn mute?"

"Fuck you."

I did some more head shaking, the skepticism still not subdued. He continued, "I've thought it through. Just hear me out. We're not stealing anything—just the drugs. When Nick discovers his shit is gone, what's he going to do, tell Rick? And if he does, do you think Rick is going to call the police and tell them he had marijuana stolen from his shop? As long as we don't damage anything, we'll be golden. Nobody loses except Nick Wainright, and I *know* you don't give a shit about screwing him over. It's a chance to get even."

I sat still as a stone, playing out scenarios in my mind. I started on the mental path to acceptance, but it was a charade. I was already there. Just like that, I had signed on. Jay needed me. "And how do we get in…without raising an alarm or damaging property?"

"There's no alarm. And our entry is actually easier than you might think. Above the back door, there's an old air conditioner. There's nothing between that air conditioner and the outside. We push it in and climb on through."

"Won't that bust up the air conditioner?" I asked bewilderedly.

"Of course it will, but I checked it out. That thing isn't exactly secure. It just as easily could *fall* out. If Rick suspects anything, he won't buy into that line of thinking once he discovers nothing is missing. I'm telling you, he won't even call it in. He'll be out a broken-down air conditioner."

Jay pounded down the rest of his pint with his confidence brimming. I played it all out again, just to be sure. I saw the back door to Rick's, hidden away in a desolate and dark back lot. "It really is ingenious," I admitted.

Jay topped off my glass and then held up the empty pitcher to David, signaling for a refill. I raised my glass and clanked it into Jay's, toasting the clever plan.

"Two things: first, I'm going to need some shots. Second, because of that, we leave the car here and make our approach on foot. It's safer and smarter that way," I whispered.

"Done and done."

22

We moved up Trapelo Road at a good pace. Despite the Jameson, the short walk to Rick's was a sobering one, my nerves suppressing the whiskey's wishes. It was close to midnight and the road was quiet except for the occasional car speeding past. The streetlights seemed brighter than ever, casting large shadows that followed us with great diligence.

My heartbeat sped up to ninth inning rate as we veered off Trapelo and took a left down Beech Street. Beech was even quieter than Trapelo, the low hum of the streetlights and the beat of our steps the only sounds we heard. I scoped out the houses on both sides, and despite a few illuminated homes, I didn't see a soul. By some stroke of luck, not a single car had passed by the time we turned right onto Maple Street, which would bring us to the back lot. We stayed to the right, hugging the back wall of the movie theater. Cigarette butts littered the sidewalk near a rear door to the theater, where I presumed ushers and ticket takers had taken their breaks. We stopped outside the door and listened for any sign of life inside the theater. We had meticulously thought out all the details. One of which was to wait until the 9:00 p.m. showing of *My Big Fat Greek Wedding* was over, even pushing our go-time back to ensure staff were gone too. Straining my ear to the wall, the theater appeared empty.

I hurried under the red emergency light above the rear door and slid into the back lot of Rick's. As we knew, a tall wooden fence encircled the lot, keeping us out of view from the houses across the way and passing cars. We hustled towards the door, but I immediately grabbed Jay's arm and slowed our pace because the lot was gravel and the tiny stones crunched loudly under our feet. The small lot was empty except for a dark dumpster that loomed silently in the corner to our left. It would provide even more cover, as it sat almost perfectly close to the door. We crept slowly to the door and stood under it, our breathing hushed, yet still loud. A light glowed overhead, but one of the two fixtures held a dead bulb, limiting the glow to a small circle that fanned out maybe six feet beyond the door.

"Look, just like I told you," Jay whispered, pointing up to the air conditioner, which hung weakly and at an angle, protruding down and away from us. The bathroom at Rick's was located right next to the back door and Jay, ever observant, had apparently noticed the air conditioner's tenuous installation. He noted that a few misplaced screws and some duct tape served as the primary support.

"Damn, a stiff breeze might knock it through," I said, becoming giddy with each passing second.

"Alright, you ready? Ten fingers," Jay said, referring to our plan for me to hoist him up. He was lighter.

"Yup," I gasped. I positioned myself below the door, took a knee and clasped my fingers together to create a web on which Jay could step. I tightened my arms to reinforce my hands and prepared to support 155 pounds of scrawny bone. Jay braced himself by jamming his arm against the door and then stepped into my hands. My hands dropped suddenly under his weight, almost to the ground, but I tightened my grip even more, straining to hoist him skyward. "Wow, you fat fuck, time for a diet."

"Shut up, higher," he exhaled. I lowered my head and pushed again, but then I saw something. I dropped him slowly to the ground.

"What the fuck?" he snapped.

"Look," I said softly, yet excitedly. Jay looked to where I was pointing and saw the chairs.

"No shit."

"I know."

Next to the dumpster, just beyond the spray of light, sat two chairs nestled side by side. Another pile of cigarette stubs lay scattered over the gravel between them.

"I guess people around here like smoking," I hissed.

"It'll kill them," Jay replied, moving to grab a chair.

He poked his arm through the open backing and hooked it onto his elbow. We had agreed to avoid touching anything, hoping to use just our arms or palms when possible. I'd seen too many episodes of *CSI*. He set the chair below the air conditioner and stepped up. "Okay, after it goes, we take cover," he reminded me. I nodded.

Jay pressed his forearms against the air conditioner and began pushing. The chair wobbled a bit and I quickly steadied it by bracing my thighs against it. As he pushed, I could see the square bulge dip slightly and knew right then that it'd go down without incident. With one final push it fell through, Jay's momentum causing him to stumble forward as well. The crash was deafening and for a split-second, I thought about running—getting the fuck out of there. Instead, I huddled next to the dumpster and waited for Jay to join me. He did and for the next minute or so, all we heard were our heavy breaths.

"Stop breathing so loud," I said finally.

"I can't help it."

Climbing though the hole was a cinch. The air conditioner had come to rest just beneath the door and made for a perfect stepping-stone. We even managed to hoist our way in without use of our fingers, instead maneuvering with our forearms and palms as planned. The familiar aroma of cooked cheese took hold of me as soon as I set my feet, and I considered hunting down a leftover slice. The inside of

Rick's was more illuminated than I'd expected. The "Exit" sign above our heads and a faint light in the kitchen cast ample light so that we could easily make out the basement stairway. The staircase was a different story. And I couldn't see an inch in front of my face by the time I hit the fourth step. We descended quietly, feeling with our feet for each step. Jay hovered behind me, his breathing constant and warm on the back of my neck. At the bottom, I ran my arm over the wall but found nothing. I moved into the room and did the same thing on the wall to my right. Within seconds, I felt a plastic switch. "I got it! You ready?"

"Do it," Jay whispered.

The room came to life before us. We were in a large room with a beige industrial carpet. A few black file cabinets lined the wall to our right, as did a small desk facing the wall. Papers and large black binders were arranged neatly beside one of those fancy green desk lights that are common in law offices. I pictured Rick at the desk, going through invoices, payroll and produce orders.

"There," Jay said, pointing to a door on the left sidewall.

We shuffled to the door, which was slightly ajar. I swung it open, and the light behind us poured into a large closet with big stainless steel shelving units like the one in my mom's pantry. Large and small pizza boxes, napkin packs, bags of plastic utensils and giant commercial-sized red cans of Pastene tomato sauce filled the shelves.

"Which one is it?" Jay asked, turning to me and pleading for direction.

I shrugged like a neophyte. "I don't know."

The ceiling was low, so I punched the panel over my head. It moved easily. I punched another. Jay began doing the same. On my fourth or fifth try, the panel moved, but something on the other side dislodged and rolled over. I punched the same panel again and heard something thump. "Here," I said out loud.

I pushed the ceiling panel straight up this time, balancing it on my fist. It swayed to the right, and the object on the other side came hurtling though the gap and then fell to the linoleum floor below. I fixed my eyes on two bricks of entangled sticks and leaves, wrapped tightly in Saran wrap and held together with rubber bands. I steadied the panel back into place as Jay scooped up the weed. About half of the top brick was missing, evident by the irregular shape at one end. The other was fully intact. "Damn, that's a lot of weed," I gushed.

"Fuck yeah it is," Jay snapped back, a grin running ear to ear. "It's almost one and a half kilos."

"What, kilos? Jay, this is weed, not coke."

"Yeah, but it's the same measuring system. A brick is a kilo, or about thirty-two ounces. There's got to be forty-eight ounces here, easy," he added.

It was a lot. I ran the math in my head. A good ounce sold for about $200. I figured wholesale might be half of that, maybe less, depending where we would come in on the food chain. Regardless, it would be in the neighborhood of five grand and damn close to what Jay needed to wipe his slate clean.

"Let's get out of here, mission accomplished," Jay said, cradling the bricks in his arm like a football.

I killed the light and we made our way up the steps. Jay stood on the air conditioner and peered out into the darkness. The coast was clear. He tossed the bricks out the opening and then hoisted himself up by the palms. I did the same and then launched myself over the chair and onto the gravel lot below. Jay tucked the bricks under his waistband while I returned the chair to its original place. Then we huddled briefly below the door. "You know, I'm not sure that air conditioner even broke. We were fucking flawless," he boasted.

I slapped him on the back. "Let's not make a career out of it."

23

Selling the weed locally wasn't an option because that would have blown our cover to Nick. We weren't necessarily worried about him, but we were most definitely worried about his supplier, to whom Nick would surely cry wolf. I didn't dare mention the caper to Bobby, or even Carmen, but I did keep an ear to the ground over the next couple of days to see if I heard anything about Nick getting his stash stolen or a break-in at Rick's. I didn't hear a thing, which was comforting. The weed went to someone my roommate Pete knew: a friend of a friend. That's how drug webs usually work. I knew Pete had a hook-up, a Boston University student with no connection to Belmont. I had to call Pete on his vacation in Chicago, and he seemed intrigued that I had come across forty-eight ounces of bud, but as soon as I mentioned Jay's name, he seemed to make sense of it all. That was Jay's reputation—*strange*. Pete made the call.

As I walked under the green canopy and then up the steps to the enormous brick apartment building on Commonwealth Avenue in Brighton, it felt nothing like college housing. The directory was extensive—at least twenty-five names—and it took me more than a minute to find the name Jeff Gilroy. I pressed the small black button and waited for the door to buzz, which it did almost as soon as I released my finger from the button. Inside, the shiny gold fixtures and soft carpet of the lobby were not what I was used to seeing in college residencies. Drug money had its privileges. I knocked twice on the door to unit 607 and a friendly, baby-faced kid, who looked sixteen, but must have been older, welcomed me.

"Are you Jeff?" I asked hesitantly.

"No, dude," he mumbled, pointing across the living room before collapsing into a huge black leather recliner. He returned his attention to a gigantic projection TV. An old episode of *Family Feud* was on, starring Richard Dawson. My surroundings intrigued me. These kids were bucking the stereotype of college drug lords. I didn't see one Grateful Dead poster or any posters for that matter, just a couple of framed prints, one of which I recognized as a Van Gogh. The furniture was show-room quality, and the two kids looked more like country club boys than weed-smokers. I wondered if tennis rackets outnumbered bongs in the adjoining bedrooms.

"You're Roy?" asked another clean-cut kid, this one in a white Polo shirt. He rose from the L-shaped sofa that matched the recliner.

"Yeah, you're Jeff? Nice place, not bad for college," I said.

"Oh, thanks. Yeah, I'm Jeff. This is Taylor." I shook Jeff's hand, but when I stuck my hand out again to greet Taylor, it remained there because Mr. Too Cool acknowledged me with an apathetic head nod, his eyes never straying from the TV. I decided he was a piece of shit.

Jeff and I settled in on the couch and exchanged a few pleasantries about his apartment and Pete. Then we got down to business. Unfortunately, my math had been a shade optimistic as he only offered $70 per ounce. In hindsight, he probably knew I wasn't in the business and in no position to negotiate. Had I thought about it, perhaps I would have researched my role better. We did a little back and forth, during which he disappeared down the hall. He returned with three full bricks, a scale and a badass bong that I almost mistook for a grenade launcher. I figured he kept his bricks in his sock drawer, right next to the Argyles.

He set his bud down on the coffee table and told me that he was already "flush" and in no bind to buy my stuff. But I was able to get him up to $75 per ounce or $3,500 because his scale showed that it was actually a little more than forty-six ounces. He sampled my weed by sniffing it and then packed the four-foot bong he called "Roger II." I didn't ask about Roger I, but assumed it was somewhere in the house or had been shattered sometime in the not-so-distant past. Jeff buried a couple of hits and then passed the weapon to Taylor, who participated with perfect disinterest. I took a half-hearted hit of my own, and then Jeff gave me a complimentary eighth of his own stuff—which he insisted was superior—and sent me on my way. I hadn't bothered to call Jay during the negotiation because we just weren't in a position of strength, and I didn't want him backing out to test the Belmont market. It was inevitable that he would take that risk and end up in even deeper shit once word got back to the Arlington cartel. Luckily, he was working at Harrington's that day, so I didn't have to worry about him messing things up.

To tie up all the loose ends, I stopped into Rick's that afternoon with Bobby. I was nervous as hell as we made our way through the front door. But I got good news in the way of cool air, which was circulating through the small wooden restaurant. More peace of mind came when I surmised that Nick didn't appear to be working.

After instructing Bobby to order us four slices, I made my way to the drink cooler, situated such that it gave me a good vantage point down to the bathrooms and the back door. I pretended to survey the rows of cold beverages, fumbling with a bottle of water and then a can of Coke as I glanced towards the back hall. I couldn't make anything out, so after deciding on a grape soda, I turned towards the hall and looked good and hard at the door. Above it, the old air conditioner was humming away. A bracketed system of two-by-fours now supported it in place. The plastic vents revealed a big ugly crack that ran vertically like a jagged lightning bolt. I did my best to hide a crooked grin and then hollered to Bobby, "Get those to go."

24

My shirt clung to my back, the sweat a natural adhesive, as I made my way up the seventeenth fairway. The seventeenth was the worst of many uphill climbs on the Oak Ridge golf course. I had been playing the course since my youth and yet, the ascent on seventeen wore me down each and every time. Oak Ridge was a semi-private course located right on the Belmont-Watertown line and thus a short five-minute ride from my parents' house. My friends and I had all been playing there since we could remember. The course was very loyal to its core patrons from Belmont and Watertown and offered unbeatable membership rates for town residents. A junior membership was $240 per year and a family slot was just $1,200. Members had access rights over the public, with the only limitation being that kids under eighteen couldn't play until after 3:00 p.m. This didn't apply to some kids, especially Bobby, who worked in the bag room.

It was a grueling match that day. Luna was a solid player, feisty, resilient and never truly out of a hole. Jay, the only one of us who hadn't taken full advantage of Oak Ridge growing up, was talented but inconsistent. Bobby was a wildcard. He could hit it a ton but was often erratic and unfocused in key spots. Golf just wasn't his thing, which was understandable since he was a star in the more legitimate sports that occupied his time. I was downright awful that Saturday, better only than Jay, who was beating it like Judge Smails.

Bobby and I were one-down when we made the will-breaking climb up the seventeenth. Jay was out of it, having hit his tee ball into the parking lot. And I was too, after muffing my approach shot from a fairway bunker. Bobby and Luna both knocked their shots on the green—Bobby's seemingly closer to the obscured flag. Jay walked a few steps ahead of me but paused as we made our way to the green.

"I suck," I said, catching up to him.

"Of course you do, there's no money on the line," he said, alluding to my reputation for elevating my play when the stakes were highest.

I blushed, feigning embarrassment, though I actually reveled in the glory of his remark. "That's your fault," I said. In light of Jay's situation, we had agreed to play a low stakes match, the losers only obligated to buy beers for a post-golf barbeque. It was a far cry from our typical $50 distance match.

"Fair enough," he admitted. "Speaking of, I got the word from Jack. It's all good. I can pick up the money tomorrow," Jay said.

"It took you seventeen holes to tell me?" I complained.

"You didn't ask."

He was right. It had been killing me all day and was part of the reason that I had played so poorly. Jay had dropped off the $3,500 for Anthony that morning, getting his balance down to a semi-manageable $2,000. Going to his dad was still out of the question, which I completely understood. In fact, I'd have fled to Tibet before soliciting my own dad on such matters. Unfortunately, I didn't have that kind of money to lend, and soliciting Luna was still laughable to Jay. So he had proposed an alternate plan—this one legal. Jack Harrington, the owner of Harrington's, was a fair and generous man with whom Jay had a good relationship. Jay had suggested that he ask Jack to front him a few paychecks. He would make up a story about needing the money for a real estate class at UMASS Boston, which fit with his pending career change. It made sense.

"I wanted to ask, believe me. It has been a distraction," I admitted.

"Maybe that's what I had in mind," he said coyly, walking off towards the green to watch the proceedings.

Luna two-putted for a par, which meant Bobby needed to make his birdie putt to win the hole and draw the match even. I crouched down behind the hole to get a good look at the break. Bobby did the same from behind his ball. It was a formality for me because I knew every inch of that green. I stayed in my crouch, watching Bobby instead of the line. His blue eyes were wide and alert and his lips flush as though he were kissing the warm air. It was his thinking pose and mine too, or so people said.

"You got it?" I asked quietly, though my voice carried in the quiet created by the pressure of the situation. He didn't even look up. He backed away before standing tall and taking a few compact practice strokes.

With his eyes trained on his putter blade, he finally responded, "Right edge." Then with confidence, he steadied himself over the ball. The late afternoon sun reflected off the club's steel blade. I heard Luna or Jay shuffle their feet behind me, and I too backed off slowly. He took one more glance at the cup and stroked the putt right into the center of the jar.

"Good putt," Luna murmured, hurrying off to the eighteenth tee. I threw my arm around Bobby's shoulders as we followed.

The eighteenth tee provided a stunning view. The group in front of us was still visible in the fairway ahead as I looked out to take in the sights. Dark green rough ran down hill and away from us before blending with a lighter green, where the expansive fairway began. Surrounded by towering spruce trees on both sides, the fairway dropped at a steady decline and then climbed slightly to a small green guarded on the right by a gigantic oak. Beyond the green, the bright white clubhouse stood like a fortress. The deck was full of vibrant colors as drunken golfers recounted their rounds, some seated under white umbrellas and others standing at the edge to take in the action on the eighteenth green.

Returning my attention back to the fairway, I watched as a man in a red shirt emerged from his cart, selected a club and hobbled to his ball. He slapped a low liner that ran fast and furious towards the green before succumbing to the hill and disappearing beneath the great oak. I turned to my friends, who were silent and standing off to the side of the tee. Silence was rare on the eighteenth tee, as golfers routinely made last second presses and save-face wagers to eek out validation for a four-hour day. With our group, the quiet had become ritual and a sign of respect. Behind the tee, a memorial stone bench sat in memory of Mark's dad Samuel Luna. He had been an honest, calm man, who was equally kind to those he met and those he knew. A master storyteller, his soothing tone and relaxed demeanor had lured listeners in, suspending them over each and every word. I reflected fondly upon the many times we had crowded him on Mark's deck, listening transfixed as he spoke. Below the bench, there was a black plaque framed by perfectly manicured grass. It read:

In loving memory of Samuel C. Luna and his unwavering dedication to the people, the spirit and the tradition of Oak Ridge. He was a friend to many but family to all who knew him.

Luna never sat on the bench, so we didn't either. He hadn't liked golf much growing up and had even said as much. Yet, his father's passing seemed to reconnect him to the game. Other than his family, it was probably his dad's greatest love, so Luna felt a sense of obligation in continuing that legacy. Once, when we were playing alone and walking up the eighteenth fairway, he had confided in me, telling me that everything about Oak Ridge reminded him of his dad—the people, the smells, the sounds. Even hitting shots from certain locations connected him to his dad. Like the bunker to the right of the ninth green, where his dad had spent four hours with young Mark, teaching him how to hit a sand shot. It was sad, but comforting because Oak Ridge was where Mark felt most at ease. There, he had nothing to prove and no ghosts to please.

Surprisingly, we all got off the tee well. Four balls lay waiting in the fairway for the first time that I could remember. Over the years, we had walked up eighteen many, many times. Pictures of the walk would serve as a perfect timeline for our lives—perhaps a certain shirt, maybe a bad haircut, even a hat signaling the year and revealing layers of being. There were no pictures taken that day, in fact, I had only one picture of the four of us making the walk.

The picture was from 1996. My dad had been playing the adjacent thirteenth and had swung by to ask me if I could drive Bobby to Little League that night. Before my dad drove away in his cart, he pulled us all together and snapped the picture, which I can still see so vividly, it seems real.

We stood arms over shoulders and all swaying to our right because Luna, who stood on the far left, had leaned in just as the shutter released. Luna was laughing because I had suggested he kneel in front, as he used to in elementary school pictures. His dad would be dead in less than eighteen months. I was next to Luna, smiling smugly with my Red Sox hat turned backward. Bobby, just eleven, was to my right, his naïve full smile illuminating the entire picture. A nasty poison ivy rash reddened his arms and swelled his little face, but clearly didn't dampen his mood. Jay was Jay, with his left hand on Bobby's head. He wore a yellow golf shirt with a missing button, lost during a friendly wrestling match with Luna that had occurred earlier that week. His eyes stared blankly to his right.

That photograph captured not just our varied personalities but also the youthful exuberance we unknowingly celebrated. It was taken at a time when little mattered beyond carefree routines and each other. Three of us were nearing the end of our formative years, our reign over innocence. And Bobby, though too young to consider his fate, was on the brink of his prime and ready to take the throne.

***

Six years later, we were walking down that fairway once again; stride for stride and in perfect rhythm. The years had brought change and the burden of being. The only sound was a light breeze penetrating the trees and the click-clack of our clubs as they bounced around with each stride. No longer kings of innocence, we walked together, but also alone.

My approach shot was a good one, or so I thought. But it slid off the sloped green and came to rest under the big oak. Luna pulled his shot left, but by some act of God—or kin—got a kick off a greenside mound and ended up fifteen feet from the pin. Jay sculled the shit out of his shot, causing a brief scare for the group ahead of us as they put their clubs away in their carts behind the green. Bobby flailed his shot right, the ball nearly striking down the big oak with a smacking thud before it ricocheted into the deadly greenside bunker. After he and Jay confirmed their irrelevance with poor third shots, I lined up a difficult chip shot that would start uphill before sliding steeply downhill towards the pin.

"This is bull shit," I snapped, standing over my ball and surveying the line. But nobody seemed concerned with the misfortune of my ball's bounce. They responded with silence.

I sensed the onlookers up on the clubhouse deck watching. Bolts of nervous energy shot down my arms. My hands grew moist and my wrists numb. I looked at my club resting behind the ball and then the hole, repeating this process five or six times. It was an effort to buy time and enable the nerves to run their course. I eased my breathing and then relaxing my hands, I let the club go weightless. All was quiet again, except for a distant bird singing a high-pitched tune. When everything felt just right—my palms dry and my fingers soft—I took the club back slow and straight, then followed through with my head down. I held my focus on the spot where the ball had lain and saw tiny clippings of grass shoot up into the air as my pitching wedge cut through the short turf. Then finally, I turned to my left and watched the ball hop, skip and then bite, settling into a smooth roll as it went up the hill and then down.

"Get in, get in!" Bobby yelled. Anticipation got the best of me too, and I slowly started to raise my club in the air, following the ball with long, quick strides.

"No! No!" Jay yelped in a hushed voice.

The ball eased to a crawl as it neared the hole, heading straight for the middle of the cup. The bird stopped singing. Then just before the ball disappeared into the black abyss, it seemed to hit something—maybe a spike mark or slight indentation in the green—and veered left, burning the left rim of the jar and coming to rest a foot beyond it.

"Huh…ugh…oh," a collective gasp billowed out from the clubhouse deck.

"Wow!" Luna said. "So close, so damn close," he added sarcastically.

Bobby took a knee, succumbing to the invisible bullet that had passed through his kidneys. I toppled over onto my side before rolling onto my butt. I remained seated and just stared at the ball behind the hole, shaking my head in disbelief.

"That's good. Good four, Roy," Jay said. He slapped my ball out of the way and pulled the pin out for Luna. "Let's go, Mark. End this thing, right here," he added.

I rose slowly to my feet and staggered over to Bobby. Luna had already sized up his birdie putt and moved quickly through his practice strokes. Within seconds, he was over the ball. It was an easy putt—lightning fast and down hill, but straight as Hugh Hefner. Luna glanced at the hole, leaning his hands awkwardly out over the ball, as he always did just before starting the club back. Bobby and I both instinctively and simultaneously issued bad-luck horns by sticking out our pinkies and pointer fingers and jabbing them in Luna's direction. Jay saw our poor sportsmanship and playfully returned the favor by aiming his own horns at us to offset the bad karma. Luna struck the ball, and in a flash, it barreled towards the hole. He had crushed it, hitting it way too hard. The ball ran right over the hole, smashing into the back lid and then popping up in the air. I swear it took five seconds to come down, but when it did, all I heard was the ball jarring around in the cup. Luna threw his hands into the air and kept them there as he walked slowly and triumphantly to Jay, exchanging a double high five with his putter dangling from his right hand. A soft applause from the deck grew louder as their love-fest celebration deteriorated into a man hug. Bobby flung his ball across the green and walked towards them in disgust. I stood paralyzed for a minute but then joined Bobby in offering congratulations.

"No Natty Light. We want the good shit," Jay insisted, smiling as we shook hands.

25

After showers and a few beers on the Oak Ridge deck, we left to accommodate Bobby, who was sick of pounding Shirley Temples. When the four of us arrived at her house, Carmen was already well on her way to securing girlfriend-of-the-week honors. She loved to play hostess. A heaping bowl of teriyaki wings and potato salad were already on the patio table. I brought the thirty-pack of Natural Light into the kitchen and found her squirting lemon juice into a bowl of homemade guacamole. I came up behind her and gave her a subtle kiss on the cheek, which she anticipated by turning her cheek to meet my lips.

"Everything looks great, perfect timing," I said gratefully.

"Thanks, you can bring this out too. The chips are in the cabinet," she instructed me.

As I placed the beer in the fridge and grabbed the chips, Jay, Mark and Bobby made their way into the kitchen. One by one, they greeted Carmen with friendly kisses and one-armed hugs. She was awkward in her exchanges, jetting out her face and keeping her arms down because of the gooey mess covering her hands. "So, who won?" she asked, cleaning her hands off at the sink. Jay and Mark didn't respond because they wanted to hear it from Bobby or me.

"*They* did," Bobby offered dejectedly.

"I should have known when I saw the Natty Light," she added, an obvious dig at my frugal tendencies.

"Whatever," I jeered.

"No worries, we have two cases of Sam Adams and some Jameson too," Carmen announced happily.

Carmen's friends, Danielle and Sara; Carmen's younger neighbors, the Corwin sisters; and Bobby's friend, Kevin, soon joined us. Jay tended to the grill, forcing Bobby and Kevin to pay close attention so that they too could someday rule a Weber. Jay took his grilling seriously; insisting on the importance of little things like poking holes in sausages, slicing dogs, toasting buns and his number one rule: never press down on a burger because while it might expedite the cooking time, it will release the juices. I tended to agree.

The food kept coming, and we kept making it disappear. There were hot dogs, chicken breasts, swordfish kebabs, hamburgers, steak tips, shrimp skewers and homemade sausages from Luna's grandmother. The only things going quicker than the food were the beers and the bottle of Jameson. Thankfully, the girls were drinking wine. Carmen's mom came home in the midst of the feast and joined us for a few drinks, fitting right in, her laid-back hippie virtue putting everyone at ease. Though I did squirm in my seat when I sensed she might propose we smoke up. That would have been fine normally, but while drinking was one thing, I didn't want Bobby bearing witness to that debauchery. I was still diligent in setting some good examples.

We stayed out on Carmen's patio for what seemed like an eternity. The only disturbance was a failed mosquito attack. It was a perfect summer night and the kind remembered forever. Luna warmed up to Danielle as he often had over the years. With her, he was able to run his standard offense—throwing deep and throwing often. Their relationship was odd, to say the least, but more importantly convenient and hassle-free. Many a drunken night had ended with them hooking up but then swearing that it would never happen again. Their escapades were like a recurring dream, though definitely not a nightmare since Luna boasted about her anything-goes policy in bed. She liked to hype her skills too, and particularly when she was drunk, which only enflamed Luna's interest and made fucking a forgone conclusion.

I monitored their situation closely, doing my best to promote the inevitable by suggesting they stay over with us. Bobby appeared especially pleased by this idea since he would be staying over too. I noticed a mischievous look in his eye and knew he would be in full spy mode, meat in hand. I couldn't understand why he wasn't putting more effort into the Corwin opportunity, but on a trip to the bathroom, he made it clear that he wasn't interested.

"No way," he said, his arrogance alarming, yet honest. "They're both cute, but they're freshman. An easy hook-up, sure, but it'll come with serious stalker implications." It was a decent and fair assessment—perhaps protective of their innocence. Bobby warned me that Kevin was game though. God bless his open-mindedness.

At one point, Jay disappeared for a prolonged period. Based on his consumption and the fact that our Jameson and ginger ales were becoming less and less tolerant of ginger ale, I suspected he might be pulling the trigger. I stumbled inside to check on him, but he wasn't in the bathroom. I called for him but didn't hear a response.

"Jay?" I yelled again, making my way into the dark living room. I noticed the lights were on in the sun porch. "Jay?" I called in a lower, inquisitive voice.

"Yeah, I'm in here," he answered.

I stumbled into the porch and found him sitting intently on the edge of the white leather sofa. The TV was on—the Red Sox ahead of the Texas Rangers 7–6 in the bottom of the ninth.

"What happened?" I asked, alluding to the fact that Derek Lowe had been cruising with a 7–2 lead just two innings earlier when we had last checked on the score. The Sox closer, Ugueth Urbina, was on to close things out, but was struggling, having allowed two men to reach base with no outs. Before I could take my seat next to Jay, Rusty Greer ripped a double down the right field line, and just like that, the Rangers had won.

"Jesus! You've got to be shitting me," I sighed.

"Fuck you, Urbina!" Jay yelled, as if he might hear him. The level of angst in his voice rubbed me funny. Jay was angry, mad as hell, and his eyes were burning. He sensed that I was studying him and straightened up, finally relaxing with a deep sigh.

"You didn't. Tell me you didn't," I pleaded.

"I *didn't.* I'm getting another drink. You want one?" He walked out of the room with his empty glass in hand. I sat there stumped, fearing the worst. Then I told myself not to worry and decided that I was being presumptuous. I was about to leave the room, but I couldn't help myself. The cordless phone resting quietly on the end table was screaming at me; it might as well have been ringing. I picked it up and stared at the "Redial" button. I tried to stop myself, but failed in record time. I hit the button, holding the phone a few inches from my ear and cringing for the voice on the other end.

A familiar voice answered. "Number, please."

I almost dropped the phone. "Yeah, um, this is F32. Can I get the line on tonight's Padres game?" I asked, having given my customer identification number.

"That game already started, sorry."

"Okay, my bad. Thanks," I mouthed unconsciously.

"JAY!" I screamed. I heard his feet growing louder as he made his way back towards the porch. Then he appeared and looked at me wide-eyed, unaware of what I now knew. "Why'd you fucking lie to me?" I asked.

"Lie about what?" he said annoyed.

"I just redialed this fucking phone, Jay. You want to tell me why Fat Andy answered?"

His shoulders dropped and he stared at me incredulously, at a loss for words. His eyes were glassy, but told a helpless story. He hung his head. Then he shook it. "I…I don't know, I was so close to even."

"You *are* even, as of tomorrow anyway, with Jack's money. Do you realize what you—no *we*—had to go through to get even?"

"Yes, I do," he mumbled, his eyes looking right into mine. "The bet was fucking nothing, $200."

"Whatever, I handed you a lot of money. Luna did too. And to top it off, you're a fucking liar," I screamed.

"I just didn't want you to worry again. I appreciate what you did, what Luna did. I do. I'm just sick of burdening everyone."

I heard more steps approaching. Luna burst into the room. "Hey, guess who is getting laid tonight?" he asked joyfully, slapping Jay on the back. "Whoa, what happened?" he gasped, noticing the game highlights on the post-game show.

"Urbina, that's what happened!" Jay snapped.

Despite his preoccupation with sex, Luna caught on to the tension. My sullen face was all he needed to see. Blown saves were a New England tradition, incapable of deflating real fans, certainly not likely to kill a great night. Luna was perceptive. He was a cop.

"I don't like this," he said authoritatively. "Roy?"

I shook my head with disgust, turning to Jay. Before Luna could say anything more, Jay jumped in. "Mark, we're not doing this. I'm not in the mood. Go fuck Danielle and enjoy the night. Please."

"No, you're wrong, we *are* doing this, Jay," Luna barked. I stuck my neck out there for you. Roy did too."

Jay just stared at the ground, but Luna continued, "I hope you didn't piss away my money."

"Wait, *your* money?" Jay shouted back.

"Yes, *my* fucking money. When are you going to figure it out, Jay? Get your life together, for Christ's sake. I'm so sick of this shit. In fact, I'm done. It's on you, Jay. I'm done holding your hand." With that, Luna threw his hands in the air, icy beer spilling from his can. He looked at both of us disbelievingly and left the room.

"Asshole...I'll give him *his* damn money, shove it up his ass too," Jay snapped confidently.

I exhaled the breath I had been holding. "No, he's right," I said with glaring anger.

Jay bit down hard on his lower lip, fighting to subdue his aggression. He spoke slowly, but his tone was still sharp. "In theory, maybe he's right. But not in the way he communicates his almighty point of view. Fuck him."

"You don't mean that," I said sincerely. "That kid loves you." My words festered, and when the time was right, I got up and Jay did too. There was nothing left to say. We returned to the patio and resumed our seats on the road to destruction.

26

I was on a mountain and the mountain was rocky, yet when I put my hand down it felt soft like ice cream. So I took a lick, and it tasted like coffee, but then I wished that I had a broomstick and suddenly, I did. I danced with it, and it grew a golden mane and roared like a lion. When I tightened my grip, it crumbled in my hands. I knelt down to scoop up the dusty remains, but my dad called for me. He was wearing a blue bow tie and mowing the lawn, but he hates bow ties, so I ripped it off him. My mom was watching and she giggled. She wore a short black cocktail dress, but she wasn't holding a cocktail at all, but rather a trumpet. She began to play it, yet all that came out was a jack-in-the box, but Jack was in a cage. The cage was large and on a high shelf beyond my reach. I climbed on a mushroom and tried to grab it and even felt the cold metal between my fingers. Just then a chef came into the room and offered me a plate of filet and fingerling potatoes. I started to eat, but it tasted like crabmeat. Next, I was on a big yellow sailboat. An audience was watching me, popcorn in hand. Then the credits began to roll, and I too was in the audience, so I rested my head on Carmen's shoulder. I nestled it there nice and good and she let me, stroking the back of my head with her soft hands.

Carmen moved to adjust her position and my eyes opened. "What are you doing?" she asked, sitting up.

"Huh?" I asked deliriously, blinded by a bright, eye-splitting light, which came rushing through the bedside window.

"You were burrowing a hole in my armpit, you weirdo," Carmen explained.

I sat up. "I think I was…dreaming. It was like this super fast, high-speed dream that just kept changing and morphing. Like that Billy Joel song about starting the fire."

Carmen smiled and kissed my forehead. Her green eyes glowed, even in the morning. I stared into them, still dumbfounded. "You're one strange bird, Roy McGrath. Next time, maybe you should ease up on the Jameson," she added, pulling her hair into a tight ponytail.

"Whatever, I was over served."

By the time Bobby and I made it home, it was 3:00 p.m., and I still wasn't right physically. We labored through some yard work—an absolute must with my parents due back on Tuesday. Bobby had beaten me in rock-paper-scissors—the best of three—and thus landed the easy task of mowing. I was on weeds, driveway sweeping and clippings disposal. Like a good sport, Bobby was careful when emptying the mower bag, which made the clippings job bearable. As I completed my tasks, I lamented the fact that I would be heading back to work on Wednesday. The pending monotony of long subway rides, hour lunches and financial models made me cringe.

Luna stopped by in his cruiser, which provided a nice break from our sweat-filled labor. He kept his engine running and pulled into the driveway at an absurd angle, his back tires protruding into my neighbor's front yard. He apologized for his blow-up with Jay and then provided some disclosure regarding the monkey sex that had occurred in Carmen's basement. Bobby was especially enthusiastic throughout the debriefing, which told me he had likely heard it all go down. I actually felt better about my own predicament after realizing that Luna was on an eighteen-hour shift that would take him through to 8:00 a.m. I couldn't have made it—no way. I would have rather cleaned toilets at Fenway Park.

After our chores were complete, Bobby and I collapsed onto lawn chairs and napped away the afternoon. But he slept the whole time on one side and awoke with an award-winning sunburn on just the left side of his face. He looked like a character from the bar scene in *Star Wars*.

We settled in for a low-key night, inviting Jay and Kevin over to help us take down the leftovers from the night before. Carmen had insisted we take them. Bobby and I went to work on the grill, and I re-emphasized the lessons Jay had so graciously revealed twenty-four hours earlier. It was another feedbag session, but this time the beers went down like shark teeth. The four of us lounged around watching the Red Sox on ESPN's *Sunday Night Baseball.* Pedro Martinez was on the mound and came out slinging, mowing down the first nine Rangers, six of them by way of strikeout. I dozed in and out of sleep as the week of self-annihilation caught up to me. But at 9:30 p.m., Jay cut short my slumber, asking me to go with him to see Anthony.

"You aren't serious, right?" I asked dejectedly. "Why haven't you gone yet?"

"I slept all day."

I sat up on the couch. "Fuck, Jay. You know that money has to get there tonight."

"I know."

"Shit, how do you know he's even there?" I asked.

"I called. He's expecting me. Besides, it's a Sunday, collection night. You know he's sitting there counting money."

"Good point," I agreed. "Alright, yeah, I'll take a ride."

As we pulled out of my neighborhood and onto Mill Street, Jay hit me with another bit of information. "I need to stop at Harrington's and pick up the money Jack left for me," he said nonchalantly.

"Fuck, you can't cash a check *now* and you sure as hell can't sign it over to Anthony," I replied anxiously.

"It's all good. Jack left me cash," Jay answered, his eyes flashing towards me.

"Oh, thank God."

As we cruised into Belmont Center, a cool breeze whipped through the car windows. Joe Castiglione's voice boomed in the silence surrounding us. "Strike three, down goes Palmeiro and the Rangers in the fifth," he shrieked.

Jay drove around to a back lot that Harrington's shared with a few other small businesses, each of which had a back entrance accessible to patrons. But nothing was open. He eased the Tempo into a space against some bushes lining the left side.

"I'll be right back," Jay said, removing a key to the deserted sporting goods store from his pocket. He got out of the car without any inkling of hesitation. As Trot Nixon came to the plate, I turned up the radio and sunk into the passenger's seat. My visit home was nearing an end, so I took a minute to reflect upon a week that had breathed life into me, developing into a series of ordinary summer days that would someday be unordinary. I fell lower in the seat, thinking about all that had happened and the swell of emotions that had surfaced.

But then I heard it. The unmistakable and harrowing sound of glass shattering. I whipped my head to the right. The door to Harrington's was gone, in its place a large opening, framed by broken glass and a black doorframe. I turned down the radio. Jay was nowhere to be found. *He had broken in.*

I grabbed my cell phone from the center console and dialed, my hands shaking. I got out of the car, inching towards Harrington's as the phone rang long and slow.

Luna answered on the third ring. "Hey."

"Mark! I'm at Harrington's with Jay…I…I think he just BROKE IN."

"WHAT? Did you say he broke in?"

"YES, I think so. Fuck, the back door is shattered. It's fucking shattered, Mark."

"I'll be right there. Stay on the phone."

"Okay, I'm going in—"

"No, stay right where you are. That might be a crime scene. Do you hear me? Do not go in. I'm close by on Dean Street. I'll be there in a second."

I stayed put, asking myself if it could have been an accident. If it was, then where the fuck was Jay?

I heard Luna's cruiser before I saw it, but then the blue and white car ripped into the parking lot, both sirens and lights off. Luna was out of the car before it came to a complete stop. He had removed his hat, but the crisp navy uniform commanded respect, forcing me to see him differently. "Where is he?"

I couldn't move my mouth and just pointed to the door. Luna marched briskly and assertively towards it with me chasing close behind. We had covered half of the sixty or so feet between the car and the door when Jay emerged through what remained of the entryway. He walked with astounding indifference.

"Jay, what in the hell is going on here?" Luna demanded, hands on hips.

"Go home, Luna," Jay snapped, walking right on by us as if we weren't there.

Luna followed him, shouting irately, "Jay, what the fuck is this? What—"

"This has nothing to do with you, either of you."

My mind was on life support. I assumed Jay had lied about Jack agreeing to front the money. But if he had just robbed Jack, breaking in seemed unnecessary. He had a damn key.

Then it came to me. Without forced entry, the suspect list would be short, meaning a staged break-in was the only way. But for $2,000, it just didn't make sense. Nothing did anymore, so I surrendered. My eyes didn't well up. My face didn't twitch. Nope. The tears just came, warm and flowing, they poured relentlessly down my face. I wiped them with my arm and then walked aggressively towards my friends. Their words were indecipherable but heated as I approached. Jay was at the driver-side of the car, peering over the hood of his Tempo, one leg inside preparing to flee.

"Jay!" I snapped. The sight of me got his attention. I was a human puddle, broken down and stripped of what mattered most—my control. Jay moved slowly from the car and took two steps towards us. Luna jerked his head towards the street to see if anyone was passing by or responding to the commotion. We were alone.

Jay stopped in front of us, looking in both directions, then behind him. He saw the same empty darkness that Luna had seen. "Guys, look, you have to trust me on this—"

"*Trust you*? I should fucking arrest you," Luna interrupted.

Jay laughed disappointedly. "You know, Mark, you don't always have to be so dramatic?"

"Easy for you to say, you've got no job to lose," Luna shot back.

"Let it go, Mark. Life isn't perfect. Not people, not careers, not relationships—none of it. Nothing fits into nice little boxes or gets due justice on a damn resume. It's life, Mark. Live it. You do it well. You're a fucking success. We know. Your dad knows. He sees you. We all do."

I had never heard Jay so articulate and *never* heard him truly stand up to Luna or me. For a moment, I forgot where I was and forgot the grim situation in which I stood. Luna's face turned to stone, but I could see it in his eyes. Jay had struck a chord and courageously said what he had probably always wanted to say. I inched closer to both of them.

"Jay, he can't just let you go. I can't either," I reasoned.

"Actually, he can. And you can too, Roy. This is all going to work out. For once, you both just need to let me be," Jay said, stepping towards the car. We stood like statues. Before settling into his seat, Jay looked up and finding both of our eyes, he stared into Luna's and then mine. He smiled like I had never seen him smile before, right into the camera. Then he was gone.

"What just happened?" I asked.

"I don't know. Get in the fucking car. I'm going to lose my job," Luna said despondently. I jumped into Luna's cruiser, and we sped out of the lot. Silence lingered. I didn't know what to say. Luna wasn't in a good place. He had witnessed a crime, of which we didn't know the full scope, but a crime nonetheless.

"I shouldn't have called you," I said finally, realizing my own culpability. "I had no idea. I didn't know what to do. I'm sorry, Mark. I didn't mean to put you in that spot."

"I know. I know. Let's just get out of here. I'll drop you at home."

"And then what?"

"I don't know. I really don't. Let's just see what happens. This can't end well," he sighed.

27

The door at Harrington's went undiscovered until early the following morning when a neighboring storeowner arrived for work. Luna's shift was just about to wrap up when the call came in, so he was one of the officers on site and voluntarily stayed for a few extra hours. He had spent the night waiting for a call: one reporting the strange scene that involved his car or one that reported a broken door and suspected burglary at Harrington's Sporting Goods.

I had spent a sleepless night alone with my thoughts, debating whether or not to call Jay. I had decided against it, but not because I trusted him. It killed me not to know if Luna would fold and report his friend. Do his job. Jay had issued him the ultimate test. When Luna came by my parents' house, it was almost noon, and I greeted him in the street. We sat on the brick steps in front of the house, and he told me what he knew.

Another officer, Detective Guy Polcari, had taken the lead at Harrington's, relegating Luna to the role of scene securer. Polcari closed Harrington's for the day and Jack was none too pleased, but apparently calm. The biggest shocker of all was that Jay showed up for work at 10:00 a.m. as scheduled. Luna avoided him like the plague at first, but figured that might be suspicious, so made small talk about what amounted to nothing.

"He was so calm. You should have seen him," Luna said, shaking his head. "Part of me wanted to slam him against the wall and slap the cuffs on. It was hard, Roy, real hard. This is against what I swore to—against my oath."

Jay had stolen $2,400 in cash from the unlocked safe, which was located in the office behind the front counter. He had left a few checks and some credit card slips. Polcari asked Jack who knew that the safe was unlocked, and Jack speculated that anyone might have assumed as much. Any one of the thirty plus employees that had worked for him over the years surely knew. Jack revealed that he only kept a week's worth of revenues in the safe, and he didn't see the point in locking it. Polcari interviewed Jack, Jay and another employee, Jill Phillips, on site, rather than inconveniencing them downtown.

"By chance, did Jack mention any money for Jay?" I asked, holding out hope that the agreement with Jack was real and that Jay had only taken what was rightfully his.

"What do you mean *money for Jay*?" Luna inquired.

I explained the severity of Jay's debt and the supposed agreement he had reached with Jack but skipped the Rick's thing. Luna wasn't surprised; he had figured Jay sugarcoated his losses the day at Suffolk.

"No, that didn't come up," Luna remarked. "Besides, if there was a deal with Jack then the idiot wouldn't have smashed through the door."

"Yeah, I know." Confirmation of Jay's lie stung, and I struggled to accept it. "I mean, that would have come up, right? Polcari did ask Jack about the contents of the safe…"

"Yeah, of course he did. We went through the receipts too. For insurance purposes, we have to account for all lost property. Give it up, Roy. He fucking lied. The money from Jack was bullshit," Luna said convincingly.

"So he robbed Jack to pay off that snake oil salesman Anthony. This is so fucked," I said, humiliated with shame by association.

"Well, he's giving the money back one way or another, so help me God. It may be off the record, but I'll be damned sure of it," Luna said sternly.

I was sick to my stomach. I didn't know Jay, not at all. I got up from the steps and walked down the front walkway. I looked to the tree across the street, the one we had all climbed as young boys. "What else, anything?" I asked quietly.

"Not much, just the typical procedural shit like lifting prints off the safe. Jay's will certainly be all over it, I would imagine."

"Because he works there," I stated rhetorically.

Luna nodded. "We also collected a few hairs near the safe and even a cigarette butt near the back door. It will all be irrelevant though. He's going to get away with this," Luna said, throwing his arms up. "I can't believe the balls on the kid," he added.

I couldn't either.

28

I was just returning from lunch when the call came in. It was Friday and four days after Jay had broken in. As I turned the corner towards my desk, I heard the phone. My desk was close to three other Junior Analysts, so I could never truly distinguish the source of most rings. This time it *was* my phone.

"Roy McGrath," I said in my professional voice.

"Are you sitting?" Luna's voice was shaking.

"Yeah, I am now. What's up?"

"You're sitting?"

"Shit, Luna, yes, what is it?" I said in a muffled voice, masking concern from my co-workers. I could hear his breathing through the phone. It was loud and disjointed.

"Remember I mentioned the hairs they found in the office?"

"Yeah, sure," I responded, not remotely alarmed.

"You figured they were Jack's, right? Maybe Jay's or Jill's even?"

"Yes, of course, Luna. I am at work. Get to your point."

"ANTHONY ROCATELLI."

I squeezed the phone. My co-workers must have sensed something was up because my face went opaque. "No!" I said in a trance-like, disbelieving whisper.

"There's more," Luna barked. "The cigarette they found…two perfect prints…and a match in the system…ANTHONY ROCATELLI."

"No shit!" I screamed, drawing the ire of the others around me.

"Roy, he wasn't alone. I think Anthony was in on it. I think he coerced Jay. He must have been there too."

I couldn't breathe. "Mark, I've got to call you back."

I stood motionless and knew immediately that I had betrayed Jay. I hadn't spoken to him all week because I wasn't ready to cross that bridge. But I had failed him and should have known that he wasn't capable of what we had pinned on him. I should have suspected another explanation. My walk became a jog as I headed to the empty conference room near my desk. I picked up the black phone and dialed frantically. And then it all played out like my crazy dream with the blue bow tie and the broomstick lion. The images flashed through my mind at warp speed.

"Hey," Luna answered. His voice echoed, but I just stared out the conference room window and focused unconsciously on the waterfront view before me.

"Hello? Hello?" Luna's patience was wearing thin.

"OH MY GOD…that crazy son of a bitch..."

"I know," Luna snapped back.

"No, you don't know."

"What are you talking about, Roy?"

Paranoia set in. "I can't talk about it now. Are you working?"

"Yeah, until 4:00 p.m. What—"

"Meet me at Boyle's, 5:30 p.m."

Anthony hadn't been there. In fact, he'd had nothing to do with it. Jay had planned the whole damn thing. Like a wily fox, he had outsmarted us all. Innocent Jay Cantwell. The slight move back towards Anthony's desk—I knew I had seen it. He had swiped a cigarette butt. The opportune trip to the bathroom—Anthony's private bathroom and certainly home to stray hairs. Then staging the break-in and planting the evidence.

The commute to Belmont was a bitch, but two subway lines and a bus ride later, I arrived. Luna was already there, milking a pitcher at a small table in the back. I took a seat in one of the wooden chairs. He poured me a beer, and I filled him in, explaining how Jay had framed Anthony Rocatelli, brilliantly manipulating him and beating him at his own dirty game. I was hesitant at first because if I was right, what Jay had done was extremely illegal.

After I explained the cigarette butt, the hair and the master setup, Luna just collapsed in his seat. It was a lot to absorb. But he gathered himself because my revelation was only the beginning. He had news for me as well.

"I'll do you one better," he whispered. "We executed a search warrant for the hardware store. We got Anthony and all the betting books. Do you have any idea how fucking big this is?"

I did. And I knew the repercussions of Jay's genius would be far reaching, extending to Big Rock and his entire family. It wasn't quite that simple though. Luna explained that there would be some legal hurdles regarding the scope of the search warrant. But he didn't make mention of the elephant in the room—a known setup would serve as the foundation for the entire investigation. It bothered me a little but only because I felt bad for Big Rock and John. Not Anthony Rocatelli, a serpent who deserved a life in purgatory. As we huddled at the small table, I focused on the seats at the bar where Jay and I had sat so many times. I wondered if we would ever sit there again.

"Does it bother you?" I asked, addressing the moral issue at hand.

"What?"

"It's wrong, Mark. Technically speaking, Anthony is innocent."

Luna thought about it while sipping his beer. Then he frowned, shaking his head slowly from side to side. Staring straight ahead at nothing in particular, he said, "No, not at all."

So I let it go.

29

After finishing our pitcher, Luna and I decided to pay Jay a visit. We were ready to acknowledge his Keyser Soze bloodline, applaud his mastery and get back to normalcy. We knew doing so in person was appropriate and necessary considering the gravity of the situation.

The door to Jay's house was open. I looked inside through the screen door, and Mrs. Cantwell's shadowy figure flashed through the front hall. "Come on in, boys," she hollered.

I let Luna go first and then followed slowly behind. A pungent citrus smell filled my nose as we hesitated briefly in the front hall. Mrs. Cantwell appeared again, in a hurry as always. She had her keys in one hand and a brown shopping bag in the other.

"How are you boys doing?" she asked, stopping in front of us, her blue eyes darting around the room. "You must miss him already. He called last night. He absolutely loves it, said he might stay. Imagine that?"

My heart stopped. Luna's wide eyes hardened under a wrinkled brow, but I shook him off discreetly. Mrs. Cantwell's eyes were too busy dancing to notice anyway. They stopped moving finally, and she scurried into the dining room to grab her purse, which was on one of the chairs.

"I'm off to catch the end of Meghan's soccer game," she called, placing the purse in the top of her shopping bag. "Help yourselves to some lemon squares in the kitchen. They're still hot." Then she slapped wet kisses on each of our faces before brushing past us. "Oh, Roy, Jay left your golf clubs in his room," she said, heading out the door.

"*Where is he*?" Luna demanded.

I shrugged the most pronounced shrug of my life before stepping past Luna and scurrying up the stairs and into Jay's room. As always, dirty clothes covered the floor and CDs were in stacks on the bureau. I sat on the edge of the bed, settling on the dark blanket that covered it.

Luna flipped open his cell phone and dialed Jay's number. "No longer in service," he said, echoing the recording on the other end. He stared at me—into a mirror of uncertainty.

I hadn't the slightest idea as to what was going on. Nor did I know where Jay was or why he had left. It struck me as incredibly odd and suspicious that he had canceled his phone and seemingly disappeared. He had told his mom something. Why not us?

"He's just protecting himself," Luna offered, breaking the silence.

"Protecting himself, from Anthony? Is he really at risk? You think that moron would piece it together?"

"Probably not, but Big Rock might. Hell, would you take that chance?" Luna followed.

"No, sir," I acknowledged.

I realized that we'd have to coax his whereabouts from Mrs. Cantwell, acting as though we knew. I looked at the pictures pinned up on a bulletin board over his desk. They formed a giant collage of his life, a work of art in which both Luna and I starred. I studied our faces and the consistency with which we each posed—my insecure smirk, Luna's mayoral smile and Jay's wooden gaze evident throughout. In the midst of the images, I noticed a perfect square void; a window made of cork. Jay's copy of the eighteenth fairway photo was gone. Just like him.

"Your clubs," Luna said, pointing to my green golf bag in the corner.

I had left them in Jay's car following the match at Oak Ridge. I glanced at the bag indifferently and reached down to grab an empty CD jacket from the hardwood floor. It was Neil Young's *Harvest.* I stared at the pinkish orange cover and the fancy script words. Then something registered in my mind, something I had seen. Without a word, I dropped the case and walked to my golf bag. The red head cover for my driver was sticking out of the half-zipped pocket that held my golf balls. I freed it from the pocket and found a white envelope stuffed inside the soft red fur. I looked at Luna, who inched closer. I grabbed the unsealed envelope and pulled out a piece of lined notebook paper. Jay's handwriting filled the page. My body shook with trepidation. I began reading with Luna leaning in over my shoulder.

Roy/Mark,

I'm sorry for the cloak and dagger shit, for the dishonesty and for putting you both in a tough spot, especially you, Mark. By now, I'm sure things have become clear. I wish I could have been there to see the look on your faces. I can see them now. I don't feel bad about what I did. Not one bit because everything evens out in the end. I suppose the money thing was wrong, but I'm sure there's insurance for that. If there's not, then I'll make it right for Jack.

Anyway, I'll be in Seattle, at least to start. My parents think this is a little vacation, but I'm thinking I'll stay. There's nothing here for me anymore. Just you guys and my family and that won't change. I'm looking forward to starting anew. I'll be thinking about both of you, cherishing all the times that we've shared. Remember, it's not an end, just the end of one road and time to go down another. Keep being the people you are, even though I will not. We'll talk soon. Burn this note like Joan of Arc.

Jay

I could hear the words as if he were speaking them. His tone was full of promise, excitement and a distinct finality. Jay was moving on. And despite his history, I knew this was real and that he wouldn't look back. I had seen the transformation in recent days—his eyes looking into mine, his exchange with Luna in the parking lot and his masterful plan. I was only disappointed that he wouldn't be around to see my own transformation. Luna's too. Mark's guard had been let down, and he had shown his true colors, a friend to the end. Somewhere up there, his dad was finally proud.

And I had come to terms with my own conflictions. I was sick of living angry and sad to be the object of so little affection. I was a good friend, loyal to a fault, and for that I was proud. I decided to make that my legacy. I would stand by the people I loved, accepting them for who they were, faults included. And I'd start with myself.

30

It has been five years now since Jay left, and my trips back to Belmont have become increasingly infrequent. Luna's in the city now and my wife, Carmen, is too. That's part of it. But something about being back there doesn't feel right anymore. There's an eerie feeling of loss. Though nobody died, *something* did. I visit apprehensively and with the anticipation of a profound sadness that is strangely happy nonetheless. Reflection is sometimes weird like that. We miss what we love. And we love what we miss.

Such thoughts of satisfying loss occupied my mind as I stepped under the familiar red, white and blue pole and pushed the heavy glass door to the Belmont Barber Shop. I caught Artie's reflection in the large mirror as he meticulously cut an older man's short brown hair. The other red leather chair was empty and had been for a few years because Artie's partner, Red, had retired to Florida. But only after his arthritic hands had become registered weapons. I settled into one of the black cushioned seats along the wall to my right. Now 4:00 p.m., the notorious Saturday morning crowd had dissipated and just one other kid waited in a chair across the room. He buried his head in the *Boston Herald*, and I was surprised not to know him. There was a time when that never happened. I glanced at the magazines on the old wooden coffee table and then reached for a worn *Sports Illustrated* with Tiger Woods on the cover. I was just about to settle back into the cozy chair when Artie finally recognized me.

"Well, I'll be, Roy McGrath," he said, stepping away from his customer to shake my hand.

I stood and extended my hand, shaking his firmly. "Hey, Artie, nice to see you," I said, sizing up his plump frame and round face, neither of which had aged. His spongy black hair was as thick as ever, rivaled only by the bushy black moustache that shaded a warm smile.

"You too, this is a nice surprise. It's been a while. So, living in the city…your dad tells me you get your hair cut downtown now," Artie said, waddling back to his customer. It was true, but a matter of convenience.

"Yeah, it's easier. But nobody cuts it like you."

"I could have told you that!" he joked. Then he stopped cutting and turned my way. A few seconds of reflection passed like a moment of silence. "You know, Roy, I sure miss all of you guys. Luna…Jay..."

"Me too," I uttered under my breath. "Me too."

I never did burn Jay's letter. In the weeks after he fled for Seattle, the full beauty of his ingenious plan crystallized. And every new detail proved more impressive than the last: the cigarette butt at the scene covered with Anthony's prints and Anthony's hair sample next to the safe in a staff-only room. At the hardware store, police discovered an envelope with the Harrington's logo on it sitting in the top of Anthony's office trashcan. Jack identified it as the envelope that had held the stolen cash. Jay had cleverly used it to deliver his final payoff. The cigarette, the hair and the envelope—it was all circumstantial, but together, overwhelmingly incriminating. The hair was especially inexplicable and indefensible. And with Anthony's record, riddled with breaking and entering charges and larceny, it was all as good as gold. In order to argue conspiracy or a setup, his defense would have had to establish a vengeful motive, which was impossible to do without acknowledging his line of work. He had no alibi either because as he did every Sunday, he was sitting by himself in his shitty back office counting money. Game over.

The authorities seized the books, and soon the whole family was knee-deep in shit. The FBI showed up too, gung-ho over the chance to take down Big Rock's regional bosses. Anthony cowered his way into a plea bargain, accepting grand larceny and some other counts against him. He signed up for four years at the maximum facility in Walpole. He got a pass on the sports booking business in exchange for full cooperation, turning on his family in a New York minute. Soon, they indicted Big Rock, but some speculated that he reached a deal too once the FBI took things over. Unbelievably, the case drags on to this day.

Jay is gone, but not forgotten. The reminders are everywhere and never modest: his favorite stool at Boyle's, second from the left; St. Anthony's church, where he spent so many mornings; and his initials, carved below Luna's and mine on the sidewalk in front of his parents' house. Jay never imposed his will and never thought about leaving his mark. And that's likely why he did. He moved silently in and out of countless lives, touching them all with his apathetic charm. He always gave more than he was given.

Eventually, he made his way down the Pacific coast to Oregon, settling in another small town, a seaside one, Depoe Bay. He always loved the ocean and empty skies too. Luna and I have visited twice and were struck by the beauty, but more so by the tranquility. Depoe Bay is the sort of place you would go to live your life without intrusion or influence. Life there is deliberate. It moves along like a slow motion replay, bringing into focus the people and the places that define and frame life there. The air there tastes different.

Jay has been home a few times for holidays—an irony of sorts—and he was there to stand beside me as I married Carmen. I look forward to his visits for weeks on end because he brings with him a slice of life I rarely see otherwise. Some people who come and go from our lives have an effect like that, an ability to balance us and bring out our best.

He is back teaching again, this time the third grade. And to no surprise, he has become quite popular, as is often the case with those who don't try. He also runs a successful summer soccer camp that draws hundreds of kids from up and down the Oregon coast. I imagine they are drawn by what they can learn and by the opportunity to be with other kids, their fellow guardians of innocence. I'm sure they are also drawn by the comforting, affable and always tolerant disposition of their host. It wouldn't be the first time.